While She Was Gone

Molly O'Connor

RP

TotalRecall Publications, Inc.
1103 Middlecreek
Friendswood, Texas 77546
281-992-3131 281-482-5390 Fax
www.totalrecallpress.com

ISBN: 978-1-59095-412-6
UPC: 6-43977-44122-5

Library of Congress Control Number: 2019902854

Printed in the United States of America with simultaneous
printings in Australia, Canada, and United Kingdom.

FIRST EDITION
1   2   3   4   5   6   7   8   9   10

To my children and
grandchildren, my many friends
near and far, you bring me joy
each and every day.

To

Michelle

Best Wishes

Molly

"Sometimes she did not know what she feared, what she desired: whether she feared or desired what had been or what would be, and precisely what she desired, she did not know."
--Leo Tolstoy, Anna Karenina

Stacey eased the mud-caked Silverado to the curb, vaguely aware of the tires rubbing against concrete. She pulled her navy peaked cap with Dominion BDB in gold lettering low over her forehead and watched the front door. The house looked the same—nothing had changed except the truck in the driveway was a newer model. The two-storey was the typical suburban home of the 1990s with red brick facing on the front and off-white, vinyl siding covering the rest. Large bay windows on either side of the recessed front door were the main features of the otherwise bland exterior. The early morning sun was mirrored in the scattered puddles left on the street by showers during the night. Traces of oil formed rainbows on their surface.

A flash of yellow in Stacey's peripheral vision prompted her to see the front door to fly open; the school bus signaled, slowed and stopped with lights flashing. Three children streamed out of the red door. A tall string bean of a girl in multi-coloured leggings and a dark green, very short pleated skirt was followed by a chubby boy with his hooded jacket wide open to the chilly March morning dragging his green backpack along the damp pavement. Walking slowly reading a book, a curly-headed lad wearing glasses and carrying a guitar case came next. Hardly able to breathe, Stacey swallowed threatening tears and watched her children—she was watching her children who she had not seen for years. She watched Brent reach back and slam the door shut while still reading. His jacket was a black and white plaid that hung half on and half off. Even though he was immersed in his book he walked confidently to the bus and climbed on after his brother and sister.

Stacey held her hand firmly over her mouth to prevent herself from yelling out—calling to her children that more than likely would not remember her.

I remember deciding to paint that door red—red doors meant good feng shui, a sign of welcome, and that joy and love dwelt within. Stacey walked out through that same door seven years ago and had not returned until this morning.

Steeled for this moment, Stacey took a deep breath and watched the bus pull away taking a significant piece of her with it. White knuckling the steering wheel, it was all she could do not to leap out and rush toward them, tell them who she was and hug them tight. Instead, she watched the bus disappear around the block carrying them away. Reaching forward, Stacey started the truck and eased it into a parking spot around the corner out of sight from the house. She reached for the truck's door handle and released the catch. Easing across the leather seat wiping tears that had trickled down her cheeks, she jumped down to the road landing on legs that almost failed to support her.

Stacey took off her cap, flung it onto the seat and loosened her salon-highlighted curls. Standing facing the truck door, she glanced at her reflection in the door's window. A full mouth set in a determined line was perfectly outlined with coral lipstick, carefully applied wide dark eyes with high arched brows stared back at her. "Okay, girl, you can do this." She slammed the truck door, turned and headed for that red door, firm steps belying her roiling stomach. She quickened her pace and walked back.

Randy's truck with Martin's Lumber Yard scrolled along the side in the company's maroon and grey lettering dominated the driveway indicating he was home. Her humorous side toyed with just opening the door and calling out "I'm home, honey." She had imagined and rehearsed a number of ways she would greet him—none of them easy; none of them stopped her tense muscles from clenching and her hands from shaking. Just do it, girl. You have come this far and there is no going back.

She paused with her finger trembling over the doorbell. "There's no backing down, girl. Just do it." Her voice quivered. Her breath hovered in a white cloud on the morning air drifting toward her finger as she pressed the button. A melody of chimes flooded her with memories—memories of answering it to guests, salespeople, neighbours and friends she had greeted time and time again. Her thoughts were interrupted by the knob turning, the door easing open and facing her was Randy. His eyes widened and his mouth froze open in the midst of an unuttered greeting. Moments later, he blinked.

"Stacey?"

"Hello, Randy."

"What ..."

"May I come in?"

Opening the door wider, Randy mumbled, "I have to go to work."

"Might want to call in sick—I doubt you will be productive after finding me on your doorstep." Stacey surprised herself at her self-assured, confident tone.

"Um, yes. Good idea."

Stacey watched her husband's awkward movements and backward glances. This was exactly the reaction she had hoped for—she wanted him off guard and confused. She needed to be in command of the situation, which was the reason she had not given any notice of her arrival.

"A cup of coffee would be welcomed. Do you still make a great brew?"

"What? Oh, yes—come into the kitchen."

As they walked along the narrow hall to the kitchen, Randy regained some composure, pushed his uncombed morning hair off his forehead and anger welled up. "Where the hell have you been? What do you mean bursting in here after seven years without a single word?"

"Some of it, I can explain."

"Stacey, you walked out of here for no apparent reason and just disappeared. You abandoned us."

"Yes, I did."

Hanging her designer pea jacket over the back of a familiar maple chair, she looked around her. Nothing had changed; everything was the same. The off-white melamine counters edged with wood trim were as familiar as her hands. The collection of cookie jars still marched across the top of the cupboards. The refrigerator was still cluttered with children's art—different art. She was surprised by how outdated and tired it all looked; the wallpaper featured tired grapevines. Randy, too, looked worn. Stacey noticed strands of grey through his thick, drab, blonde hair. Small lines of crow's feet made his eyes seem smaller, sadder.

Randy watched a woman he thought he knew intimately, who had been his wife for eleven years but lived that life for only four. He saw a stranger. She had an air of confidence and authority. The Stacey he knew was timid and yielding. This woman was smartly dressed, stood erect and seemed taller than he remembered.

"You didn't answer my question. What have you been doing for seven years?"

Stacey recognized the aggravated tone, the domineering male alpha growl.

"That's not what you asked, but get us a cup of coffee, sit down and I will tell you why I am here."

Randy filled two mugs; placed one before this person who had shared his bed—this person he did not know—this person who sat across the table from him. He noticed her perfectly manicured hands and that she still wore her wedding ring.

CHAPTER 1
Seven Years Earlier

Stacey wiped away the steam on the mirror after emerging from her quick, hot shower; the glass misted again and again. The ghosted image looked back from the bathroom mirror. Lacking in colour and expression, it reflected a twenty-two-year-old woman with tired eyes and long, mousy brown hair—straight and lifeless with weary looking eyes and tired hair. Rivulets ran down the glass beside the mirrored tears running down her face. Drawing in a big sigh, Stacey fought for the energy to get on with her day. Happy baby sounds drifting down the hall brought a weak smile to her face. Dougie, her chubby nine-month-old, was happily babbling away in the playpen surrounded by his toys. Her two older children, Lois, four, and Brent, three, went to nursery school three mornings a week, Monday, Wednesday and Friday. Today was Friday. Randy, her husband, would soon be home for lunch. She threw the wet towel into the laundry basket, pulled on a T-shirt, underpants and jeans, stepped into a pair of scruffy slippers, picked up the basket full of soiled laundry and headed for the laundry room. She blew Dougie a kiss as she passed him in the kitchen.

Sorting the darks from the lights, Stacey thought about her life, who she was and where she was. *I am still young, only twenty-two and already locked into a life of drudgery. That's what I get for getting knocked up at seventeen. I guess I should be grateful that Randy Martin even married me. He certainly makes it a point of telling me often enough. I don't know why I am so unhappy. Randy is a good provider. I have three beautiful children and a nice house. Isn't that what every woman strives for?*

Stacey started the washing machine and went into the kitchen. She smelled it before Dougie announced "poo." Sweeping him up, she nuzzled his cheek. "Off we go, stinky boy. You need a diaper change." Dougie squirmed as Stacey carried him to the bathroom and laid him on the change table. She carefully removed the soiled diaper and tossed it into the toilet. As she always did, she tickled him and sang as she wiped his bottom clean. Squeals of laughter filled the air as "Tar-ar-a-boom-de-ay" accompanied great lifts of his legs and noisy blows to his belly. Once he was changed, she stood him next to the toilet as she rinsed the dirty diaper and flushed away the contents. Dougie loved to watch this and always waved as he announced, "bye bye, poo."

She took her sweet-smelling boy to the den, turned on her favourite talk show, sat in the green plaid rocking chair and cradled Dougie. Before long, his little face went slack and he drifted off to sleep. Stacey blew stray blonde curls off his forehead, eased out of the chair, careful not to wake him and carried him to his bedroom. She laid him in his crib and sat his sock monkey in the corner to watch over him.

"Sweet dreams, my pet." Stacey blew a kiss toward her chubby cherub.

A deep sigh escaped as she turned and headed for the kitchen. When she and Randy painted the kitchen yellow, it was intended to cheer her up when she was working in it, but lately, it seemed to aggravate her. It seemed hostile somehow. Randy would be home shortly and he complained bitterly if his lunch was not ready. She glanced at her Timex and quickened her step. She would be hard pressed to have something prepared before he got home. Opening the refrigerator, she grabbed a carton of eggs, a tomato, a package of bacon, green onions and a block of cheese. Once the bacon was in the microwave, she set about making an omelette. She heard the side door open, then shut. Stacey imagined him removing his coat and hanging it on a back hall hook. As the egg mixture flowed into a waiting pan, every muscle tensed as Stacey heard his approaching steps.

"For Christ's sake, Stace—isn't my lunch ready? You'd think the least you could do was have it on the table when I get in. What is it you don't understand about lunch hour? It takes me fifteen minutes to get home and fifteen to get back. That means I only have a half hour to eat and relax for a bit. All you have to do is look after the house and kids, for God's sake."

Stacey piled his plate high with crisp bacon, well-buttered toast and a steaming omelette.

"What! Breakfast food again? You know, for once, I'd like to come home to a hamburger and a mound of hash browns."

"It's laundry day and Dougie needed some attention." Her excuse felt feeble. Her excuses always felt feeble.

Randy ignored Stacey and dug into his lunch. He picked up the TV remote and turned on the news. He didn't acknowledge the generous slice of jellyroll she put before him. He ate every scrap, grabbed the morning paper and left the kitchen. Stacey knew he would sit in the bathroom reading the sports pages and all the hockey news for the remainder of his lunchtime.

Randy was heading back through the kitchen when he demanded, "Get a sitter for tomorrow night. We're going to Phil and Roberta's to watch the hockey game." The door slammed and he was gone.

As Stacey cleared the table, she thought about what had just transpired. Shaking her head, she went to put a load of laundry in the dryer and one in the washer. "Mom, Mom, Mom" came persistently at her from Dougie's room. Her little man was wide awake and demanding release. As she headed for his bedroom, she heard a car pull into the driveway—Lois and Brent were home. She heaved Dougie onto her hip, strode to the front door and waved at Emily Fortain. They took turns car-pooling. This was Emily's week—her daughter Anne was the same age as Lois and they were 'bestest' friends.

"Time for a coffee?" Stacey called to Emily. Emily waved out the window of her eight-year-old, four-door, red sedan shaking her head.

"Can't today. Gotta take Dad to the dentist." Emily's father had lost his driver's licence after suffering a stroke; her mother had passed away two years before. Stacey admired how Emily coped with a young daughter, an upwardly mobile executive husband and a sick father. She was always upbeat and in control.

My life is so much easier, yet I can't seem to find the kind of joy Emily does. What am I doing wrong?

Stacey waved goodbye as Emily reversed down the driveway. She ruffled Brent's unruly mop of curls as she helped peel off his blue plastic raincoat. It had rained the entire week only letting up mid-morning. After hanging their coats, she gathered up their backpacks and ushered them into the kitchen.

"Hot dogs, I want hot dogs." Brent knew that Friday was hot dog day.

"Annie got a budgie bird and she is going to teach it to talk. Can I get a budgie?"

"We will have to talk to your father about that. Wouldn't you rather have a canary that sings?"

"No. I want it to talk." Lois, a miniature version of Stacey, with the exception that she had fair hair, eyed her mother with a longing and pleading expression.

"You know, having a pet comes with responsibility. You will have to keep the cage clean and make sure there's always food and water in its dishes. That's if Daddy allows you to have a bird." Stacey knew Randy would. He adored Lois and bowed to her every request. He was a devoted father. "Lois, you know that if you do convince Daddy to get a bird, it can't be just your bird. You have to share. It has to be the family's pet."

Lois thought about that and finally agreed with one condition. "But I get to teach it to talk." She pulled at her tight braids as if that settled the issue. Stacey looked at that small face set with determination and confidence—they may be look-alikes, but Lois was a distinct contrast to Stacey's timid personality.

The afternoon sped by including a brisk walk to the park, an hour's playtime and finishing the laundry. The children opted for a Muppets video and promised to keep an eye on Dougie, who had settled in his playpen, while Stacey made lasagna for supper.

Randy often stopped for a beer with his coworkers on Friday so supper would be late. When he came in, he went right into the family room, swung each of his children into the air and gave them a big hug. A promise to go to the pet store in the morning to see the budgies sent squeals of joy soaring sky high. Even Dougie, who had no idea what a budgie was, was loudly joining in.

"So did you get a sitter for tomorrow night?" Randy was tying a bib on Dougie.

"Didn't have time. I'll do that this evening."

"What do you mean you didn't have time? What do you think, kids? Mommy has all the time in the world. She stays at home doing nothing all day. You would think she could find time to do the one thing I asked."

"You didn't ask—you ordered," Stacey muttered to herself. The conversation around the table centred on the children and the plan to buy a bird, cage and food.

Dougie upended his bowl and lasagna spilled onto the floor.

"Gees, Stace, weren't you watching him?"

Stacey was at the stove getting Randy a second serving. Stacey cringed. His words were like sharp slaps to her face; she felt battered and bruised. If ever she could please Randy, it seemed she could never live up to his expectations. She was a failure in every sense of the word. Hardly sitting, Stacey attended to her family's dinner needs, serving, cleaning faces, removing dishes and bringing dessert.

Randy finished first and, without so much as an 'excuse me,' left the table shouting back, "Hurry up, kids. I'll be in the rec room."

Every evening, Randy played with the children while she tidied the kitchen. After the kitchen was clean, she routinely bathed Dougie while Randy snuggled in next to the older two to read them a story. All clean and in his pyjamas, Dougie faded as his mother crooned him to sleep.

"My life is the same every night except when we go to Phil and Roberta's. Even that scenario is the same—the guys each grab a beer and a plate full of snacks, then hunker down to watch the game. Roberta and I watch a movie on the bedroom television." Stacey tucked Dougie into bed, then went to the phone and arranged for a sitter.

Randy, carrying a 12-pack of Molson's in one hand, pushed the doorbell with his other when he and Stacey arrived at Phil and Roberta's two-storey Tudor style home. A shadow figure appeared on the other side of the frosted glass door and Roberta opened it with a welcoming smile. Roberta towered over Stacey. She was big boned, full figured and had a mop of unruly, dark hair that was untamable—she was a definite contrast to Stacey's diminutive stature. Stacey handed a plate of cheese and crackers to Roberta as she followed her friend into the house. No sooner had they reached the kitchen than the two men made off with the beer and snacks and headed for the TV. Roberta rolled her eyes and nodded in their direction as she guided Stacey into the master bedroom offering Stacey a glass of red wine.

Phil and Roberta had one son, Frank, who at nine-years-old was showing promise as a hockey player. Phil was one proud father and was forever extolling the possibility that he was raising a future NHL player. Oddly enough, Randy had no such expectations for his children. Stacey and he both agreed that whatever they turned out to be was fine with them.

"Phil is taking me to a resort for Valentine's Day. He arranged the whole weekend, got a sitter for Frankie and booked a romantic get-away. Are you and Randy doing anything special?"

"Not likely. Randy is not into special occasions."

"Oh, well, flowers and chocolates and a cozy evening at home works too."

That is not what happened. Stacey bought a bottle of wine, a Valentine card and a special sweater Randy wanted. After the children were in bed, she changed into her sexiest nightgown, lit a candle and joined Randy in the recreation room. She turned out the lights, turned off the TV, poured the wine and snuggled into Randy's arms. They made passionate love and Stacey forgave Randy for not buying her a gift or flowers.

The next time Emily drove the children to nursery school, she stopped in for coffee. "Honey, what is wrong? You seem so down."

"Nothing—well, it's just that I can never seem to get it right. I'm such a dunderhead—that's what Randy calls me. I feel like a failure. Nothing works. I think I am doing the right thing, but it never pleases Randy. This is not how I figured my life would be. When my dad had the accident and died, a part of me died too. He was my buddy, but more than that, we were a team. For months after he was killed, not a day went by that I wouldn't cry and wish him back. My poor mother had to go out to work to make ends meet and since I was in school, we seldom spent time together. She and I were never as close as my father and me, but we both were miserable when we lost him. Life was never the same again.

"You know I wasn't dumb in school—the only stupid thing I did was get pregnant at seventeen, so I never finished my studies. Randy was working already so we got married and here I am twenty-two-years-old and a mother to three kids. I just can't seem to cope with being a wife and mother, or so Randy points out all the time. I always wish I had been able to finish school and have had a career before rearing a family."

"Whoa, honey, life doesn't end just because you got married. You can still get your diploma. Go back to school. Get a job. Do whatever you like. Be somebody."

"Sure—like Randy would put up with that. His parents would never let up on how the lumberyard supported the family so well that Randy's mom was a stay-at-home mother and that is the way it should be. I read all the trade magazines Randy has delivered, so I think I am fairly up on the products and service offered by the business. I suggested that I could help part-time at the lumberyard doing the books and you should have heard Randy laugh. He told me, flat out, that I couldn't do that. He pointed out, yet again how I couldn't even manage the house the way he wanted. I thought I might be helpful by offering, thought I'd be able to contribute. Maybe I can't."

"That is ridiculous. Of course, you could. Honey, you have got to stop letting Randy railroad you. You know, Stace, I would bet my black ass that you could do this. Go back to school and do something to feel better about yourself."

Emily was insistent that Stacey could fit schooling into her life. She told her about night school classes designed to help people like Stacey who had, for one reason or another, dropped out of school. She wasn't alone. There were lots of people that had to leave school without graduating. Emily had spawned an idea—Stacey considered going to night school. In fact, the more she thought about it, it was the perfect answer. Getting her high school diploma would be fulfilling.

"If I proved I could get an education, maybe Randy would appreciate me more. If I could somehow go back to school, then I would be a better mother and be able to help my children with homework."

"Then you might look into it?"

"I just might."

Wednesday morning, Stacey dropped Annie, Lois and Brent at their school and left Dougie with her cousin, Edna. She had made an appointment with a career counsellor. Her meeting buoyed up her spirits as she learned that there was a wide range of courses she could take to get her high school diploma and college equivalency and they were also at convenient times. Stacey was jubilant at the thought of completing her education. Armed with brochures, she broached Randy with her plans.

"Are you out of your mind? There is no way you could do that. For God's sake, you can barely keep up with changing diapers." Randy chucked the brochures in the garbage and went to watch the game.

He's right. I was stupid to think I could do it, she thought to herself.

The next day, Stacey overheard Randy on the phone talking to Phil. "No, I didn't support her crazy ideas. What does she need to go back to school for? I make a good living and will inherit the family business, so it's not about money. All she has to do is manage the house and look after the kids. She doesn't need a degree for that. Don't you let Roberta put ideas in her head either." Randy's cautioning tone was because he knew Roberta was taking some computer courses.

How dare he discuss my idea with Phil. I just want to improve myself. The more Stacey thought about Randy's reaction to her wanting to go back to school, the angrier she got. She decided to mention it again.

"Randy, I think I'd like to take some courses and get my high school diploma. I have enough money from my inheritance to hire sitters…"

"You know, Stace, it's all about you. What about the kids and me? You're my wife and their mother—that should be enough. Besides, how would it look for my wife to be taking children's courses? You have to think about whose wife you are. Frankly, I don't want to hear about this again."

Stacey walked away and locked herself in the powder room. "Really, what does being a mother and a wife have to do with it? Nobody ever tells me how good I am at that. Surely, there should be some gratification. It's all work and no pay. Sure, the children are affectionate and their hugs are special. I adore my children and love my husband. I just don't feel I'm worth anything. I feel like a housemaid, a caregiver, a drudge. I hate my life. There, that's the truth. I hate my life. For all the thanks I get, I could be anybody—at least hired help gets paid." Stacey was brushing her hair and talking to herself in the bathroom mirror.

The following week, Emily listened to Stacey vent about how she felt.

"I just feel so down about everything. I know I am being ridiculous, but I can't seem to get out of the doldrums. It's more than feeling sorry for myself. I simply have to force myself to get through the day." Once spoken and shared, Stacey knew it was true.

"You know, honey, the problem with you is you really lack self-esteem. I've known you for years and I swear you think less and less of yourself every day. I shouldn't be saying this, but you need to get a grip on things. Everyone needs to feel good about what and who they are. The way you are going is self-destructive—you are heading into the depression zone. You need to stand up to Randy and make him stop making you feel like a lowlife. You're not stupid. You're smart. Remember who got the highest marks in math at school? That was you, girl. That's not being stupid."

"Yes, but that was years ago. I've changed."

"No, you haven't. Stacey, can I ask you something?"

"Sure—shoot."

"Frankly, if I were in your position, I would pack up the kids and leave. Have you ever thought of that? Randy has no idea how to be a husband and friend. You need that. You are still young. It is not too late to start over."

"Em, that is impossible. Randy and his family would take the kids. They have all the power and resources to do that. I have no education, no job and no way to support the children. Randy would take control and deny me access. I'm trapped. Besides, how could I leave? I love Randy."

"Sometimes, love isn't enough. A marriage is a partnership with equal support for each other."

"Randy is a good father and provider."

"Well, I think he is abusive and you deserve better."

"Oh, no, Randy would never hit me."

"Abuse does not have to be physical—all those demeaning remarks are pure and simple mental abuse. Stacey, he *is* intimidating you. At the risk of our friendship, I need to say something. In my opinion, Randy married you to avoid gossip and to protect his family's name. He took advantage of you. You were seventeen, heartbroken over your father's death and dealing with a mother who was dying of terminal cancer. He was five years older than you, from a wealthy family and good looking. You fell for him but couldn't see the chaff for the grain."

"Emily, that is not true. Randy loves me."

Later that week, Stacey opened the oven to check on supper. Smells filled the kitchen with spicy, savoury flavours. When Randy came home, he looked over her shoulder, peered into the door, then turned to the children.

"Hey, what's wrong with your mom tonight? She sulking because she's too stupid to remember that tonight is supposed to be spaghetti night?'

"Randy, I just thought a change would be nice."

"No, a change is not nice. A change is stupid. Isn't that right, kids?"

"I wanted to try this recipe for chicken-pot-pie…"

"On spaghetti night!"

If he had run over her with a truck, Randy could not have hurt her more. Stacey heated some leftover spaghetti and slapped it on Randy's plate—could she never do anything right for this man?

After the children were in bed, Stacey put on her jacket.

"Where are you going?"

"I need to go for a walk."

Somewhere deep inside her, a knot twisted and gripped her intestines. All the bright colours of the world were cloaked in a mass of grey matter and each breath she took was forced and tight. She needed to get out of the house. She was suffocating. Generally, she cowed and just accepted her place in the household, but the events of the past few weeks festered and constantly crept into her thoughts. Randy was her love, her reason to be, but he didn't complete her—he undermined her in every way. That was the problem—Em was right. Randy intimidated her. He never told her he loved her.

She found herself striding down the street muttering. "How will I ever find what I'm capable of if I don't try? How will I ever be happy? Right now, I feel beaten, defeated. I don't know how to stand up to Randy."

The evening turned from dusk to dark, softening the edges of night. As Stacey quickened her pace along the orderly subdivision with uniform patches of green grass, the velvet night wrapped itself around her, soothing her shattered nerves. A gentle breeze whispered through her mass of lank hair and swept away some of the feeling of doom. She drew her jacket tight around her and hunched her shoulders as if to ward off the misery she felt. To others, her lifestyle would be envied. Randy's father owned one of the largest lumberyards in Ottawa and when she and Randy were married, he bought them a modern two-storey home at the end of a cul-de-sac in a bustling subdivision in a highly desirable neighbourhood. Right now, she was putting distance between herself, that house and her husband. The night air sharpened and cleared her mind and a plan began to form— a drastic plan. She needed to change her life or there was no reason to continue, no reason to want to live.

"Oh, my God! How can I even be contemplating suicide? But if things don't change, I'm apt to do something drastic. I am no longer a fit mother and can never measure up as a wife. What if I do something dreadful in front of the children? Oh my God, I think I am losing my mind. I need to change my life," Stacey muttered to herself as she shuffled along the street.

When she returned home, Randy shouted from the family room, "Hey, dunderhead, don't forget that tomorrow night is hamburger and fries night—I don't want to come home after a hard day's work to find some fancy-dancy recipe you think you want to try on us."

In the following days, Stacey noticed that she started to shake and beads of perspiration broke out on her forehead when Randy was due home. Instead of looking forward to him coming as she should, she dreaded it. She thought more and more about how he degraded her to the children. "This is a destructive situation. There's no way I can go on like this—I need a break. I need to get away. I need to regroup and prove to myself that I can cope, that I am not worthless. I need to be able to breathe."

The internet became her source of information. Stacey searched and searched for cases of verbal abuse to try to find an answer to her dilemma. She read about a number of cases where women became submissive and depressed. She learned of disastrous outcomes, but she also found women who took charge and changed their lives. None of them did it without making sacrifices and tough decisions. Randy's constant haranguing cut deep and hurt to the point that Stacey started to throw up before he was due home. Her nerves were frayed to the breaking point. Somewhere deep inside her, Stacey knew there was only one way she could change her life. She wasn't sure she had the strength or will to carry it out.

Three weeks later, she got up on a Saturday morning, fed the children and settled them in front of the television to watch a purple Barney. After giving each one hugs and kisses, she stood in the doorway taking in the scene. Lois in her Dora pyjamas, Brent in Superman ones and Dougie in his teddy bear ones. A picture to remember. She then wakened Randy—it was his day off work. He was to be in charge of the children while she and

Emily helped at the school, or that is what she told him. Instead, hidden in her car was a packed suitcase—she was leaving. She left a note in Randy's beer fridge that she knew he would not find until late in the afternoon. As soon as Dougie was down for his nap, and the other two were busy, he would grab a beer before putting on the hockey game—that would be when he would find it and learn where she really was—gone.

Randy,

I love you and the children but cannot continue to live like this. The car is at the airport in the employee parking lot at the back. You can pick it up. You will find the extra set of keys in the desk drawer. I will not be back until I am ready—it could be months. Kiss the children for me.

Stacey

Chapter 2

I can't believe I am doing this. Where did I find the nerve? I could never find the courage to confront Randy and explain to him how cruel he was with his disparaging remarks, yet here I am running away from my home and my children. I am so frightened that I am making the biggest mistake of my life, but what else can I do? I know Randy is a good provider and a wonderful father, but he makes me feel so inept and inadequate. He ridicules and defeats me to the point that I don't want to continue my life as it is. My nerves are so frayed — twice I've stood in the bathroom holding a razor contemplating slicing my wrists. Yet I didn't. Every time I think about leaving my babies permanently, I can't do it. Right now, I want to turn around and forget this whole idea, but on the other hand, getting away for a short period might give me time to rethink how to deal with Randy. If I turn around now, I know Randy will never let me forget that I left. He won't see the reason as valid. He won't understand my need to improve myself in order to be a better wife and mother. He will taunt me forever.

I need to learn to stand up for myself. I need to find some way to achieve some success so I can take a little pride in myself, or find out Randy is right and I am worthless. If that is the case, I will return and take his demeaning comments as deserved. At least, I will have a nice home and be near my children. But I can't accept that I cannot find something that will prove I am not as stupid as Randy thinks I am. When I left the car at the airport and caught the bus downtown, I could hardly breathe. The pressure in my head scared me. But I took two super strength Aspirin and continued with the plan.

Chapter 3

Stacey knew decidedly that Randy was possessive and that he would go to any length to drag her home. He and his father would consider the fact that she left to be a direct personal affront and a threat to their status in the community. They would use every means possible to track her down. Randy would check every flight to find her destination. He would consider her escape an act of defiance and she knew that to his way of thinking, no wife of his was going to get away with that kind of stunt. Stacey took all this into consideration when she planned her get-away. She was like a fugitive running for her life.

She boarded the transit bus at the airport terminal for downtown Ottawa, got off at The Lord Elgin hotel and walked to the bus stop pulling her suitcase behind her. She paid cash for a ticket to Toronto. All her possessions were packed into one large suitcase and she carried her laptop computer. When she reached Toronto, she hailed a cab and got out at Union Station where she caught the train to Sudbury.

All her determination and resolve started to dissolve. Stacey's inner voice was trying to convince her that her decision was the right one, but the doubts crawled over her skin like a crowd of fleas, biting, biting. She sank lower and lower into her seat, her thoughts crowding her into the corners.

Five hours later, after sitting numbly unaware of the sights and smells around her, she was nearing Sudbury. For some reason, the seat beside her remained vacant, a good sign. The train slowed as it reached Sudbury. The rhythmic thrum of the wheels slowed, then squealed as the brakes caught as it pulled into the terminal. She steeled herself to disembark and watch for a sign that said 'Lois.' She had created a new person and was now

Lois Brenton-Douglas. She had used her children's names to become her new self. She needed to completely disappear for a while—she couldn't go back until she felt she was ready. She needed to become self-assured or face the reality that Randy was right. The only way she could do this was to resign herself to being a new person, a person different from Stacey Martin. She felt the only way she stood a chance to succeed was with a total identity change, so, for now, she was Lois—Lois Brenton-Douglas.

Using Craigslist, she had applied for a job as a live-in nanny in Sudbury, far enough away from Ottawa where she could be that new person. Stacey Martin had sent a glowing reference email. She was interviewed by phone and she was hired. Stacey had opened a new email address, goneaway@gmail.com, for fear of being tracked, and cancelled her other one. She was going underground and didn't intend to surface until she was rid of the fears and trials of life with Randy, or until she realized it was futile and returned like a whipped dog.

Stacey, now Lois, bent and looked out each window as she eased up the aisle to the exit door of her car holding her hand to her forehead to shield her eyes from the glaring setting sun. That was when she realized she was still wearing her wedding bands. She stopped and pulled them off and shoved them into the pocket of her slacks. Once again, she watched out each window as she walked up the aisle. She was looking for someone holding a sign; this would be her employer.

As the passengers in front of her stepped from the train, she saw the sign, 'Lois's held high by a tall, broad-shouldered man. Stacey, now Lois, experienced a moment of terror, of regret. What had she done? She had left her darling children and a responsible husband and changed herself into another being. She knew if she turned back now, there would be no forgiveness and Randy would use it as a constant reminder of how irresponsible and scatterbrained she was. She had put herself in a position with no choice but to move forward—she was trapped—this time a different trap than living with Randy. There was no turning back now. She straightened her back and stepped off the train.

Nodding her head to the porter as he indicated her suitcase, she took a deep breath, stepped to the pavement and headed toward the 'Lois's sign wheeling her case.

"Mr. French? I'm St..er.. Lois."

The sign came down and two large hands completely covered her outstretched one. A smile beamed as he looked into her eyes. The warmth in their depth welcomed her without words. He reached for her suitcase.

"Norm—call me Norm. Helen and I are so glad you accepted our offer."

His British accent was cultured and mellow. Lois had spoken to Helen by phone but not Norm. Helen had no trace of an accent, so she assumed Helen had met and married a Brit. She noticed Norm's buff jacket was of the softest leather and he wore neatly pressed navy chinos. The smile that spread across his broad face eased some of her tension, but waves of nausea brought bile to her throat. Swallowing repeatedly, she followed this large man.

"The car is right over there." Norm was pointing to a maroon SUV in the parking lot as he strode with a firm grip on her suitcase. Lois noted two child seats firmly anchored in the rear. "This will be the car you will be driving. Are you okay with an SUV?"

"Yes, I.. er.. Stacey had one." It felt weird, yet, somehow adventurous to be speaking of herself in the third person. She had embarked on a new life and become someone different. It was going to take some getting used to and carrying it out was her greatest concern. She had become the lead character in a play, a play about a new person and a new way of life. The drama was happening, and the lead player had her parts to play.

"Helen has planned a bit of a welcoming party, mostly to get the children excited about your arrival. She thought it was a good way to get them to accept you easily. Hope you don't mind. I know you must be weary after travelling all this w

"No, I think that's a great idea and frankly, ...
after sitting for so many hours. Have Barby an ...
nanny before?"

"No. And you will find Helen a little reticent about someone else caring for her children. She has been a stay-at-home mom, but when we moved to Sudbury last year, she decided she wanted to get back into the workforce. She's an engineer, a specialist in environmental issues. Sudbury has so many opportunities for her talents and the offers kept coming in. She probably told you I own the local Independent Grocers, so I work long hours. Helen needed something beyond the four walls of home—something more stimulating."

"I can sure relate to that. And you don't mind her going back to work?"

"Hell no, taking care of a household is just not fulfilling enough for her. One needs to explore all the paths life offers. She is a wonderful wife and mother, but she is also an experienced engineer. It's all about balancing the two. And that's where you come in. She feels she has been lucky to have had the three years at home, but now she is ready to tackle a new job, with your help, of course."

Lois thought about the narrow life she led as Stacey and how much better it would have been if Randy held the same views as Norm. She could be with her children, enjoy being Randy's wife and be a complete person.

"The train station is in Sudbury Junction, ten kilometres from Sudbury but convenient for us as we live this side of the city in a fairly new subdivision called Hidden Ridge. We are minutes from home." Norm turned the vehicle onto a main highway and eased into traffic.

"Barby is a caution. She will talk your head off and her little mind is always at full speed—a duplicate of her mother. Grant is quieter but a deep thinker. He is the follower and Barby the

er. They are twins but very different. Helen and I are so
essed to have them. They are such a joy. I don't mean to say that
they are perfect. Like all children, they have their quarrels and
little tempers, but that is to be expected. We respect their
differences but fall prey to displaying that they are twins and do
dress them in matching outfits. It helps that they are opposite
sexes." Ten minutes later, Lois had heard all about the twins,
Helen and her experience as an engineer and Norm's store. She
was glad she did not have to answer questions about her life and
just listened as Norm talked endlessly.

The car pulled off the main road into a new subdivision and
Lois stared at the upscale homes. The area was definitely new
with large houses on good-sized lots. Newly planted trees
softened the starkness of the sidewalks giving the street a false
settled look, but it was evident that the subdivision was still
growing and under construction. Norm turned into a long
driveway leading up to a large, two-storey, stone-fronted house,
with a deep veranda spanning the entire width of the front. The
waning sun cast a rosy glow over the sky and the stone turned a
soft pink. The smell of freshly mown grass wafted through the
car window. As the SUV drew closer, she saw the front door open
and a tall, slim woman and two children stepped out. The small
boy clung to Helen's knee and an equally small girl stood off to
the side sucking her thumb. The twins were three years old and,
according to a previous telephone conversation, very, very
attached to each other. Both children took after their father with
shocks of thick, dark hair and broad, ruddy faces. Waves of
emotions swept through Lois—she already missed her own
children with a fierceness that was choking her. What had she
done? How was she going to be able to do this? Being a nanny
was a stepping-stone, but each and every day, she would be
reminded of her own family. She was afraid she was going to
throw up. The car stopped and she automatically opened the door
and stepped out on legs that almost failed her. Lois bent over,

and took a deep breath, inhaling deeply so she wouldn't faint.

"Are you all right?" Norm held Lois under her elbow to steady her.

"Fine, I'm fine, just a little light-headed from too much travel. I will be okay in a few minutes. I need to breathe some of this clear northern air."

Norm carried her suitcase in one hand and took charge of Lois's laptop as he guided her forward. Helen stepped down and grasped her hand. "Welcome to your new family. I hope Norm didn't talk your ear off on the drive in—he is an awful gabfest." Stacey/Lois noted that this was said with affection, not criticism.

Turning away, Helen herded her son and daughter in front of her. "Barby, Grant, say hello to Lois. She is going to be your new, very best friend."

Lois liked that approach and knelt to their level and smiled at each one. "I'm very pleased to be your new, special friend. Do you want to hear all about my ride here on a big noisy train?"

Without hesitation, that invitation led each twin to grasp one of Lois's hands and steal her away from their parents. Lois led them to the bottom step and sat down with a child on each side of her. The vertigo was still making her a little dizzy so she needed to sit and used the moment as an excuse so she could recover. Norm and Helen shared a glance of approval.

She had told the Frenches that she wanted to continue her education and they had helped research the courses available through the adult training programs at the local college, Cambrian College. Helen would be home most evenings, so Lois would be free to attend school. Her duties included looking after the children, doing laundry, general tidying and preparing meals. A housekeeper came in weekly to do the housework and Norm looked after the outdoors.

The twins listened to the animated story about Lois's travels with lots of questions.

"Did the engineer blow the whistle?"

"Many times—whenever it was going to cross a road."

"Did you walk around or did you sit still the whole time?"

"I only got up once to use the bathroom."

"There is a bathroom on a train?"

Helen walked over and spoke to her children. "Remember we planned a special—"

Barby jumped up and pulled Lois by the hand. "Come and see. Come and see."

Helen's welcome party was a huge success with a dinner of macaroni and cheese; lots of festive balloons decorated the dining room table. Of course, there was cake and Norm made toasts with lemonade glasses raised high. The twins, tired after being allowed to stay up beyond their usual bedtime, were tucked into bed with kisses all around. Stacey, now Lois, was accepted by the children as their new best friend. The day had been physically and mentally trying, so she excused herself early to go to her room. The bright, airy room was painted in three tones of buttercup yellow blending to deep gold that picked up the tones of the duvet cover splashed with daffodils and daisies. The cheeriness of the room failed to lift her spirits as she thought about her actions and the frightening direction she had taken. Stacey faltered and decided to renege on her arrangement wanting desperately to return to Ottawa. She felt vacant; she could feel her children—she knew they would be crying because she was gone. Her own eyes were spilling tears. There was no way she could continue with this charade. Then she imagined Randy's voice yelling, "What a crazy, dumb thing to do. You are really one stupid dunderhead." She imagined him condemning her and declaring her an unfit mother and demanding she leave. She had left but on her terms. Lois wiped her eyes and blew her nose, looked at the back of the closed door directly across from the twin's bedroom, stood up and resolved to carry on with her new life—to find out that she was far from being a dunderhead.

Downstairs, Helen and Norm cuddled together in the

recreation room watching the late news. Helen shoved aside the magazines scattered across the deep tan leather sofa, drew her knees to her chest and laid her head across Norm's legs.

Norm twisted her mass of shoulder-length, ash-blonde hair. "What do you think? Will you be able to leave the twins with Lois and totally place your trust in her ability to look after our family?"

"It is as if I am abandoning them. What kind of mother abandons her children? Oh, Norm, this is so hard, but I honestly feel that we made the right choice, not only in my decision to go back to work but in choosing Lois. I must say, I was jealous when the twins attached themselves to her and followed her around like they were stricken with puppy love. Well, I will have to get over that, won't I?"

"She seems so reticent, so withdrawn. I asked her a few questions about herself and got limited answers."

"Norm, you know she confided that she has a troubled past. We need to give her space and let her resolve the issues she left."

"Yes, I know, but wouldn't talking about them help?"

"Not everyone wants to share their problems. Let's give her support and let her know we are here if she decides to confide in us. Let's take her at face value, make her feel welcome and valued."

Chapter 4

What delightful people! Helen and Norm are amazing, friendly and welcoming and the children are so sweet. They seem to appreciate my efforts, but they are not my children and this is not my home. I miss my babies so much. Oh, where are the tissues? I can't stop crying. Randy is right—I am a dunderhead. I have to tell Helen and Norm that I can't stay. What will I tell Randy? Will he throw me out and demand a divorce? Yes, he will and he will take the children—I know he will. His parents will use every contact and provide gobs of money to legally steal my children. I doubt I would even be allowed access. Oh, how I wish Randy were more like Norm and supportive of me.

I've got myself into this tangled mess and am caught in it like a fly in a spider's web. I am scared to death to return and terrified of staying and of what lies ahead. Why did I ever think I could pull this off? I need to get real and either do this or not. I need to be Lois absolutely and completely. I made it this far, so regardless of the outcome, I need to try. And I need to improve myself. Then maybe, maybe, I can return with some self-confidence and explain to Randy why I left. If I feel better about myself, then I am less likely to be intimidated by his remarks. There needs to be a frank discussion as to why I took this drastic step. I have to continue this charade—I have to try. Lordy, this is so much harder than I thought it would be.

Chapter 5

The first month in Sudbury was a mixture of finding her way around and getting through the hours of despair and anxiety. Missing her family had her reaching for the phone time after time, but she always caught herself knowing the only choice now was moving forward. Days blended into weeks and being Lois came easier. Filling out the forms for registering at school, she almost blew her cover as she was not concentrating on being Lois, and almost wrote her name as Stacey Martin. She got around the issue of providing documentation by claiming she had lost her wallet and the replacements hadn't arrived yet. She hoped it would not be requested again.

Often, when least expected, the faces of her children flared up in front of her. Her heart would skip a beat and tears brimmed to the surface. She found that when the twins did something that Brent or Lois had done, her stomach muscles clenched and it was all she could do not to scream. Every minute of every day, she thought about her children and had to convince herself all over again why she had walked away. It was far from easy. Several times when Helen called her, she didn't respond. Then the realization that she was Lois made her blood race to her head, making her dizzy and disoriented. It was hard work being another person, emotionally draining and tough—very tough.

Terrified that her children would forget her, she cried herself to sleep night after night. But each morning, she rose with new resolve and was determined to finish what she started. Within a few weeks, she fell into a rhythm and pattern; being Lois became routine and her role easier. By the third week of September, her days were full. Going to school had reawakened her desire for learning and she found she was good at most subjects—not a dunderhead after all. She decided that once she completed her high school, she would consider enrolling in the community college and take a business course. If not in Ottawa, it meant she would be away for two years—two long years. However, she hoped she would be strong enough to face up to Randy and return at the end of June.

Only one person knew how to contact her and it was through email. She had no idea that Stacey was now Lois or where she lived and worked. That way Stacey could not be found, but she needed to know her family was okay. She was thankful she had Emily and had, at least, regular updates on her children. Emily even emailed pictures when she could manage to take them. She was the only one who had Stacey's new email address. Stacey sent birthday and Christmas parcels through mail order, so Randy had no idea where the parcels came from. Stacey needed Randy to know that she was still alive, still his wife, and still mother of their children. She knew that Randy would pester Edna, her cousin, and Rachel, her friend, but he did not know Emily. She was sure he would not even consider her as anyone other than a person who drove the children to school. Emily told Stacey that Randy had hired a nanny/housekeeper who drove them, so there was no need for contact with Emily at all. She called Emily once a month to see how the children were doing. Emily always made it a point to discreetly question Lois about Brent and Dougie—Lois and Annie were still *bestest* friends. Every time she called, Lois almost quit her job and returned to being Stacey but somehow managed to talk herself out of it and remain Lois. She was beginning to feel some pride in her schoolwork and her fondness for Barby and Grant made the situation tolerable—they were happy children, healthy and full of energy. During the day, there was little time to do anything but tend to her duties. The hours turned into days, the days into weeks. She was so engrossed in becoming Lois that sometimes hours went by without her thinking about her life before

Sudbury. She was Lois, nanny to Barby and Grant.

Helen and Norm accepted Lois into their fold more than pleased at how everyone blended and became used to each other. The children waved 'goodbye' to their parents each morning without creating a fuss and within days adjusted to the new routine. Helen praised Lois in a way that Randy had never done and Norm expressed his appreciation whenever she tried new recipes. He always asked what she needed from the store, so Lois soon learned to plan the meals ahead so she had fresh ingredients. She decided to enroll in a cooking class on Saturday mornings. She had seen one posted on the school bulletin board.

Lois's marks at school were exemplary. Her schedule worked so well that her inner voice affirmed it was meant to be. She excelled in math and held her own in communications. The years away from the classroom were not a problem because all the students were adults that had returned to school for whatever reasons they had. Life fell into a routine that was comfortable and rewarding. Life in Ottawa drifted farther away.

Helen and Norm were told that Lois left Ottawa to escape an abusive relationship. She told them she had never been a friend, only an employee of Stacey's so was not interested in staying in contact. They accepted her reasons without question, so Stacey was able to easily slip into the identity of Lois. Emily had told her that there was gossip about her disappearance. Some said that she had run off with a man. In fact, that seemed to be the general consensus—the talk was not kind to Stacey. She heard that Randy was hiring a private detective to find her. This alerted Stacey, now Lois, to the fact that the only way she could avoid being found was to officially change her identity and her name. She gave this considerable thought. She knew that if she did not legally change her name, she was in jeopardy of her true identity being discovered—this made her uncomfortable and nervous. There were several problems she had to deal with, the main one being that her driver's licence was for Stacey Martin. Legally changing her name was a step she was reluctant to take, but it seemed the only solution—if she was going to be Lois, she needed to be Lois. She could always change it back when she returned to Ottawa.

After making discreet inquiries through the school counsellor, she hired a lawyer, Sam Cody, who understood that her identity was not to be revealed under any circumstances. He, too, believed she was escaping an abusive relationship and needed to be protected. In many ways, it was true—verbal abuse can be as debilitating as physical abuse, just not a visible injury.

"Lois, have you ever been fingerprinted?"

"No, not that I know of. Why?"

"If we do that now, and there is ever a search, it will come up as Lois Brenton-Douglas. It is just an extra precaution that I suggest you take."

Within four months, the legal process was complete and she was officially Lois Brenton-Douglas with all the proper documents, including a birth certificate and passport. Her personal banking account was transferred to a numbered company (the lawyer's) and then deposited into a new account under Lois's name. The lawyer was even able to get a new driver's licence immediately. It was the single document that she had feared would give her away if Norm or Helen had ever asked to see it—they hadn't. She had never had a police check for her job as a nanny and decided that having it on file was a good idea, at the same time she had her fingerprints registered. She felt like a new person—she was a new person. Stacey Martin was now officially Lois Brenton-Douglas, newly minted.

"Lois, I need to tell you that I am moving to Toronto. I will take your files with me for confidentiality. Should you need to reach me, I will keep the same email." Sam Cody shook Lois's hand. "I am so glad I was able to resolve your concerns so quickly. I do hope the rest of your life, your new life is safe, satisfying and successful."

The Frenches looked on her as a member of their family and the daily routine became quite normal. Helen accepted some work assignments that required travelling so Lois became the other mom. Or, that is what Norm called her instead of the children's nanny. The children called her by her name, Lois. The neighbours waved when she was out with the twins—the family and neighbourhood accepted her. She was transformed into a new world and new life.

One neighbour, Francis, stopped by one morning in mid-October with her daughter Betsy. Wearing a thick, knitted throw over a stylish maroon sweat suit, Francis flashed a winning smile, her whitened teeth stark against her Asian skin. Betsy had the same black hair as her mother and wore a jean jacket undone to reveal a Winnie The Pooh T-shirt.

"Hi. We live at the end of the block. I see you with the twins at swimming. Betsy is in the group ahead of them—we are usually leaving the pool as you are settling into your seat. I thought you might like to meet one of your neighbours. I'm Francis and this is Betsy." One hand was extended; the other held a plate of freshly baked brownies.

Francis and Lois bonded immediately and became close friends, finding they liked the same movies and both loved to cook. Lois could not help but chastise herself about how easily her new life fell into a comfortable pattern. She had her own room; she had a close friend, she was attending school and Sudbury became as familiar to her as Ottawa. When she drove downtown, she returned to what she thought as 'going home.' "In many ways, this is too easy—I even go hours without thinking about my former life. Does this mean I am a bad person when what I want to do is make myself a better person?" She often talked to herself when she was in the car alone.

She had not altered her appearance. Her long straight hair still sported bangs that drew a line above her thick arched eyebrows. She still wore casual slacks and t-shirts. Then, quite by chance, she caught sight of former neighbours from Ottawa at a shopping mall. She was easing the car into a parking spot when she saw them opening the entrance doors. Her breath caught and she realized that she was so easily recognizable. Her immediate reaction was to slide down in her seat to hide. That is when the realization hit her that it was not enough to move away and change her name. She was going to have to look different too. Otherwise, she risked being seen and recognized.

She booked an appointment at a salon that Francis recommended. She had her lank, stringy hair cut in layers, got a soft perm, had it restyled and added highlights to give it an overall lighter look. The contrast, from having always worn her hair long or pulled into a severe ponytail, was a remarkable change with curls that softly hugged her cheeks. Her eyebrows were plucked to a fine line that accented her blue eyes and gave them a lift. The image the mirror reflected was hardly recognizable, especially since the bangs that had been a part of her look since grade school were gone. She left the salon and headed right to a fashionable clothing store, and by the time she got home, she was loaded with parcels containing a new wardrobe and a collection of cosmetics.

"Holy cow! Lois, you look incredible. I hardly knew you. I am going to have to put a leash on Norm."

Helen's comments were exactly what Lois needed. The difference *was* remarkable. She was still the same but different, almost reborn. She had changed enough that anyone seeing her would not think she was Stacey. Her new look gave her such confidence that her posture changed, she moved in a commanding way and her voice took on a firm tone.

The twins made her tell them every detail of the transformation.

"Ouch! They just pulled out the hair in your eyebrows?"

Lois's laugh echoed off the walls as she answered question after question. It was the first spontaneous laugh since long before she left Ottawa. A fashion show was demanded and her transformation was turned into a celebration. Grant had to be assured that she would still look that way when he woke up the next day. Norm's long low whistle was the grand finale to celebrate the new Lois.

"You know, Lois, you have been with us for five months and I see a remarkable difference in you. I hope it's because you are happy here. I know your circumstances for leaving Ottawa were difficult and I want you to know that you are safe here." Norm reached for another sausage to add to his plate of pancakes.

"Sometimes, I *am* afraid. There are things I seriously miss about my life in Ottawa, but you and Helen have made me feel so worthwhile, valued and, yes, safe. Thank you for that."

Norm glanced up. "The thing is, Lois, you are worthwhile and valuable, as a matter of fact. Because of you, the house runs smoothly and Helen is upwardly mobile in her job. Barby and Grant adore you and both Helen and I are so proud of your progress at school. Please, let us know if there is anything that is a problem. We want you to feel you are a member of the family, always."

That night, Lois cried herself to sleep again. It was too soon to return to Ottawa, but she was desperate to see her children. Her greatest consolation was that she knew Randy would make sure their life was the best he could make it under the circumstances. Even though he was a lousy husband, he was a great father. She knew if she went back, the emotional abuse would begin again probably more-so since she *now* gave him cause. She knew she was not yet confident enough to stand up for herself. She knew she would cower and become, yet again, insecure, miserable and depressed. And she knew if she saw her children, she would never be able to leave again. She knew she needed to be proud of who she was—to have that much-needed self-confidence. She wanted her children to be proud of their mother—she needed to be proud of herself. The months had flown by—the next few seemed much more doable than when she first arrived in Sudbury. She consoled herself, knowing she had made progress as Lois, but she was not convinced that she would feel the same as Stacey. The few months she expected to stay were her hope of being stronger and more self-assured.

She had left Ottawa mid-August and now as March came in like a lamb, spring was in the air. Lois thought about her garden and knew her tulips would be poking their heads through the moist, dark soil.

"Barby, Grant, let's see if any flowers are up."

Lois held each of the twin's hands as they walked down the front steps. She had dressed them in Wrangler denim jeans and Pokémon t-shirts. Dew laying heavy on the grass made their rubber boots slick with moisture. She directed the twins to a protected portion of the front garden where a wee bit of green poked through the earth. She showed the twins and explained that the little green shoots would get bigger and bigger every day and within a few weeks turn into flowers. "They are tulips."

Two excited children met their mother when she came home. "Come see, come see—we have two lips."

"Of course, you have two lips. You have always had two lips."

Lois was laughing at the puzzled expression on Helen's face as she clomped out in her steel-toed work boots and brown coveralls a twin grasping each hand. The children pulled her outside and to the garden.

"Oh, tulips, of course, how silly of me. Spring is coming and Daddy has lots of pretty flowers in the gardens."

"They grewed, they grewed." Grant turned to Lois. "They grewed."

"Yes, they did."

Chapter 6

Watching the twins with their mother makes me so homesick. I remember showing Lois each flower as it poked its tip through the soil every spring. She was enthralled with how each grew. Even at four, she was learning to identify the different plants by their leaves. I can hear her scolding the weeds when she saw them and would pull them from the ground, always asking me first if she was right. I can hear her little voice: " You nasty thing, sneaking in and stealing the food the beautiful flowers will need to bloom. I don't like you."

I am not sorry I left Ottawa, but I struggle each day being away from my dear children. I fight constantly feeling distressed and depressed from missing my children, my home and my husband. The schoolyear is drawing to a close. I am not sure I am ready to face Randy yet, but I do know that I do feel better about myself. I know I am capable and not a complete dunderhead as Randy would have me believe. Helen and Norm have made me realize that I do know how to manage a household—they are so quick to praise all the things that Randy criticized. How I will convince Randy that I am capable and his life is better because of me, I have no idea. Right now, I doubt I can, but I have come a long way in nine months, so maybe I will be that much better in another three. Oh, it will be so good to hold my babies. I want to return to being a mom and help them learn things, to teach them as I am now teaching Barby and Grant. There is no way the twins are a substitute for my three.

Chapter 7

"Lois, I need to talk to you." Helen led the way through the house with her brisk, long stride and ushered the twins into the den. They had returned from an evening drive by the lake. "Children, get a book and I will be with you in a minute. Lois, come into the kitchen." Helen's long legs were clad in black designer boot jeans topped by a coral bulky-knit sweater.

Lois felt her stomach clench and her throat constrict making breathing difficult. Had she done something wrong, something for which Randy would have chastised her? She started biting her bottom lip as she followed Helen.

Helen poured each of them a glass of lemonade and set out some crackers and cheese. "I need to ask a big favour. Norm and I have been talking about taking a holiday this summer. We are thinking of going to Greece. We have found a house on the Mediterranean. The thing is, Norm and I will want to take in some of the culture and to take advantage of tours offered for day trips. Museums and art galleries are not three-year-old stuff and we definitely want to take the children with us. Are you able to go? It would just be the best thing for the twins if they had someone they knew and trusted with them. It would free up Norm and I. We could have family time and adult time."

Lois was too shocked to reply. She stared at Helen with eyes wide, holding her full glass frozen at her lips.

"All expenses paid, of course." Helen waited expectantly. Her request seemed to hang in the air for what seemed like forever.

Suddenly, a huge smile exploded on Lois's face. "I can't believe it! Greece, oh my goodness, of course, I will go. I'd love to go. Oh my goodness, you're not kidding me, are you? I thought you were going to fire me."

Helen laughed at Lois's enthusiastic response and gave her a big hug; she assured her the offer was genuine and the last thing she would consider would be firing her.

"We are planning on going the second week of July and returning the first week of August in time for the twin's birthday. My mother is flying in from Victoria for the week. Do you want to take your holidays at that time?"

Lois had not considered that she would even still be in Sudbury over the summer—it meant she would be away from Ottawa for a full year. She had not even given holiday time a thought. She paled and gulped for air. Helen saw the sudden change, recognized Lois's fear and quickly made a suggestion.

"Here's a thought. I know Ottawa is out of the question. Norm and I often rented a cottage on Manitoulin Island before the twins were born. It is very beautiful and peaceful there—a great get-away—wonderful food and with a pristine lake, ideal for swimming. I have pictures. Do you want to see them?"

When Helen mentioned swimming, memories of her mother (Stacey's mother) came flooding back. Richard Stockton, Stacey's father, had died in a tragic workplace accident—a girder fell from a crane and crushed him. Stacey was fifteen at the time. Her mother, Eleanor, received some insurance and a pension, but she still had to work part-time as a clerk at the Home Depot to make ends meet. Money was tight and Stacey had to give up her favourite sport, competitive swimming. She now took the twins to swimming lessons but had no time to swim herself.

Losing her father, whom she adored, and having her life change drastically at such a vulnerable age, was what led her to find the attention of Randy so welcome. He was older and even at twenty, settled. Pregnant at seventeen, she and Randy married. Shortly after, Eleanor was diagnosed with lymphoma that spread quickly to her vital organs. She passed away just weeks before baby Lois was born never having seen her granddaughter. At eighteen, Stacey was still feeling the loss of her father and had to deal with yet another significant loss: her mother. Lois was a fussy baby and demanding. To Stacey, that year was one big blur. Randy was amorous and sexually demanding. Stacey found comfort in his embrace and was soon pregnant with Brent. Two years later, Dougie was born. She had no time to be anything but mother and wife.

Yes, Manitoulin sounded perfect and getting back in the water appealed to her. It was as if that would wash away the bad things in her life. Her new life, Lois's life, was certainly developing into a positive experience. Greece, then Manitoulin, two exciting adventures offered within a three-week span, not to mention the special people who were now a part of her life. Lois asked if she could consider the offers overnight.

She knew she was not ready to face Randy, but if she accepted these holiday weeks, it meant making a commitment to continue her role as Lois and being a nanny. If she took advantage of the Frenches' generous offer, she would not be able to hand in her resignation—she felt that she would owe them another year to compensate. It meant spending another year in Sudbury, another year away from her children, another year away from Randy. She was restless and slept little that night as she weighed her options. She couldn't return to Ottawa with any doubts about who she was and her ability to be a whole person, a person who benefited from her accomplishments. Knowing she still had a long way to go before that confidence level was achieved, Lois accepted Helen's offer to go to Greece. The next time Lois went to the mall, she stopped at the bookstore with the twins in tow, bought a book for them and a book on key phrases in Greek. With a child holding each hand, she headed to the sports store to buy a swimsuit. She drove home singing and smiling the whole way. The twins, buckled into the seats in the back clapped and sang along. The joyous mood continued all through supper. Helen was detained, so Lois got Barby and Grant ready for bed.

"Sorry, I'm late getting home—I hope you got my message. I don't know if you saw the news, but a storage tank at the Petro

Station sprung a leak early this morning and I was called in to do an environmental assessment. Will you still make it to class on time?" Helen threw her keys on the counter and grabbed Barby for a big hug. Grant clutched her leg. The twins were bathed and in their favourite soft yellow pyjamas with twin teddy bears hugging.

"Yes, I got your message. I'll just make it to class on time. The twins have finished eating and are ready for bed. Thanks, Helen, I'm off then."

Lois was privileged to be able to use the van for personal use as well. She pulled into a parking spot at Cambrian College, grabbed her purse and books and stepped down onto the pavement wearing tailored black slacks and a maroon turtle-necked sweater.

"Lois, hi. Walk you to class."

A tall young man, who carried a good portion of his height in his legs, strode over to stand beside Lois. Peter was a classmate, another adult learner. He reached for her books and tucked them neatly under his arm. His well-worn jeans were faded but clean and pressed. He wore a denim blue windbreaker with Watkins Equipment embroidered above the breast pocket. Sparkling eyes and a broad smile set off his regal nose. A lock of rich brown hair fell onto his forehead. "Man, that math assignment floored me. Were you able to get all the answers?"

"I have to admit that I am finding the math easy. My difficulty is physics."

"Now, I love physics. Maybe, we should pair up to do homework."

Lois recognized what she thought to be a 'come-on' and flushed. What if he knew she was married and a mother of three? Once arriving in Sudbury, Stacey had removed her wedding bands and tucked them in the lining of her cosmetic bag along with a few snapshots of the children. Casually dressed in jeans and a red windbreaker, her tiny frame reached slightly above his elbow. She definitely was not going to encourage his interest. "That is not likely because I work full time and the only spare time I have is for school."

"You must set aside time for homework. I'm suggesting we link up for that—I could help you and you me. We could even do it over the phone."

Lois was still hesitant. The last thing she wanted was to give the impression that she was available. "I could use help with physics, but it has to be strictly homework. I could likely help you with your math too. We could give it a try. What is Walkers Equipment?"

"Oh, that." Peter noted her looking at the logo on his shirt. "We sell large equipment for construction and earth moving needs. I am a heavy-equipment mechanic."

"My dad worked with large cranes and bulldozers. I learned to drive one when I was thirteen. I used to go to work with him on weekends because he often had to do overtime. He let me work the bulldozer for small jobs. Crazy, eh! But you know what—I loved that big machine—learned to manoeuvre an excavator too."

Lois turned to Peter and stuck out her hand. "It's a deal then."

Peter shook Lois's hand. "Now we are officially committed. Let's meet at break and organize our homework schedule." He held the classroom door open for Lois and handed her the books. He was seated at one end of the classroom and she at another. As she made her way across the room, Lois thought about Peter's warm smile and how his brown eyes lit up at the same time. *Careful, girl, this is dangerous territory.*

At break, Lois met Peter in the hallway where he had grabbed space at one of four tables, each occupied by students poring over their books. "Listen, Lois, before we go any further—I don't want you to get any wrong ideas. I am not coming on to you by asking for help. I am happily married with a six-month-old son. I realized I might have given the wrong impression. Sorry if I did."

"Actually, I'm relieved. I *was* a little concerned and am not interested in dating either so I'm glad." She offered no further explanation. "I usually get to my homework about 9:30 every evening. After the kitchen is cleaned up from supper, and the twin's messes are straightened out, I go directly to class and do my homework when I get home."

She noted Peter's puzzled expression. "I'm a nanny."

The phone homework worked well, but Lois and Peter found that both subjects required visual interpretation, so Peter invited Lois to his place on Saturday morning. She could attend her cooking class that was over by eleven, then meet Peter. "Mary and Jack will be here, but we can work in the quiet of the living room."

The following Saturday, she told one of the other people in her cooking class that she was considering taking a holiday on Manitoulin Island.

"Oh, my God, when? Did you know that the Manitoulin Hotel is offering a special cooking course? It covers fermenting, brewing *Kombucha*, baking bread and food preservation. It also is going to feature cooking local fish and produce. I'd so die to go!"

Lois smiled and said she would check it out.

After class, following Peter's directions, she found herself driving through a part of the city she had never been in. She drove through an industrial area passing one grim warehouse after another. When she turned a corner, she passed houses with driveways of black cinder, taken from the slag heaps. There were few trees and very little grass—it seemed so barren, felt so lonely. There were indeed lots of paved parking lots. Peter had told her to watch for a playground and to pull into the first drive after it—his apartment building was on the left—unit 5. It was not hard to spot the playground—it had the only sizable grassy area. She turned into the lot that served three triplexes and pulled into a spot on the left. Unit 5 was on the ground floor and before she could press the bell, the door flew open.

"Hey, saw you pull up. Come in. Here, let me take your books. Just throw your jacket on the chair."

Lois followed Peter, who was wearing grey sweatpants and a red T-shirt into a large, airy living room that overlooked the parking lot. Toys were strewn across the floor and Lois carefully crossed the room to where Peter stood holding out a chair. She set her books on a card table near the front window that was obviously going to serve as their workspace. Lois turned to meet the eyes of a woman almost as small as Lois, with a pale complexion and light blonde hair. She was balancing a sturdy, equally blonde baby on her hip. Lois swallowed hard as thoughts of Dougie overwhelmed her and tears blinded her momentarily.

"Sorry, I didn't mean to startle you." Mary's smile was bright and welcoming.

"No, I was just taken aback when I saw Jack. He reminded me of another child I used to look after." It took all Lois's strength not to reach for Jack and hold him tight. "He was about the same age the last time I saw him." Lois choked back the tears and reached for Mary's outstretched hand. "I hope it isn't a bother for Peter to help me with my homework."

"I think it is a mutual help situation. Besides, I am the creative type, not in the least bit practical so have absolutely no concept of either subject. You two work away and Jack and I will watch a movie in the bedroom—great to meet you, Lois."

"And you, Mary." Lois watched as Mary turned and left. It was as if she were watching Dougie disappear. Swallowing tears, she sat down and pulled open the physics text. She needed to divert her attention.

The rest of the morning and well into the afternoon flew by before Peter and Lois realized that working together was a wise decision. By the end of the day, Lois had a good grasp of momentum and Peter made a major step forward with calculus. Mary, having tucked Jack in for an afternoon nap, brought the studying pair a plate of cookies and milk. They celebrated the success of the partnership with raised glasses. Lois had a late afternoon hair appointment and left with just enough time to make it. Her stomach was tied in knots and tears threatened to spill as she thought once again of Dougie. *I've made a serious mistake. I cannot continue to be away from my children. I have to go back to Ottawa.*

When she looked in the mirror at the hairdresser's, she saw Lois, not Stacey. She saw a confident, straight back and a face with clear, sparkling, blue eyes. Her conversation was that of Lois, not Stacey. *I like who I have become. If I go back, Randy will undermine everything I have gained. No, I'm not ready yet. Maybe, once I've graduated—yes, I need to graduate. I need to be able to hang my diploma. I need to stay longer.*

She left the salon, and along the mall caught a glimpse of a travel agency. She stepped inside and found a brochure featuring Greece. As she walked along the mall toward the luggage store, she saw her reflection in the store windows. She saw a small attractive woman, stylish and portraying a confident air. *O mirror, mirror in the mall, if you only knew.*

Chapter 8

Now I am confused about who I am. Am I Stacey or Lois? They are so different. It is like being in a play and I am playing the lead. As I lie here on this soft bed in a room of mellow yellows, it is like being centre stage and I am a character called Lois. I like being Lois. I like who she is. But, I am really Stacey, the mother of three beautiful children and live in a house most people would envy and have a husband that is a good provider. Yet, he made me feel worthless. As Lois, I have nothing, am living a lie in someone else's house pouring my affections out to their children instead of my own. But Helen and Norm compliment my efforts—they praise the little things I do, they are supportive of my schooling and the twins have accepted me as their very own. They make me feel important and worthwhile.

I do so miss Lois, Brent and Dougie. Dougie will be walking now, saying a few more words and I missed that. Lois will be full of her daily happenings, and Brent will be growing. Oh, I can't continue this charade. I have to go home. Randy will be furious. What will he do? There is no question—he will be angry and I expect he will lash out at me with the most derogatory remarks. No, I am not ready to counter that. I am not strong enough to face him. I need a little more time. I will finish out the school year. Then if I have good grades, I will feel better about myself. A few more months, just a few, then I will return—at least then, I will feel I have accomplished something. This trip to Greece will broaden my education—travel is a great teacher. Randy has never travelled. I will have done something he has not, and I will be better for it.

Chapter 9

Norm and Helen handled all the travel arrangements and by the time they left for Greece, Lois had completed her year at school, garnering top marks in all the subjects but physics—in that, she got a decent pass grade. Peter, too, did well. Mary had planned a celebration party, but Helen and Norm pre-empted it with a dinner celebration at Idyllwylde Golf and Country Club where they were members. Peter and Mary left Jack with a neighbour and joined them. Francis, who was also invited, was grinning at Lois from across the table. The twins were at Francis' house with Betsy's father in charge. Lois looked at the faces around the table and couldn't help thinking about her new identity and how lucky she was to have found this life so far away, one that was extremely different from her life as Stacey. How she wished she could have had this kind of support and love with Randy. Never would he have considered celebrating her accomplishments. Emily would though and Lois knew she would call her in the morning.

"To Lois and Peter, may they continue to reach their goals and may we join together next year to celebrate their graduation from college." Norm's bass voice was raised in bravado as if he was a proud father. In fact, he had become very fond of Lois and considered her family. He liked her choice of friends and was pleased that Helen had thought of inviting them all to celebrate and share together. As he looked around the table, he realized that his world had grown and become richer now that Lois was a part of it.

The next morning, Lois drove to a motel on the western edge of town where she knew there was a pay phone. She had three different locations she used in case her calls were traced. The phone rang and rang. "Please be home." A breathy "hello" was picked up on the other end. "Emily, it's Stace."

"Hey, I had to put my parcels down before I answered. This keeping the larders filled is a full-time job, especially now that Dad is living with us."

"Do you have any idea how lucky you are to have a husband who supports you the way yours does?"

"Yes, I do, and I tell him so on a regular basis. I only wish you were in the same situation. So how did your exams go?"

Stacey (Lois) filled Emily in on her marks, her celebration party and her friends without saying where it was. Emily brought tears to Lois's eyes when she told her how Dougie was not only walking but trying to run to keep up with his brother and sister. She told her how Annie and Lois were having their first sleepover at Emily's house that night and how Brent had started taking piano lessons. "He has a love of music and sings like an angel." Lois thought about calling her daughter at Emily's house but decided it was too risky. Emily promised to take pictures and email them.

When she hung up, Lois sat there willing herself to be hundreds of miles away—in Ottawa. "Damn you, Randy." Stepping away from the booth, she wiped misty eyes and ran smack into Peter.

"And who is Randy, may I ask? And why are you crying?"

Lois was flustered and stood shaking her head. Peter gathered her into his arms and held her firmly. "It is none of my business, but if you ever need to talk, remember that Mary and I are here."

It felt so good to be comforted. If only she could share her dilemma, but Lois knew that was not possible. She stayed in the comfort of Peter's arms until she had almost composed herself, then stood back. Finding a tissue in her pocket, she blew her nose.

"Nothing like the shoulder of a friend—thanks."

"Lois, shit happens in everyone's lives. You don't have to bear it alone, you know. Sometimes, talking it through helps."

"Yeah, I know. Thanks, but no thanks. I sometimes miss my

former life, but this one works for me right now." With that, she found a weak smile and asked what he was doing there.

"The owner has a bulldozer that's on the fritz and I am going to see what the problem is. Want to come along?"

"Now that sounds like a plan." Adjusting her purse shoulder strap, she hustled to keep up with Peter's long stride, wiping her damp eyes on the sleeve of her green cardigan. Accumulated dust and dark beige walls along the hallway of the motel crept into her psyche and smouldered. Lois was glad when Peter held open the door to the outside. Brilliant sun startled her and a soft breeze caressed her cheek. Letting the door close on its own, Peter headed across the parking lot to a bulldozer with Lois close behind. He checked the engine and asked Lois to climb up and try to start it. Between the two of them, they found and solved the problem.

"You weren't kidding when you said you knew your way around bulldozers."

"Like I told you—I was playing with them when I was thirteen."

"I sure wish I could afford one. This baby is for sale. There is so much work out there for heavy equipment, but I would never be able to even get a down payment."

"I'm sure you do not want the headache of owning your own company."

"Lois, that is exactly why I am back at school. I want to take a business degree and make something of myself. My dad struggled as a barber to make ends meet and I was fortunate enough to get an apprenticeship and get my mechanics papers. I happened to dig big equipment and lucked into this job. I don't want Mary and our children to struggle the way my parents did. The only way I know of doing that is to be my own boss." Peter wiped greasy hands on a grubby towel he had tucked into the back pocket of his jeans.

"Then that would be awesome."

All the way back to Helen and Norm's, Lois thought about what Peter had told her. A plan began to form. When she got home, she cornered Norm at his desk.

"Norm, you own your own business. Can I pick your brains?" Lois asked question after question.

Helen was calling from the den for Lois to see something on the internet. Reluctantly, Lois excused herself from Norm and headed across the hall. Helen showed her the resort on Manitoulin Island where she and Norm had stayed. It was rustic, set in a pine wilderness and close to a sparkling lake. Lois was enchanted. Right away, Helen picked up the phone and between the two of them booked a small cottage. Lois straightened her back and shook off the doubts and guilt that had started to set in. She was determined to do this. Now she had two holidays to look forward to. It was a good thing she bought new luggage.

Driving from Sudbury to Toronto made for a long day, but Norm wanted to leave the SUV with a dealership near the airport to get a remote starter system installed. He had arranged to have someone from the auto service department meet them at Pearson Airport. The work would be done while they were away and their flight would be met on their return. Lois was always in awe of Norm's organizing skills—this way he avoided paying for parking and had his vehicle serviced when it was not in use. It meant no one was inconvenienced. He by text and the transfer of the vehicle was seamless.

At Helen's insistence, everyone was casually dressed to be comfortable for the long flight. Lois wore white slacks, a soft knit, pale green shirt and multi-coloured sandals. The twins were dressed in khaki shorts and neon green t-shirts in order to spot them easily if they wandered off. Lois managed to keep them under control while Helen and Norm checked in at the Air Canada counter.

Barby whispered in Lois's ear, "why is that man wearing a ladies' skirt?" and while Lois was trying to explain different customs to Barby, Grant was pulling away wanting to explore the airport. They were beyond excited about the assortment of passengers they saw and the prospect of flying in a big airplane. Booked on a late evening flight meant the children would likely sleep for most of the trip. Norm and Helen took the twins over to the viewing windows to see the planes while Lois checked in. She kept looking around to see if anyone might recognize her, but thankfully, didn't see a soul she knew. They had early boarding privileges and once they had stashed the carry-on luggage, it was a full-time chore to tone down the two little ones' voices to a tolerable pitch. It was a ten and a half-hour flight and Lois hoped the children would settle down soon. Once in the air, a stewardess introduced herself.

"Hi. I am Felicia. I think I can find chocolate milk and cookies. Anyone here interested?" She was looking directly at Barby, who broke into a great big smile.

"Me-me. I would and so would my brother. We are twins, you know?"

"Wow, twins—that makes it extra special—I think I will have to find two cookies each."

Barby yelled across the aisle to Helen to announce their good luck. Lois hushed them and explained that smaller voices would be appreciated by the rest of the passengers. Grant started to bounce up and down as the plane rose higher and higher. It was a good thing his seatbelt restrained him. Once again, Lois had to explain airplane etiquette. The milk and cookies were devoured and the children were fascinated by the lights getting smaller and smaller and eventually disappearing altogether. The drone of the plane had a soothing effect on the twins and they soon settled down and fell into a deep sleep. Several hours into the flight, Lois too, dozed off. She was wakened by a gentle nudge to her shoulder and a finger pointing out the window. The plane was descending over the Mediterranean, the noonday sun high in a cloudless sky. Lois caught a glimpse of three cruise ships—

miniature on the expanse of blue-green water. A quick trip to the bathroom and a splash of water on her face brought Lois wide awake and her excitement rose as she watched the decent into Athens. The twins had moved over to be with Helen and Norm, so she had the window to herself.

Chapter 10

There is no way I could have passed up this chance to see Greece and, when we return, spend time by myself on an island. I have never had a holiday before. I guess I am being selfish, but won't the experience broaden me and make me stronger? As Lois, I have made strides toward being independent and have far more self-confidence than I did ten months ago. Stacey would never have taken the initiative to be who I have become. I feel I will soon be strong enough to counter Randy's verbal abuse. I am beginning to think that I can stand up for myself. Helen, knowing I was dealing with inner conflict, suggested that I might seek counselling, but there is no way I want to talk to anyone—I would simply fall apart and lose all the confidence that I have gained. For me, it is better held deep inside.

Every day, I have to convince myself to continue this charade. Every day, I wipe away tears missing my children. Then I wash my face, apply Lois's makeup and put a fake smile on my face before heading downstairs to begin another day. I tell myself I need to finish what I started. When I become Stacey again, I have to take all the critical gains that I made as Lois. What scares me is that sometimes almost half a day will race by and I have not thought of my babies. I hate this about myself. How could I forget them for even one single minute? A holiday in Greece will give me time to reflect and plan for my return to Ottawa and how I will counter the verbal abuse I know Randy will throw at me. I will need to be strong, strong enough to cope with being berated and undermined. I do feel stronger and am almost capable enough to stand up to Randy. I do miss him and the children so.

Chapter 11

Arriving in Athens, the heat of mid-day and the din of the crowded terminal was overwhelming and suffocating. Edging through the throng, they gathered their luggage from the carrousel. The twins had small cases and were told that they were almost four now and were old enough to take some responsibility, so they had to look after their own suitcases. Valiantly, they toddled across the tiled floor to the exit. Norm, pushing a luggage cart, set off to exit the terminal and secure a taxi. Helen, Lois and the twins followed as far as the curb. Norm left the cart with them as they waited curbside. It became a bit of a challenge for Norm to find a cab that would take them to Rafina where their cottage was booked. Each time he asked a driver, he was directed to a cab farther back by a pointed finger with the simple explanation "Miko" until at the back of the line, he found him. Miko not only spoke English but was familiar with their destination. They were also fortunate that Miko had a van with working air conditioning.

"Yes. We go to Rafino. Hey, kids, you get in. Miko will buckle you up. You have names, yes?" He talked non-stop, his accent fascinating the children.

"You talk funny." Miko ruffed Grant's hair and lifted him into the seat, fastened the seatbelt—he had already installed the child safety seats Norm had brought from Canada as baggage.

"You will like Rafina. There are many restaurants that specialize in kalamarakia, mareedes, galeos with skordaya and other things from the sea. The best restaurant is Agoni Grammi; it is owned by my cousin, last one on dock. You love fried fish, beer, ouzo and wine? Afternoons, you can drink and relax and not worry—very cheap. Tonight or tomorrow, spend in Rafina. Then other day, take catamaran to Mykonos—is quick trip.

Beautiful place—many tourists—many fishing boats, so can buy freshest fish and the biggest crayfish. Rafina is good place to be—no pollution—you get taxi to Athens and see sites, and then come back for swim and dinner—all in one day—is easy. Taxi company is owned by my cousin." Miko's rapid-fire conversation brought smiles to the passengers.

Forty-five minutes later, the car pulled into a shaded laneway. Helen gasped in awe. "Oh, this is beautiful, far better than the pictures."

"You pick best place—is owned by my cousin Nikita."

"Miko, you have many cousins in Rafina?" Norm was laughing.

"Yes, many—you meet my cousin Reta—she has bakery—best bread. Other cousin Rafael has hotel—best wine. Many cousins from my father's sister."

"Well, we sure lucked out hiring you. Can you take us back and forth to Athens when we need to go and take us back to the airport when we leave?"

"Is no problem. I be here. My cousin Luca owns taxi company—he make me your personal chauffeur."

Norm gave Miko all the particulars, got his contact information and paid the fare giving Miko a generous tip. The children had already run off to the shore with Lois closely behind them guarding their safety. Helen was watching when Norm came up beside her and put his arm around her waist. He kissed her cheek and they both smiled watching their family explore.

That evening, they walked the streets and boardwalk of Rafina, stood and watched the sun sink into the ocean, visited the bakery where Reta gave the twins a cookie each while she fussed and fussed over them. "So, lucky you—much luck twins, and one of each—so lucky."

Norm selected a bottle of wine and Helen bought a bucket of mussels and dipping oil to go with the black olive bread they had purchased from Reta. At the groceteria, Norm picked up peanut butter, white crusty bread and milk for the children—the perfect comfort food for the end of a long journey. They were totally disoriented from the changes of the day that had started from Sudbury and ended on the Mediterranean. The salty air smelled different, the vegetation was unrecognizable, and the architecture different, not to mention the time difference.

"This is just what we all needed—a complete break from our lives at home. Norm, your choice was perfect." Helen reached for Norm's hand, then gave him a big noisy kiss on the cheek. Everyone laughed.

Norm and Helen ventured off to Athens on three separate days taking a city tour one day and visiting galleries, tourist spots and museums. The third day, they took tours of vineyards and caves. Each day was jamb packed with culture and adventure and they arrived back in Rafina ready for a glass of wine and sat to hear the children's stories. Lois and the twins had daily adventures exploring the beaches, the wharves and the part of the old town that was like a village. The local residents were enchanted by the twins, who made friends with everyone they met. The children were quick to recognize where they wanted to stop and visit on their walks. Barby and Grant always made a beeline for the bakery. Then pulling Lois by one hand while eating their cookies held in the other, they dragged her to the wharf. Grant loved the big boats and begged to go on one. They were fascinated by the fishermen unloading their catch. There were always large hands waving to them and broad smiles of greeting. Grant begged and begged to go on a boat. Midweek, they took the ferry to Mykonos with Helen and Norm. Crossing the straight was smooth and the water a brilliant turquoise. The twins hung over the railing as the ferry off-loaded watching a multitude of cyclists roll away. They finally disembarked and walked the hilly roadways until the twins had to be carried. They slept all the way back to Rafina on the boat.

Before they walked back to their cottage, they decided to eat in the village. The twins were rested from their shipboard sleep and full of energy. They feasted on fresh-caught seafood at Agoni Grammi, Miko's cousin's restaurant, and yet again, watched the sun set over the sea. Norm and the children did a countdown as the golden globe sunk below the horizon. Wandering ever so slowly to their holiday home, the twins skipped ahead singing a Greek folksong.

"How did they learn that?"

Barby stopped singing long enough to explain that the old auntie at the corner taught it to them. A puzzled expression on Norm's face had Lois explaining that the two of them had adopted the old lady who always sat on a chair in front of her house and called her auntie. Since she couldn't converse with them in English, she sang that folk song to them every day. By day three, they were singing right along with her.

"You never saw such a radiant smile when they did. It was as if she had just received the most precious of gifts."

"I am sure she did." Helen smiled and blew a kiss to each of the twins. "The villagers consider twins good luck and when there is one of each gender especially lucky—I agree—we are so lucky."

When the children were tucked into bed, Lois said her 'goodnights' declaring that it was one of the best days of her life. Helen almost asked her what the others were but decided that she wouldn't. Lois had still not revealed a great deal about herself, but Helen felt that she would when the time was right. She knew Lois often sobbed herself to sleep and was still deeply troubled.

The weather had cooperated and Rafina had been the best choice of locations, a small city, with charm galore. Lois had mastered enough Greek to function and the twins grasped the concept immediately. When they walked through the village, they were greeted by villagers and returned the greeting in the local dialect. Reta always ran into the street with a cookie for each twin, kissing each on the forehead for luck. On their last day, the entire family went to the village saying farewells to their new friends, many of them Miko's relatives. Reta insisted they drop by her house for wine before they left. When they got to Reta's house, the back courtyard was filled with the same people they had spoken to during the day, as well as Miko. A table was laid with a feast and before they knew it, music was playing and a celebration began. The twins danced right along with the village children and Lois was always trying out the different dance steps with one partner after another. Exhausted and happy, they returned to the cottage having made promises to return to Rafino.

In order to make the twins stop grumbling about leaving *their* beach, *their* village, *their* friends and *their* wharf, Helen started telling them about the plans for the birthday party and that their grandmother was coming. "If you stay here, you will not see Grandma and will not get any presents from her." Lois smiled at the psychology used to change their focus.

"Will Grandma be there when we get home?" asked Barby.

"No, but four sleeps later, we will go to the train station to get her. In the meantime, we have to get the house ready and pick flowers for her bedroom." Elaborating on the plans, Rafina was soon set aside and the twins were anxious to get home.

On the Saturday of their return, Lois purchased a remotely operated toy bulldozer for Grant and a giant stuffed dog for Barby as birthday gifts. She was busy wrapping it in her room when Helen knocked on her door saying she had a visitor. Immediately, she froze thinking it was the police or a private detective. However, it was Mary. Her mother had fallen and been taken to the hospital. She wondered if she could leave Jack with Lois for a few hours while she went to her mother. Helen did not mind and the twins were fascinated to have a toddler in the house. Mary's mother was to be released from hospital the following day and would require care, so it was arranged that Jack would visit during the day with Barby and Grant for three days and take part in the birthday celebration.

Helen's mother's train arrived on schedule. Her two grandchildren were more excited about seeing the big train than her.

"Nobody can be more interesting to almost four-year-olds than a train." Mrs. Daly accepted her greeting, or lack thereof, with grandmotherly understanding. "My, how they have grown!" She hugged her daughter and waited patiently while the twins waved goodbye to the train and watched until it was off in the distance. Helen held the twins hands, but they pulled away and charged toward their grandmother.

"Thank goodness, today is their birthday because they would not have been able to wait another day." The twins had been allowed to stand on a bench to wave at the train as it left the station. Helen explained to her mother while the children were out of hearing range that Lois was preparing everything and the house would be decorated as a big surprise when they got home. Norm was leaving work early to join in the festivities.

"Well, I am looking forward to meeting this marvellous Lois person. You rave about her all the time."

The afternoon was a big success marked by shrieks of joy. The children were smeared with chocolate cake and ice cream, on their faces and clothing. Lois felt pangs of regret as she had missed Lois and Dougie's birthdays. Brent's was in two weeks. She had sent gifts, but not being there had made for two challenging days. Emily had filled her in on as many details as she was able to find out from Annie. Christmas had been more than trying, but being part of this family and hectic activity had made it bearable.

Chapter 12

Did I wake up to me screaming or was I dreaming? I remember now; there was a gigantic birthday cake with one candle. Then it changed to six candles, then one, then six. It started to whirl and topple on top of me. Even in my sleep, I felt guilty for missing Lois and Dougie's birthdays. What kind of mother am I?

I need to get a grip on myself; I need to be able to look in the mirror and see a strong Stacey. I am stronger, but I am stronger as Lois, not Stacey. Can I return to being Stacey and still be this confident? I did graduate with excellent marks; I do manage this house and these children easily, so what am I afraid of? Facing Randy? Yes. I can feel the trembling start the minute I think of his disapproving stare. I dread walking back into that poisonous environment. Yet, I know it will be up to me to make the effort and to deal with the issues directly. Randy has to realize that undermining my every move is dangerous and the sting of his words are as bad as physically striking me. In some ways, I wish he had hit me. Then there would be visible marks to prove how he mistreated me. At least now, I do believe that I became morose and depressed because of Randy's constant verbal abuse. I needed his support but got criticism instead. How can I make him see it for himself? How can I explain how he hurt me emotionally and how debilitating that was? How do I get him to even listen to me? Would he ever go for counselling? Not likely.

Chapter 13

Lois was leaving for Manitoulin the following morning. She had checked out the cooking school and managed to get the last vacancy. She was excited to be off on a holiday by herself, her first time on her own. Her head was still spinning with thoughts of heavy machines, Greek Islands and noisy twins. She was looking forward to being alone and the quiet of the peaceful countryside. Norm dropped her at the bus station on his way to work.

The miles slid by, the highway slicing through wilderness, dense stands of pine trees, rock-faced hillsides, stately maple trees and patches of wildflowers. Lois leaned against the bus window letting her thoughts wander to her children. *How much have my children grown? Is Dougie talking in sentences? Are they remembering to brush their teeth? How can I forget how each one looked tucked in and angelic as they slept? How can I be so selfish as to run away and make a separate life for myself?*

"What am I doing?'

Not realizing she had spoken out loud, she was surprised when her seat partner turned to her with a puzzled expression.

"Excuse me, were you talking to me?"

"Sorry. No. I was deep in thought."

Lois took note of the lady occupying the seat beside her. The term 'lady' popped into her head as she noted the trim, elegant woman, probably in her late sixties, dressed in a matching skirt and sweater set of sky blue; small single pearl earrings matched a strand at her throat. She was peering at Lois with questioning eyes, so blue they matched her outfit.

"A pretty young thing like you should not have such deep concerns. Are you travelling to be with family?"

"No. I am going on a short holiday on the island."

"That is where I am going too. I live there. I taught there for many years. Where are you staying?"

"I've rented a little cottage near Gore Bay."

"Oh, Ethel Blakely rents out cottages. Are you in one of hers?"

"In fact, I am."

"You must get her to tell you some of her native stories—she is well known for her wit and can tell Ojibwa stories for hours on end. She also makes the best fish stew on the island."

"Really? I love to cook and am taking a cooking class at the inn while I am there.

"Oh, my dear, I am one of the tasters for the cooking school, so we will see each other again. I'm Lucille Bailey, but you can call me Lucy."

Lucy reached for Lois's hand; a broad smile of deep red lipstick spread across her freckled cheeks. Traces of rusty threads mixed with grey framed her long narrow face in a short, curly bob. Her hand, too, was heavily freckled; the warmth was equal to her smile.

Lois told Lucy that she lived in Sudbury. Lucy did most of the talking, eager to tell Lois all about Manitoulin.

"Manitoulin Island is a place of mountains and mists. We treasure our unspoiled natural beauty that takes one's breath away. It is a place of legends and warm hospitality. Did you know it is made up of the largest number of freshwater islands in the world? There are numerous lakes and fishing is a favourite pastime."

The conversation continued until the bus pulled into Little Current. Lois had not thought about her children from the moment Lucy began talking. The trip flew by with her seat partner pointing out features of the landscape.

"You can imagine how difficult it is maintaining the causeway in winter; the snow blows across it almost as soon as it is ploughed. Winter driving is a challenge. But, at this time of the year, we enjoy the best of the best. A good number of folks from below the border come here for the fishing and to relax, of course. Tourism has both saved the island and threatened it at the same time. The ecosystem is fragile here. The wildflowers and vegetation are hardy because of our harsh seasons yet suffer from pollution that is increasing due to more car traffic."

"My hobby is photographing wildflowers. Oh, we are pulling over. Are we here?"

"Yes, dear, there's Ethel over there standing beside that gleaming old red station wagon—that old thing is her pride and joy."

Lucy waved frantically until she caught Ethel's attention and was rewarded with a smile that lit up Ethel's dark face. There was no mistaking her heritage with her strong, angled facial features and dark, thick braids that hung to her waist—she was definitely aboriginal. Tall with a firm, athletic body, she also looked the part of a resort owner in her green plaid shirt and faded jeans. Lois noticed she was wearing beaded moccasins. As Lois and Lucy stepped down from the bus, Ethel quickly moved across the pavement to greet them.

"Can I presume I have no secrets from you, Lois? Lucy does like to tell all."

Easy laughter broke the ice and as Lois waved goodbye to Lucy, who headed for a silver SUV, she turned her attention to Ethel, who had gotten into her truck. Lois climbed aboard, now happy that she was also wearing jeans and a plaid shirt. She had felt a little self-conscious when she met Lucy and was afraid the island folk dressed as eloquently as Lucy, but now she felt just right.

Ethel shifted the manual gear shift and pulled onto the road to Gore Bay.

"Your cabin is all ready for you and the weather forecast is looking good. Being Saturday, I always treat my guests to a dinner up at the main lodge. I hope you do not mind fish stew."

"That is perfect, especially when Lucy raved that it was

absolutely the best. Do you keep the secret of your recipe, or might you share? I am taking the cooking classes at the inn and am so excited about learning about preparing dishes from your culture."

"One of the sessions is taught by me and one of the dishes I introduce is my fish stew. Now, aren't we going to have fun? You need to be aware that it is a fair hike to the inn from the camp and I cannot drive you there. However, I can give you a bike to use while you are here."

"That is just the ticket—I am also interested in photography and want to venture out in the early morning to catch the special light that plays on the landscape at that time."

"I can certainly give you some ideas about where to go. Do you like to catch fish?"

"No, I just want to hike, bike and swim."

"Well, you have come to the right place for sure. Here we are."

Ethel put on the right-turn signal and turned into a tree-lined drive. The driveway opened into a field of wildflowers and four log cabins stretched along the waterfront. Two large Pyrenees dogs came loping up to the wagon as they approached.

"That's Ike and Sam. Hope you do not mind dogs, especially big ones that think they are lap pooches."

Lois laughed and assured Ethel that she was likely to spoil them rotten.

The cabin was exactly like the pictures, bright, compact and comfortable. Lois quickly put away her clothing and headed for the main house to find the bike Ethel had promised. She walked along a path strewn with pine needles and bordered by wild thyme. The pungent scent of this native herb made Lois realize she had to find a grocery store and stock up on necessities. Ethel, aided by Ike and Sam, who kept winding themselves between her legs, wheeled an old Raleigh out of the garage, dusted off the seat and pointed Lois in the direction of the local convenience store where Lois could get groceries.

"Mind you, don't eat too much for lunch. I expect to fill you to the brim this evening."

Ethel's words followed Lois as she struggled to keep her balance. She had not been on a bike in years. Soon, she was navigating at a good clip enjoying the wind in her hair and the sun on her back. *The last three weeks have been life-altering. I earned my college entrance and I have been to a foreign country. I may never go back to being Stacey again. Maybe I should kidnap my children and raise them as Brenton-Douglas's.*

Even though her head was playing mind games, Lois knew she would never deprive Randy of his children—her children—their children. There had to be a solution.

A box truck whizzed by her almost toppling her into the ditch. She hopped on one leg until she came to a stop and stood shaking for a moment afraid to strike out again.

"They say when you fall off a horse, you need to get right back on or you never will—same with a bike, I think."

Lois spun around to see a grinning face peeking from beneath a peaked cap. Laughing brown eyes were watching as she composed herself and was about to confront this lanky stranger. He was straddling a bike of his own with his work boots planted firmly on the road.

"Rod Frazier—I heard you checked in at Ethel's. Maybe you should close your mouth, so these pesky black flies don't fly in."

Lois was too flabbergasted to say anything. She took in the blue denim shorts and faded T-shirt with VHF on it. Before she uttered a word, Rod apologized and told her he was Ethel's go-to guy. He lived next door.

Finally finding her voice, Lois said, "Oh, hello."

Rod then insisted on riding along with her to the village. There was little traffic and the two rode in silence. Lois needed to concentrate on keeping her balance. She was not unhappy to have the company as she was a little insecure as to the directions she had been given. Rod told her to lean her bike against the large boulder outside the convenience store and insisted it was safe to leave it. Lois flashed him a big smile and made her way into the store. When Lois came out of the grocery store carrying a bag crammed to the top, he was waiting for her.

"Here, let me take that." He reached for her parcels and set them in an old-fashioned carrier on his bike. "Better this way. You are having enough trouble balancing without carrying groceries."

He was right and Lois was grateful. As they rode back to the camp, Rod filled Lois in on where to fish, where to hike and where to bike. Taking his leave at her door, Rod told her he would see her around and left. Lois watched as his bare legs made short work of the path and he disappeared into a grove of trees. Turning, she stepped into the cabin, quickly put away her purchases, grabbed an apple and some cheese, filled a water bottle, slung her camera around her neck and went out to explore. A gentle breeze sent small ripples in regular formation again and again to the shore. Lois shed her sandals, left them by the path and waded into the shallow water. She thought of how Lois and Brent would love to be splashing about and Dougie, held up by his arms, would kick his feet getting her soaked. She stumbled ashore and fell on the grass wracked in deep sobs.

Wrung out from tattered emotions and crying, Lois made a commitment. "I am going back to Ottawa. I will have my holiday, finish the cooking course and, once I get back to Sudbury, I will tell Helen the truth and leave. I simply cannot stay away any longer. I may not feel as confident as I would like, but I can do it. Yes, I can. Wow, now that I have made my mind up, I feel as if a mountain has fallen off my back. I am going home. I am going to see my children. Randy is another matter, but somehow I will deal with him and his family." She talked out loud to herself as she dried the tears, blew her nose and headed back to the cabin.

"I'd better get the most out of the next few days." When she reached the cabin, she donned her swimsuit and headed for the water. Within minutes, she was stroking smoothly and evenly.

The motion was liberating and affirming because it was one of the few things she knew she did well. The swim washed new life into her and she returned to the cabin to get ready for dinner with Ethel.

Going up to the main lodge for supper, Lois had a bounce in her step and a smile on her face.

"Well, miss, you look like this island is working its magic on you." Rod held the door open to a wide screened porch that stretched across the entire front of the building. "One thing you will soon find out is that we need to be behind screening as those vermin mosquitoes will descend on us as soon as the sun drops into the lake."

Lois wore white capris and a red sleeveless blouse. She had slung a deep blue windbreaker over her shoulder thinking she might need it after dinner. Ethel appeared from behind a large door made of stripped cedar saplings and greeted Lois with a smile. "You mind, you watch out for this lad. He is a first-class Romeo."

"I don't know about that, though I am ever so grateful that he came to my rescue this afternoon."

"Oh, no, his Sir Galahad role—even worse." Ethel laughed as she flung a t-towel over her shoulder and turned to return to the kitchen.

Rod directed Lois to one of the deep-seated willow branch chairs with lush cushions in native designs. Guests started to arrive and everyone met over a glass of blueberry wine. There were six people for dinner and the conversation was lively. One couple, Bud and Sara, in the cabin beside Lois's, had been out fishing and caught a largemouth bass. Bud insisted that he caught the bass single-handed and his wife countered his every word. The contradictory banter was rapid and full of a warmth that only a couple deeply devoted to each other can share without being offended. Chatty conversations continued as everyone made their way inside and were seated around a large hand-hewn table.

"Ethel's father made this table from a huge pine that was felled when the highway was brought in. Many people have shared stories and food around it."

"This food is amazing! I am so excited about the cooking classes and to learn how to make this fish delicacy is a pure bonus." Lois was ladling a second helping into her bowl. "I'm sure glad I'll be biking, or I would gain too many extra pounds and with my height, it all goes sideways."

Everyone laughed and agreed the food was outstanding. The evening ended with Ethel playing her guitar and everyone singing camp songs they all knew. After a few glasses of wine, or, if preferred, a few beers, the voices got louder and more energetic. Rod walked Lois back to her cabin, then quietly disappeared into the dark. Lois stood at the door breathing in the pure night air.

"My life is about to take another about-face. I hope I have the strength to stand up to Randy and to make our marriage work. He needs to understand how debilitating his degrading comments and attitude are. I *will* suggest counselling, but I am sure he will refuse that. I need to treasure every minute here and strengthen my resolve." She spoke to the night sky and, once this pronouncement was uttered, turned and headed for her bedroom. The night air was heavy and hot, but when she turned on a fan, the sweet smells of earth and water filled the room. Lois threw on a too-large, shocking-pink tank-top and fell on top of the sheets. The cedar plank walls and soft blue curtains that drifted and swelled in the fan-induced breeze lulled her into a deep sleep.

Dawn shot light into Lois's bedroom and she jumped up, pushed the curtain aside and scrambled into a pair of jeans and a long-sleeved jersey. She grabbed a pair of socks and her running shoes, reached for her camera and headed out the door. Morning light and shadow were precisely what she wanted to capture.

There was a small cove about two kilometres away and she wanted to see if that perfect shot was waiting for her.

She had only cycled for a few minutes when she saw a doe with two babies in the middle of the road. The fawns were busy nursing and the mother did not seem to be alarmed that Lois had dismounted. Slowly raising the camera and adjusting the focus, Lois zoomed in to take picture after picture. She edged slowly forward, stopping to take more pictures. The fawns stopped nursing and stared at Lois with deep, dark, curious eyes. A flick of the doe's ears and a leap in the air sent them out of sight into the brush.

"Oh, my, not my usual subject, but who could refuse that gift? I think I might have at least two excellent shots."

Back on her bike, Lois rode straight to the cove that Rod had recommended, leaned the bicycle against a tree and strode to the edge of a cliff, not a steep cliff but definitely a height above the cove. The sun was rising quickly and Lois wanted to take some photos before it lost its pink glow. A dead tree hung over the water casting an interesting shadow effect. After a few clicks of the shutter, Lois glanced into the bush and spied a clutch of purple. Upon investigation, she found a patch of water iris. They were snuggled in a marshy matt of grass. Stepping gingerly onto dry patches, Lois edged close enough for shots aiming deep into their intricate throats that were like oriental artwork. Lost in her moment, Lois stepped back sinking one foot deep into a gummy quagmire.

"Shit. Now I've done it. Not only is my foot soaked, but I smell like rotten sewage."

Carefully manoeuvring herself out of the boggy area, she rinsed her shoe, foot and leg and carried on with one wet appendage. Heading toward the pathway, she spied bugloss, one of nature's most intricate blossoms. One discovery led to another—in all she found and recorded ten different species. Totally engrossed in framing her subjects through the camera's lens, the morning slipped away before she knew it. She had little time to get back to the resort before rushing to get changed and over to the first cooking class; a distinct bounce in her cycling was keeping time with the song in her head.

Chapter 14

"Oh, what a beautiful mornin'. Oh, what a beautiful day." My goodness, I am singing out loud. I haven't done that since I sang to the children. I am so glad I took the extra time to put myself together—I now know I will return to Ottawa and I am excited thinking about seeing the children and Randy. Yes, I miss them all, and the sooner I confront the issues that drove me away, the better it will be. Even though I go through periods of being self-conscious and shrink to being the old Stacey, I know I have changed and it is the strength that I have achieved as Lois that will have to support me when I return to being Stacey. I can just imagine the expression on Randy's face when he sees the new me. I certainly don't look like the mousey Stacey who left, and I don't feel like her either. I feel important. Yes, that's it! One year away, and I have become much more sure of myself. When I look in the mirror and see the change in myself, I take on the persona of Lois; I must not lose that.

I can't let Randy undermine all the work I have done and what I have accomplished, while I have been in Sudbury. I need to retain some of my selfishness and do some things just for me. When I get back, I am going to join the Masters Swim Club. Yes, it is time I did something for myself. I have been doing little things for myself for the past twelve months. And it feels good; it feels right. Yes, Randy Martin, you are going to meet your new wife. Oh, I can't wait to gather each of my darling children in my arms and hug them to death. And they will learn to eat a variety of foods; I am not going to let the cooking classes go to waste.

Chapter 15

Propping the trusty bike by the inn walkway, Lois found her way to the kitchen. Several people were standing around, and three more trailed in after Lois.

"Good afternoon, ladies and gentleman"—indeed, there was only one male participant. "Please, line up behind the counter as I call your name. I am Chef Alf Basson. I will be your instructor plus we will be honoured to have two guest cooks: Judy Spence and Ethel Blakely. There are a few rules you must follow and take heed of kitchen etiquette. Working together in a kitchen requires that you respect efforts of each and every one of your classmates. So, as an introduction, starting with the person to my right, I want you to introduce yourselves and tell us a little about your interests."

Once that was completed, Alf gave a little background on himself. "I graduated from the prestigious Cordon Bleu fifteen years ago and was immediately hired on to a cruise ship line as a sous-chef and gradually moved to become *the* chef. I did this for seven years working cruises in the Caribbean and Mediterranean. Having explored numerous ports, I decided to apply for a position with the Marriot Hotel chain and worked at three different locations over six years. Needing to get away from that cruise/hotel mentality, I looked for a location that was very different. Good fishing was my number one requirement; the thrill of landing a bass or pike is my utmost challenge. I signed on here for one season and now after two years, I have no intentions of leaving–ever. Manitoulin has become my home. Enough–let's start. Today, you will learn how to make Kombucha tea. This delicious beverage is a staple on the island because nature provides so many natural berries and herbs to infuse into the brew and thereby many flavours can be introduced."

Lois raised her hand. "Is Kombucha alcoholic?" Alf nodded.

"Good question. Because it is a fermented drink, there is a certain amount of alcohol produced but usually in minimal amounts. I mentioned 'ferment.' Does anyone know how we will do that?"

A shout-out of "yeast" answered his question.

"Yeast-based, yes, but once one batch has been made a 'starter,' it is reserved for the next brew. It is called a scoby. Directly in front of you, mid-table, you will see a one-quart preserving jar—pick it up. What do you see?"

"A gelatin blob on the bottom."

"Right. That is a scoby—the starter."

All eyes were on the amber coloured blob that seemed to quiver when the jar was moved.

"Behind you on the counter, you will see kettles. One of the requirements for superb Kombucha is making it with pure spring water, not chlorinated or treated tap water—thus the three ceramic water crocks, also on the counter. They are filled with fresh spring water. By the way, one of the reasons Kombucha is so widely available here is because there is abundant sweet water on the island. So fill your kettles about half full and plug them in."

Eager classmates bumped each other as they headed for one of the crocks. Apologies were expressed as each one lined up to complete this task. Lois noted the stainless steel countertops were gleaming and utensils were carefully sorted into distinct groupings. Each student was assigned a station where the utensils lay.

"Okay. Now while the kettle is heating, I want you to put 1/4 cup of sugar into a jar beside the one with your scoby. You will find what you need in the cupboard above your crock. Once your kettle is simmering—it doesn't have to come to a full boil—pour some over the granules and stir until the sugar is dissolved. Add two tea bags, also in the cupboard, to the sugar mixture; add enough water to the jar leaving about two inches at the top. Now, we will let the tea steep for twenty to thirty minutes. While we are waiting, I want each of you to select a fruit from the refrigerator, one that you savour. Wash it and chop it up into fine pieces until you have about 1/4 of a cup."

Lois stood with three of her classmates staring at the selection. There were raspberries, blackberries, blueberries, apples, peaches, plums and rhubarb. Without hesitation, she reached for the blackberries.

"You will see several sheets of labels on the table. Please, put your name on one and stick it on your jar. Kombucha takes seven to fifteen days to mature. We will sample yours on day seven."

The silence in the kitchen was only punctuated by pens scribbling on paper as each wrote their name and put the label on their jar.

"Class, your tea should be ready, so, please remove and discard the tea bags in the refuse can under your counter space. Now you must pour in the starter being careful not to slop. Tip your tea jar to a slight angle and the scoby jar bit by bit until the starter slips easily into the tea. Slowly now, ah, there that does it. Perfect, not a splash."

Everyone looked quite pleased with themselves and watched the blob of starter slowly sink to the bottom of their jar of tea looking somewhat like a big fat slug in brown liquid.

"Now, add your fruit. You can also use mint, lemon or other flavouring, but since Manitoulin produces all of this fruit, I like to have my students use them. You will notice coffee filters in front of you. Place two firmly over the top of your jar and secure them with the elastic band, also in front of you. Voila, c'est tout. Please set your jar on the counter against the backboard where it will not get knocked over and can ferment for the rest of the week. Please, clean up your area and put the now-empty scoby jar in the dishwasher. Take a short break before we learn how to make some appetizers to share with a glass of wine to celebrate our first day together."

With a big grin on her face, Lois stepped onto the back deck just through the kitchen back door. She breathed in the fresh air and turned her face to the sun.

"What do you think so far?" Lois turned to the heavyset, brown-eyed lady beside her. Her gravelly voice indicated she was a smoker. "Andrea." She reached out her hand.

"Too early to tell, but I think it will be great." Lois leaned on the railing after shaking Andrea's hand.

"Ladies, please don't lean. The railing is in need of repair and I am not sure it is safe. Carpenters are coming next week to fix it." Alf spoke with concern a frown on his face.

When the class resumed, they made barbequed meatballs, not on the barbeque but using Alf's personal BBQ sauce. Alf's choice was a tasty barbecue sauce that he claimed got a little spirited from adding beer. The barbecue sauce is simmered slowly until it's reduced and nicely thickened.

Alf set each student a chore—two people were to combine the ground beef with rolled oats, egg, and milk. Three others made a mixture of salt, pepper, flour and paprika. Each one took a handful of the meat, moulded it into small round balls and rolled each ball in the flour mixture, then added the meat to a pan with the shortening that had been heated to a boil. Once browned, the balls were removed, drained and placed in a casserole dish. Using the same shortening, they sautéed onions until translucent, added them to the casserole and covered the dish to bake for half an hour.

"Oh, my, the smells wafting through the halls are heavenly." Ethel opened the kitchen door. She was a wearing traditional native leather jerkin and reams of beaded necklaces. Alf greeted her with a bear hug and tugged her braid. He then introduced Ethel. "This elegant lady is one of the best cooks on the island, next to me, that is, and she will share her expertise on Wednesday." Turning to Ethel, Alf asked what brought her there that particular day.

"Nosy, I guess. Lois is a guest of mine and I saw my bike resting against the tree near the front veranda, so I decided to pop in. I won't disturb you and will be on my way."

Blowing air kisses, Alf watched Ethel wave at Lois, then exit through the swinging doors. He then turned to the class.

"Now, cooking is nothing without presentation. Appearance sparks the taste buds into action, so it is important to present food like you are an artist." Alf demonstrated how to arrange cheese, crackers, some veggies and fruit on a platter. When the arrangement was complete, he removed the casserole dish from the oven, dumped the meatballs into a serving bowl, and surrounded it with rounds of a crispy, toasted baguette that he had had one of the students prepare.

"Now ladies and gentleman, pour yourself a glass of wine and eat up. Before you leave, I want everything cleaned up spit spot. That is the rule for every day—spit spot."

Lois heaped her plate and pulled a stool to the counter. "I am famished. I forgot to eat breakfast and lunch and this is so delicious." She ate her fill, then gathered her plate to the dishwasher, picked up a cloth and started wiping down the surfaces. Alf oversaw the cleaning process offering advice where needed, then shooed everyone away with air kisses.

"Tonight I go fishing—tomorrow we cook fish."

Exhilarated by her first cooking class, Lois peddled quickly back to her cabin looking forward to a cool dip in the lake. She was now completely competent on the bike, loving the wind in her face and knowing that it was terrific exercise. Sliding to a stop at her door, she leaned the bike against the wall, dismounted and after running her fingers through her hair and shaking her head, she went inside. Minutes later, with her towel over her arm, she stepped out the door to find Rod leaning against a tree. He, too, was wearing a swimsuit and carrying a towel. Lois frowned— this was not meant to be a social time. She liked to hit the water full out and drive her body to its limit. She found swimming energized her and left her mind clear and devoid of emotional baggage.

"Hey, beautiful, thought I'd join you. Okay with you?"

Lois hesitated, then assured him he was welcome even though she was not enthusiastic about it. She hit the water with a shallow dive and with strong strokes was soon far ahead of Rod, who was still edging his way into the chilly lake. Rod was not a strong swimmer and muttered to himself, "not too smart, asshole. Not only did you intrude, but you now look like a jerk."

Turning at about the half-mile point, Lois stroked back. The tenseness was gone and she was one with the water. She repeated the route and had the oddest feeling she was not alone. It was almost as if there were a presence in the water matching her stroke for stroke. Every now and again, she stopped and looked around to find she was really alone. She swam for about an hour before heading for the shore. Rod was sitting sheepishly on his towel watching her.

"Okay, I think I just made a huge fool of myself. But, if you needed rescuing, I would have risen to the challenge."

"More likely I would be the one doing the rescuing. Sorry, Rod, but this is my meditative time and I dismiss the world once I am submerged."

"Understood."

Rubbing the towel vigorously up and down her arms, Lois started to laugh, then laid her towel beside Rod's and stretched out.

"I had the strangest sensation out there. It felt like I was not alone, like someone was swimming alongside of me, but each time I stopped and looked, I was all alone."

"Danny."

"Pardon."

"Danny—Danny Ford—his ghost."

"Like I am supposed to believe that one."

"The island is full of ghosts; the natives call it the Spirit Island. When the moon is full, two headless British redcoats are often seen lounging by their campfire as they were two centuries before. A band of Hurons surprised them and decapitated them. It is said that their spirits just won't rest. But our most famous ghost is Danny Ford of the famous Ford Motor family."

"You're spoofing me."

"Nope—it's a fact. Young Danny was a bit of a rebel and contrary to his family's wishes went off and married a local—a daughter of the tugboat captain. So, you can imagine the indignation of the Fords. Danny and his bride used to escape up here to their lodge, the Ford family lodge—used to be over there." Rod leaned forward and directed with a pointed finger indicating that Lois look to the far shore where the land rose to a majestic point. "Danny was a restless one: always trying crazy schemes to get attention. He found some sticks of dynamite, lit one and threw it out the window of the lodge. Stupid thing to do and the explosion wounded him. As his buddies and his new bride were taking him across the lake to the mainland for medical attention, he fell overboard and drowned. There was some skepticism about this as Danny was an excellent swimmer. But, nothing was ever proven to the contrary. His being an avid swimmer was probably why he joined you today. You are an excellent swimmer, too."

"Rod, you are totally creeping me out."

"Heck, you could run into one or two of the old trappers or seamen that are roaming about—you just never know when they will pop up. They are harmless ghosts, in fact, downright friendly."

"Okay, let's change the subject, not that I believe one word you are saying."

"There is a good movie in town tonight. Want to go?"

"Frankly, Rod, I came to Manitoulin to get away from city things. I appreciate the invitation, but I have a good book and am looking forward to losing myself in it."

"Am I beating myself up by wanting to pursue you for a date?"

"Pretty much. You are an extremely nice person and I enjoy your company, but I have no interest beyond that. Sorry, I don't mean to sound insensitive. I like you, but I am already involved. I'm way flattered though."

Rod shrugged, gathered up his towel and left her lying there.

Chapter 16

Now, wasn't that flattering? I haven't had anyone make a pass at me since I was seventeen and Randy came into my life. Well, old girl, I guess you must be improved by one hell of a lot. Wow, kind of fun. Anyway, I wouldn't for one moment even consider two-timing. Randy is the love of my life. Once I get him to understand why I left and he makes an effort to be more supportive, I will have the best of everything—wonderful children, a devoted husband, a beautiful home and a happy life. Let's hope so anyway. I know it is not going to be easy, but I feel certain that I can stand up for myself and whenever he makes a derogatory comment, I will merely draw it to his attention and demand an apology.

Maybe I will be able to convince Randy to come to Manitoulin next summer for a holiday. My goodness, I don't think he has ever taken a holiday. Perhaps he will like fishing. I will have such fun telling the children about the ghosts on the island. Maybe Helen and Norm will bring the twins to meet Lois, Brent and Dougie. That is, if they ever forgive me for deceiving them. They are such marvellous people and I do love Barby and Grant. Yep, Stacey Martin, now Lois Brenton-Douglas, you have made a mess of things. Even though I dread telling them the truth, it will be good to get everything out in the open.

Chapter 17

At first light the next morning, Lois grabbed her camera and making sure the strap was secure across her shoulder as she hopped on the bike, she headed for Bridal Veil Falls. She hadn't worn a wedding veil, just a smart beige suit. They had gone to City Hall to take their vows and register their marriage. Her mother invited Randy's parents for a small celebration at the Elgin Hotel. There was little or no connection between Stacey's mom and Randy's. In fact, Stacey felt her mother was being snubbed. When she reached the falls and climbed down the steps to the river, she once again broke into tears. She had propped her bike against the railing and walked down the steps to a ledge that led to the falling water. The water fell in a transparent sheet so like a wedding veil. Mist clouded in patches and the only sound was the falling water. Lois sank into deep reflective thought and tears, once again, streamed down her face.

Through her tears, Lois could see a clump of watercress. Quickly, she stood, wiped away the tears, lifted her camera and stepped forward to capture the deep green leaves framed against the falls.

"That could be a beauty."

"Yes, it could." A voice behind her made Lois turn her head to see Lucy leaning over the railing above her. "You're an early bird."

"Well, so are you. I am always on the lookout for special morning light that brings out the colour and intricacies of wildflowers."

"I have a nice thermos of coffee and scones with Hawberry jelly. Want to share?"

"Now, that is an invitation impossible to turn down."

Lucy was in a "tell everything about Manitoulin Island" mode again and Lois had no choice but to listen.

"I'm sure you know that this island has the most freshwater lakes of any island in the world. Situated on Lake Huron where it joins Georgian Bay, it is part of the Cambrian Shield. This limestone cliff gives way for the water to tumble over twin falls. It is a popular tourist destination as well as a favourite of the locals. If you follow the trail along the river for a kilometre or so, you will see where the salmon come to spawn."

Lucy and Lois said their goodbyes as each headed in a different direction. Lois was anxious to get to her cabin and change for her cooking class. Several days later and several cooking classes completed, Lois was relaxed and comfortable with who she had become.

The highlight of the week was the day that Ethel taught the cooking class her special recipe for fish stew. Every afternoon, feeling fulfilled and happy, Lois took her time enjoying the bike ride back to her cabin. Every evening, she took to the water for a swim. The perfect ending to a perfect day.

Lois struggled with mixed feelings as she biked to her final cooking class. Her holiday was almost over and she knew she would leave Manitoulin the next day to face two difficult situations. She had made a new and positive life for herself in Sudbury. She loved Helen and Norm and the twins. Her confession was apt to hurt them deeply, destroy their trust in her and her resignation would leave them in a difficult spot. Then she had to face returning to Ottawa and her own family. The question she also faced was, would Randy welcome her return? Pedalling faster and faster as her thoughts were reeling, Lois almost lost her balance as her tire hit a rock. Slamming on her brake and coming to a complete stop, Lois started to shake.

"I have to pull myself together. I put myself in this position because I ran away from Randy. I have created a horrible dilemma that has and will hurt people I love."

The blare of a horn had her scrambling to the side of the road as a dump truck swerved to miss her.

"Oh, my goodness, I have just avoided two accidents. Hope that old superstition of things coming in threes does not come true." The loud horn had brought her back to the moment and the fact that, if she did not hurry, she was going to be late for class.

With her heart racing and breathing fast, Lois managed to get to the kitchen, tie on her apron and stand behind the counter as Alf stepped in the doorway.

Standing there, she recalled the second day. Lois had watched and learned how to gut and prepare a Northern Pike.

"Did you catch this, Alf?"

"Not this one. I did hook a few small ones but put them back to grow some more. I have to admit; I had to buy this one."

That day, Lois learned how to cook the fish so the texture remained firm and the delicate flavour made the taster salivate. It was served with local wild rice cooked just enough to release the nutty sensations. Added were slivers of leek and hot peppers with a generous slab of butter. Alf explained that wild asparagus lightly braised in olive oil and dusted with finely chopped garlic was a treat to the taste buds. Blueberries were in season, so two students were tasked to prepare a sauce to pour over slices of white bunt cake. The classes ended with each student sitting to eat a serving. Alf poured a Pinot Grigio explaining how the light bouquet of citrus and flowers blended with the fruity flavour to enhance the taste of each part of the meal. Lois left that afternoon eager to return the next day as Ethel was the guest chef.

The time on the island was rapidly racing away.

The last night of her holiday, like every evening, she swam until every fibre in her body was relaxed. When she went to bed, it was to sleep a deep sleep waking refreshed and positive. Her decision to return to Ottawa still caused her to be anxious about how Randy was going to react. Standing in front of the mirror, she saw Lois, not Stacey. "Please, have the strength to go through with this and stand up for who I have become and don't fall prey to Randy's negative comments. You're a good mother—you're a good wife—you're a good person."

Early the next morning, Lois set off with her camera and while looking for the perfect subject, muttered away about her decision to return to Ottawa constantly convincing herself that she was worthy and strong. "The fact that I have made this decision proves that I can do it. I know I can. I will have to be strong."

She found clusters of bayberries spotted with dew that the morning light caught and threw a rainbow effect into each droplet. Adjusting her macro lens, Lois took picture after picture that was nature's work of art to her camera lens. She also captured images of intricate spider webs glistening, each strand wearing dew like a diamond necklace. On returning to her cabin, she wolfed down a speedy lunch and headed off on her bike for the final cooking class.

"Ah, my favourite pupils—today, you will not only learn how to prepare a barbeque feast, but also we will all share a special meal, drink wine and you can all tell me how wonderful I am. No? Well, that is not necessary, but what is, is that we get started. I am going to divide you into groups of two and each group will prepare a different dish to make a complete meal." Alf designated tasks by pointing and handing each pupil a recipe. "We will start with cream of tomato soup with hot oatmeal rolls, followed by spare ribs done on the barbeque and served with Caesar salad and a mixed bean salad—then we will finish the feast with hot applesauce cake topped with ice cream and Hawberry jelly. Now, hurry to your stations. We haven't got all day. We will celebrate your last day with me by eating till we are ready to explode!"

Lois was paired with Bob, the only male student, to prepare the ribs. Lois read the recipe and started to wash the meaty back ribs and wipe them dry. She then placed them in a pan with onions and garlic, a cup of white wine, a tablespoon of vinegar and enough water to cover them. Setting the element to a medium heat, she set them to slow cook for thirty minutes. She and Bob were also making the oatmeal rolls and Bob was busy measuring the ingredients. Lois busied herself making the barbeque sauce. Alf put on some jazz and while everyone was concentrating on their chores, bodies were swaying to the rhythm. "A good cook loves good music and jazz is good music, right?" All heads nodded.

Lois noticed that the ribs had been simmering for twenty-five minutes and asked Bob to light the barbeque. The smells were heavenly and she kept inhaling big deep breaths as she removed the simmering ribs, poured some of the liquid into the sauce makings and discarded the rest. Laying the meat, meat side up, on a baking sheet, Lois brushed a generous layer of sauce on them and headed for the deck to put them on the barbeque. Bob was checking the propane tank and didn't hear Lois approach. Suddenly, he stood up ramming his heavy frame into Lois. Completely off balance, she stumbled backward into the railing. The unstable railing gave way and Lois fell backward onto the rock garden below. The sound of breaking wood and Bob's screaming rent the air.

"Holy shit! Lois, are you okay?" Bob looked over the edge to see ribs scattered everywhere and Lois lying still. "Oh my God, she is hurt. Help, help someone."

Alf was the first to reach Lois and saw immediately that she was unconscious and bleeding from her head. He felt for a pulse while yelling instructions. "Call an ambulance right away and get me some blankets and towels."

Andrea raced down the hall of the hotel into the first room and grabbed bedding and towels. When she got back, she handed them to Alf. He covered Lois and gently lifted her head and placed towels beneath. He held her limp hand rubbing it trying to stimulate some response but felt the heat ebbing away. "Lois, Lois, stay with me, please."

The class milled close with expressions of dread masked on their faces. The shattered railing at their feet, spare ribs and red sauce splayed across the rock garden mixed with the blood flowing from Lois's head.

"Oh, my God, is she going to die?"

"Don't be stupid. She is only knocked out."

"She just has to be okay."

Comments were buzzing back and forth while Alf tried everything he knew to revive Lois. Suddenly, the reality of the possible injuries Lois might have endured made the entire group fall silent. Glances went back and forth; some shook their heads, and some bit their bottom lip, wrung their hands and looked terribly uneasy.

Within minutes, the piercing wail of the ambulance broke the heavy silence. Bob, who had been waiting at the road, waved it to the back of the inn and stepped aside as the doors flew open. One medic rushed to Lois and the other ran around to the back of the vehicle and threw open the back doors. The medic that ran to Lois noted that she was lying on her right side. He knelt next to her head where he could do a quick assessment of the injury. Without breaking his examination, he asked questions.

"How did she fall?"

"I knocked her over—I didn't mean to do it. I stood up too quickly. She was carrying the ribs to the barbeque. I jumped up and knocked into her—next thing I know, she fell against the railing and it broke. It gave way. All I could see was Lois falling and the ribs flying everywhere. Then there was red. I don't know if it was barbeque sauce or blood. Oh, my God, I hope she is okay! She is alive, isn't she, Alf?" Bob was distressed, talking too quickly, wringing his hands and pacing back and forth.

Turning to Alf, who still knelt near Lois on the other side, the medic asked him to hold her head steady as he eased a rigid collar around her neck. His partner reached over and placed a surgical pad over the wound to stem the bleeding. His partner left and arrived back with a backboard. Carefully, the two medics straightened her legs and slid the backboard tight against her back. One medic stood up and, using his mobile radio, called for air transport.

"Yeah, I have a victim GCS3—fall from a height, female about 110 pounds, unconscious, breathing rapidly. There is no response. Suspect brain injury and might be dealing with a spinal injury as well. The local hospital is not equipped to handle this— send a chopper. Good. I will switch to Provincial Communications and talk directly to the chopper."

"Hey, guys, I am glad the dispatcher alerted you. You're on your way? Good." Turning to his partner, he informed him that air transport was on the way.

"Okay, folks, please stay back. We need to transfer her to the gurney and monitor her until the helicopter arrives. What's her name?"

"Lois," a chorus of bystanders called out.

The two medics gently, yet firmly, rolled her onto the backboard. "Okay, 1-2-3, lift." With efficient fluid teamwork, they lifted Lois with the backboard onto the gurney and wrapped her in warm blankets. Within minutes, they had inserted an IV to keep her fluids up to stabilize her blood pressure. A soft moan surfaced from the gurney.

"Lois, can you hear me? My name is George; I am a medic. You had a fall. We are waiting for a helicopter to take you to the hospital in Sudbury." Even though he got no response, the medic continued to check her pulse and speak to her. He checked her eyes to determine if there might be swelling of the brain, then turned to his radio.

"Getting soft moans and slight motion. What is your ETA? There is a parking lot next to the hotel, but there are too many cars parked there, so I think the road would be your best bet. Fifteen minutes—okay, I will get the road cleared and ready for rendezvous."

George then instructed one person to go to the corner and stop traffic from entering the roadway and another to stop vehicles several hundred feet down the road. He and his partner eased the gurney slowly down the side of the hotel being careful not to jar Lois. All the time George kept up the one-way conversation. "Lois, we are moving you to the front of the hotel. Can you hear me? The chopper will be here very soon. You've had a fall. Can you hear me? We are sending you to the hospital in Sudbury. It is just a few minutes in the air and a team of doctors are on standby to help once it lands."

Speaking into his communications receiver to the chopper crew, George gave them the specific vital signs—"weak pulse, rapid breathing and still uttering soft moans. No response to my questions."

The students from the cooking class stood by in awkward silence, a few holding hands for reassurance, as they watched their broken classmate being lifted and wheeled away. Bob was busy directing traffic, which prevented him from thinking how he had been the cause of the accident. Alf reported to the owners of the inn what was happening as soon as the gurney was in the control of the medics and he was no longer needed. Everyone gathered in a cluster when they heard the ambulance arrive, straining to watch Lois. Hushed remarks blended into the summer breeze that was wafting through the evergreens.

The throbbing of the chopper blades soon made conversation impossible and everyone watched wordlessly as Lois was loaded on board and handed over by the two attending medics to the chopper medics. In less than five minutes, the door was closed and the helicopter lifted off. The silence that seemed to prevail was broken by Bob uttering in a demented scream, "I've killed her! Oh, my God, I've killed her!"

Alf wrapped his arms around Bob's shoulder and, with the assistance of Andrea, eased him into the building and sat him on a stool in the classroom. The rest of the class followed. The tension in the room filled every corner.

"I am sure she will be okay. There is nothing else we can do today except clean up the ribs from the garden and throw them into the garbage." Alf realized that no one wanted to finish the class, so he instructed them to get busy cleaning up. He knew that by keeping active, the shock of the events would diminish. Once the classroom was tidy, he handed out recipe booklets and certificates plus a gift-wrapped jar of Hawberry jelly and their Kombucha. It was a solemn group that left the inn. Alf promised to keep them informed as to Lois's condition.

The hotel had notified Ethel and she arrived at the hotel right after the ambulance had left. She helped Alf fill out a report and called Helen and Norm. By the time the chopper landed on the helipad beside the hospital, Helen and Norm had hastily left work and were on their way to the hospital. They pulled into the parking lot right behind each other. They exchanged worried looks and together dashed for the emergency entrance.

Lois had been rushed from the chopper to a treatment room and, with precision movements, transferred on the backboard to the hospital stretcher. The trauma team took over as the medic shouted out to the team what had transpired. A nurse wrote down everything said as doctors, residents and nurses, rolled her gently on her side to remove the backboard. They cut away Lois's shirt and jeans, wrapped her in blankets and took her vitals. She seemed to be regaining consciousness but appeared confused by the activity and voices surrounding her.

"Hello there." The doctor standing beside Lois was speaking in a gentle voice. "I am Davis Dorset, a physician. You have had a bad fall. Can you tell me your name?"

Lois blinked at the glaring light, focused on the figure standing beside her and tried to shake her head.

"Oh! My head hurts."

"Yes, you had a nasty fall. Can you tell me where you were born?"

"I'm sorry, I don't know. I can't remember."

"Okay, then, can you tell me where you went to high school?"

"I'm sorry, I can't remember that either. Why am I here?"

"Do you know where you are now?"

Lois grasped the sheets and tears ran down her cheeks. "I don't know anything. Who am I? What happened?"

The medical staff recognized that panic was setting in and that Lois was stressing. "Easy, easy, everything will be all right. You fell. You hit your head when you fell and are experiencing a temporary loss of memory. It is not uncommon, so to help you relax, we will give you something to calm you and let you rest. I am sure your memory will start to return shortly. We need to do some further tests, so don't be alarmed. Everything will be okay."

Chapter 18

Right now, I wish my head would stop throbbing and I would like to lie on my right side instead of on my back. The ceiling is all I can focus on and I can see a stand with a bag of something that has a tube running into my wrist. Thankfully, the nurse put a warm blanket over me because I was shivering uncontrollably. It is white like the sheet and the walls—it's a marshmallow world. Okay, I remember that song. Now it is running around in my poor aching head.

Oh, I want to turn over, but I can't because my whole body hurts. It all happened so fast. Last thing I remember was walking across the deck to Bob. Then I was air born. The next thing I remember is a doctor leaning over me with a bright light shining into my left eye. He kept asking me questions I couldn't answer and others I could. For the life of me, I do not remember the easiest ones such as where I went to school. Where did I go to school? He asked my mother's name. What kind of person can't even remember their mother's name? Oh, this is so depressing. I keep trying to think of where I lived before Sudbury. I know I have been here a year and am twenty-three, but other than that, I have no idea how I got here or why. Oh, dear, here I go again. Tears are pouring down my face and onto the pillow—I simply feel so frustrated. The doctor assured me that this is not uncommon. I sure hope he is right. It is terrible not knowing who you are or where you came from.

Chapter 19

Norm grabbed Helen's hand and together they rushed to the emergency desk asking for Lois. It seemed to take forever for the file to be located. Then the attendant was less than helpful. They were instructed to take a seat and wait. Neither sat—they both paced. The twenty minutes they waited seemed like hours. Finally, a soft padding of shoes approaching them made them pause. A green smocked man with a thick head of flaming red hair approached them.

"You are Lois's relatives?"

"No, but we are the closest thing as she has no relatives that we know of. She lives with us. I'm Norm French." Norm shook the doctor's hand and introduced Helen.

"She is regaining consciousness but is quite confused as to who she is and where she is. This is not unusual under the circumstances. She is drifting in and out of wakefulness. We have her sedated and under constant scrutiny. Right now, you need to know that her injuries are not life-threatening and, although there appears to be severe bruising on her face and shoulder, there does not appear to be any broken bones. However, her head did receive a serious blow and she probably has a concussion— right now, we are taking her for an MRI. We should have the results within an hour. I suggest you get a coffee and return about that time and we will have a better understanding of her injuries."

Much relieved to get even this information, they were still very concerned. Norm ushered Helen to the cafeteria. Their coffees grew cold; the silence between them hung like a heavy curtain. When they returned to the reception area, the doctor was waiting. He informed them that Lois was stable, had no broken bones and he would do a further assessment and a CT scan in about twelve hours. He told them that she was resting but heavily sedated, so they would have to wait until morning to see her.

The hospital staff monitored Lois constantly for the rest of the day and overnight for concussion. Helen and Norm arrived early the next day and were allowed a few minutes with her. Helen grabbed Norm's arm to steady herself when she saw how pale and fragile Lois looked in the hospital bed. When Lois saw them, she immediately smiled weakly and reached for Helen's hand.

"You gave us quite the scare. Do you know me?"

"Of course."

The doctor had filled Helen and Norm in on the amnesia, so they were delighted Lois knew them. During the night hours, Lois had remembered her name and also recalled the minutes leading up to the accident. She also told the doctor where she lived in Sudbury but was not able to remember her high school or where she grew up. Bits and pieces were coming back, but she still had major gaps in her memory.

"Why can't I remember anything? I must have told you all about me when I arrived, right? But I don't remember having that conversation."

"We didn't. You were quite secretive about your past. We only know that you came from Ottawa, or at least that is what you told us."

After a few minutes, Helen and Norm consulted with the doctor, who informed them that he had called in a neurologist, Dr. Frosst, for his opinion.

When Helen and Norm left the hospital, they called Ethel to fill her in on the news. They needed to arrange to collect all of Lois's belongings. Ethel said she would let everyone at the inn know what was happening and she was going to Sudbury the following day, so she would bring all Lois's things.

That afternoon, Helen met with Doctor Frosst at the hospital in Sudbury.

"She seems to be recovering exceptionally well, regaining strength and keeping light food down. She is going to be mighty sore and will have one glorious black eye. However, there are some complications. There is still the concern of memory loss. She can recount everything she did on Manitoulin and is adamant that she needs to get home and back to work to take care of your twins. Oh, yes, she talked and talked about Barby and Grant. What is a major concern is that she can't seem to recall anything prior to living in Sudbury. This is very puzzling as she has a clear memory of everything in the past year. It is early to tell, but there is a rare disorder that is triggered by psychological trauma. Simply put, the patient loses all memory prior to a traumatic event. Dissociative disorders are usually caused by trauma in the recent or distant past, or with an intense internal conflict that forces the mind to separate incompatible or unacceptable knowledge, information, or feelings. In dissociative amnesia, the continuity of the patient's memory is disrupted. Patients have recurrent episodes in which they forget important personal information or events, usually connected with trauma or severe stress. The information that is lost to the patient's memory is usually too extensive to be attributed to ordinary absentmindedness or forgetfulness. Dissociative amnesia was formerly called 'psychogenic amnesia.' Do you know if Lois has been under any stress that might trigger this kind of response?"

"We do know that she came to Sudbury to escape a difficult situation. She never talked about it, but both Norm and I assumed it was an abusive relationship. Frankly, we had no idea what she was running away from—it could have even been a financial issue. We have no idea. She did come with glowing recommendations from her former employer."

"Yes, the primary cause of dissociative amnesia is stress associated with traumatic experiences that the patient has either survived or witnessed. These may include such major life stressors as serious financial problems, the death of a parent or spouse, extreme internal conflict, and guilt related to serious crimes or turmoil caused by difficulties with another person. The prognosis for recovery from dissociative amnesia is generally good. The majority of patients eventually recover the missing parts of their past, either by spontaneous re-emergence of the memories or through hypnosis and similar techniques. A minority of patients, however, are never able to reconstruct their past; they develop a chronic form of dissociative amnesia. The prognosis for each specific patient depends on a combination of his or her present life circumstances, the presence of other mental disorders, and the severity of stresses or conflicts associated with the amnesia."

"We do know that she told us that both her parents are dead and she has no siblings. What can we do?"

"Dissociative amnesia is most commonly diagnosed in young adults. The amnesia appears to be caused by traumatic or stressful experiences endured or witnessed such as physical or sexual abuse, rape, combat, abandonment during natural disasters, death of a loved one, or by tremendous internal stress. The prognosis is determined mainly by the patient's life circumstances, particularly stresses and conflicts associated with the amnesia, and by the patient's overall mental adjustment. I would like Lois to go home tomorrow and resume some of her light daily activities. Try to introduce what you know of her past to her and record her reaction. I would like to see her once a week for the next month. Likely, this whole issue will resolve and she will be as good as new. The concussion also needs to be monitored, so she should not do activities that require any physical exercise or lifting. In other words, she needs plenty of rest for a few days, but she will regain her strength rapidly."

"I will contact her former employer and see if we can get more details about her. My mother has agreed to stay on for another week, so that should help Lois settle in and give her time to resume her responsibilities. Being home with us should help also."

"It is always better to be in familiar surroundings."

Helen returned to Lois and told her she would pick her up the next day to take her home. "The twins are so anxious to see you. They have missed you each and every day."

Buoyed up by knowing she was going home, Lois fell into a deep sleep when Helen left.

Smells of freshly baked bread wafted out the door as Lois arrived home. Barby and Grant stood shyly inside, not knowing quite how to greet her. They were dressed in matching red pants and yellow t-shirts with Sudbury Tiny-Tot-Swim on a large splash of water. Lois squatted down balancing her back against the hall wall. Both rushed to her, then backed away. "Is it okay to touch you? Does your head hurt? Why did they shave off your hair? Do you have a hole in your head? Do you have to stay in bed? Did you hit your eyes too?"

The questions came fast and furious as the twins took in the state of their nanny, her shaved and bandaged head and her blackened eyes. Lois chuckled and as she slowly eased herself to her feet; she gingerly walked to the living room and sat on the sofa. Lois motioned the twins to sit beside her as she answered their questions.

"I am thrilled your grandmother is staying for a few days because I will have to be very careful in terms of how much I do and besides, I am stiff and sore. Too bad it is not Halloween ' cause I think I would have the winning costume without wearing a costume."

The twins giggled and nodded their heads.

"Here is something you need to know—falling on rocks is not fun. It really, really hurts. I hurt my head and some other parts as well. My black eyes are from the fall too."

"Will your hair grow back?"

"Yes, it will and will cover the place where the stitches are. The doctor will take out the stitches in about a week, but I will always have a scar. But the good thing is, I will get better and, with your help, in a hurry. Grant, you know how you always hold up your arm to show me how you have muscles? When someone has a nasty fall like I did, muscles get hurt too. What is it?"

The twins were smiling and jumped down from the sofa, dashed across the carpet, left the room and returned with their hands behind their back.

"Here." Barby shoved a folio forward. On the front was "Get Well Soon."

Lois opened it to find sheets of coloured pictures with happy faces and flowers and handprints each one with 'get well' written in childish print. She reached for each twin and hugged them close. "These are the most beautiful pictures ever. Wow, this is the best homecoming present."

Helen's mother appeared around the corner, welcomed Lois home and announced that the bread was fresh out of the oven. Always a stylish dresser, she wore an elegant taupe pantsuit even though she was baking. She had an uncanny ability to stay unscathed with no flour or stains on her clothes. The smells of the fresh bread followed her. Something resembling a stampede occurred as the family raced to the kitchen. Lois followed carefully taking her time; she was a little dizzy. She made it to the kitchen and sat at the table savouring the smells and the loving atmosphere. After eating a small portion of the freshly baked bread, she realized that the trip home had left her exhausted.

"I have to go to my room. I am still somewhat fragile."

Over the next few days, she gradually gained strength pushing herself a little more each day. The doctor proclaimed that the physical wounds were healing nicely, but they were still concerned about her memory loss. Helen tried to reach Stacey, but her email was not working and Helen had neglected to get her last name or a phone number.

"How could I have been so careless as to not get that information? Sometimes, I wonder just where my head is." Norm nodded in agreement.

"You are too trusting and when Stacey was so adamant that Lois would be a good nanny, you simply accepted her word. Details are not your forte—except when it comes to engineering problems."

Lois remembered distinctly arriving in Sudbury; she remembered meeting Norm at the station and the drive home, but everything before that time was blank.

Chapter 20

In the hospital, the voices of the doctors and nurses wakened me. It felt as if I was in a void, apart yet present—there was a roar of voices, or at least it seemed like a roar. Everything was amplified. Once I was lifted from the gurney to a bed, the nurses checked me regularly, but I was so sleepy that everything is a blur. Helen and Norm were there when I woke up the next morning and told me that I would be going home and that Helen would be picking me up, so maybe my memory is fine. The questions the doctor asked about my past keep running through my mind, but for the life of me, I cannot remember anything before coming to Sudbury. Apparently, I used to live in Ottawa. I have no idea where and can't remember anything about that city except I know it is the capital of Canada. 'Traumatized,' that is what the doctor said. He explained that my past must have been dramatic enough for me not to want to remember. Whatever could be so bad as not to want to remember? I turned everything out of my wallet trying to find some documentation that might answer some of the questions—nothing.

Right now, I don't care. I missed the twins and Helen and Norm. I'm just happy to be home, to be able to sleep in my own bed and be with the people around me that I trust and love. The doctor predicts that whatever I have forgotten will likely surface in time. Something entirely unexpected will probably trigger it. Fine. I think I will just take each day as it comes and not let it worry me. Oh, I couldn't wait to get out of that hospital and see the twins. Grant was so impressed with my whopping black eyes—not sure I share his delight. I look a fright and every inch of me hurts. Even the powerful painkillers the doctor gave me are of little use, so I'd rather not take them if I can avoid it. Somehow, the pain is comforting—it makes me know that my body is healing.

Chapter 21

Eager to resume her duties and to let Helen's mother return home, Lois took on more and more small chores and was soon competent enough to do everything. By the end of the week, she could stand for longer periods of time without getting dizzy. Peter and Mary had sent flowers but had put off visiting until her second week home. Lois assured them that they must bring Jack or the twins would never forgive them. Mrs. Daly had left cookies galore and fresh cinnamon buns when she left. Sitting around the kitchen table Lois, Peter and Mary rapidly caught up on each other's news.

"I am going nuts." Peter slapped his hand against his forehead leaving a red mark. "Do you remember the bulldozer that we worked on? Well, the owner is offering it at an amazing price and I have a contact that has agreed to rent it for some work, but I can't get the bank to give me a loan as I have no collateral. I also have a line on a grader I heard about that can be bought for a steal. I am disappointed to miss out on these opportunities. It could have been the first step toward having my own business."

Lois sympathized but seemed somewhat distracted. When Peter left and the family visit was over, she asked Norm if she could talk to him. She told him about what Peter had said.

"Norm, this may sound foolish, but what would you think if I approached Peter about a partnership? He wants to start a company that rents out construction equipment. For some reason, I know a lot about big machinery. I have some money invested in Mutual Funds—where it came from, I don't know—but I do have a considerable sum. There is a weird gap in some of my Sudbury actions, like where that money came from. However, I need to think ahead. You won't need a nanny forever and I plan to stay in Sudbury. If what Peter says is true, there is a huge demand by construction companies for heavy equipment. A partnership in this kind of venture might be the right timing for me and the right thing for both of us."

"Lois, to begin with, how come you know anything about heavy equipment?"

"Now, there is a pointed question— I don't know. I just know I am familiar with operating and running a bulldozer and an excavator. How come? I have no idea, but this is obviously a link to my past, lost when I lost my memory."

"Perhaps it is a sign that it will come back a little at a time. Now, back to your question. Owning your own business is a formidable venture—when it is successful, it can be one of the most rewarding things in life, but so much can go wrong and it can be highly stressful. We do know that you have dealt with something traumatic before arriving in Sudbury. I'm not sure it is a good idea to subject yourself to another situation that might add further stress. On the other hand, I don't want you to miss out on what might be a timely opportunity. I'd advise you not to make any rash decisions, but it might be a worthwhile exercise to have Peter draw up a business plan and a financial proposal with all the numbers, et cetera. He will benefit from the exercise and I don't mind helping. I will go over it and meet with the two of you to discuss it."

"Oh, Norm, that would be fantastic. I like and trust Peter and Mary, but without the proper guidance, it could be a disaster."

Lois phoned Peter right away.

"But, Lois, how could you do it and why would you do it?"

"I cannot be a nanny forever and I have a little money. I am not committing, but I think we should talk."

Peter worked well into the late hours and was at Norm and Helen's house early the next morning. Lois and the twins were still in their sleepwear, Lois wrapped in a blue housecoat and teddy bear slippers; the twins wore matching green shorty pyjamas. Helen and Norm were dressed for work. Helen was in her jeans and T-shirt and Norm in a neatly pressed, brown dress pants and a short-sleeved, beige shirt ready for the day. Norm laughed at Peter's early arrival and eagerness.

The smells wafting from the kitchen had Peter begging for a cup of coffee. "I worked nearly all night. A pick-me-up is what I need."

"This kind of enthusiasm and early hours are crucial to surviving the pitfalls of owning your own business."

"I got so excited when I started adding up the numbers that I couldn't wait to share them."

"Are these numbers correct?" Norm was running his fingers down the columns of figures on the spreadsheet in front of him.

"They are accurate but likely modest. I didn't want to make any wild claims that might not be realistic."

"And your projected working capital is accurate too?"

"Yes."

"If Lois goes ahead with this, how will you protect her investment?"

"Lois indicated that she would like to be a full partner. She suggested putting up the money and holding a lean on the grader and bulldozer interest-free until the company paid them off in full, at which time the ownership would transfer to the company."

"This may sound insane, but I think you two have a great idea. I am going to put you in touch with my financial accounting wizard and my business lawyer with a clear understanding that if they think this is a bad idea, you both walk away."

Both Peter and Lois were nodding their heads and smiling. Without thinking, Peter grabbed Lois, swung her around and gave her a big hug.

"Watch it! You big lug—I hurt! And, I don't want to be wearing your coffee!"

Norm recognized the need for expediency because the machinery needed to be acquired before someone else heard about them. He made appointments with his contacts for the following day. By the next day's end after running the numbers over and over again, Peter and Lois were on their way to owning a heavy-equipment rental company.

All the talk of heavy equipment had Grant asking endless questions of Lois. She showed him with his toy excavator how he could move sand around the sandbox and create roadways for his cars and trucks. Grant had the heavy equipment bug as did Lois.

After the accountant had gone over the numbers and given his nod of approval, the lawyer agreed to write up the partnership agreement. Peter put a tentative offer and hold on the dozer and grader. While he was waiting for the legal work to be done, he contacted contractors that might need heavy equipment. Lois insisted that anybody renting their equipment must sign a rental agreement that made them liable for any accidents and misuse of the machinery. The lawyer drew up the necessary paperwork for both the partnership and the rental agreements. The contractors that Peter contacted indicated that there was more work than expected.

"So, madam partner, what will we call the company? Brenton-Douglas Barto or Barto Brenton-Douglas?"

"Too wieldy. Why not BDB Heavy Equipment Rentals?"

"Hey, you get one more letter than I do!"

"Tough—take it or leave it."

"Just kidding. I like it—wow, my stomach is flipping butterflies and I am borderline sick with nerves. This is such a huge step. Mary says I was tossing and turning all night."

"Strange as it might seem, Peter, I am totally the opposite—it just seems so right. I don't even feel that putting nearly all my money on the line is a risk. I am so, so confident that we are making the right decision."

The next month was a blur of finding a location, setting up banking, logo design, going over all the business details and scheduling rental times for clients. They decided to continue with their current jobs and operate BDB via cell phone. The motel owner that sold them the bulldozer offered a six-month, rent-free yard at the back of the motel and Walker offered their repair facilities and tools at a nominal hourly rate. Lois took a refresher course in heavy equipment operation and passed her licence with exemplary marks. There was no question of how competent she was—she handled the giant machines like a pro.

"You know, kids, this endeavour was as if it was meant to be." Norm's voice projected one of authority. "All the pieces are coming together in rapid order." Mary, Peter, Helen and Lois were seated around the kitchen table at the French's at Norm's request. It was the first official day in business for BDB and already the equipment was booked for two entire months. Everyone was focused on Norm standing at the head of the table. "I wanted us all together this extraordinary evening to let you know that Helen and I are behind you all the way. As a memento of this special day, we want to present you each with a small gift."

The twins, with Jack crawling behind, approached the table— Barby handed Lois a gift-wrapped parcel and Grant handed Peter an identical one.

"Really, this is not necessary –"

Peter was cut off by Helen. "It would not be nearly as much fun if it was necessary—go ahead and open them. 1,2,3, go."

Paper was torn away and Peter slapped a navy blue cap with BDB in gold lettering on his head. Lois was slipping on a bomber jacket with the company name. Camera at the ready, Helen was recording the partners as they stood in corporate caps and jackets with silly grins on their faces.

"Now, we are so totally official." Lois hugged Norm, then Helen, then Mary and finally Peter. "You know, I may not remember my past, but this evening will be engraved on my memory forever as one of the best nights of my life."

"It is not over until it is over—we are going to the club for a celebratory dinner complete with champagne. Francis is coming over to sit the children."

The news of BDB spread through the dining room at the golf club and people kept coming over to their table to wish them success.

A small pasty looking man with mousy brown hair leaning on a cane edged close to Peter. "Andrew Ford," he said as he reached for Peter's hand. "I own Dominion Construction and Paving. We are resurfacing all the roads leading onto Manitoulin next spring. Could keep your equipment busy for the better part of a year if the price is right. Can you come to my office to talk to me tomorrow morning—early–at seven?"

Peter stood up to introduce himself, but Ford slapped his business card on the table and moved away. His raspy smoker's voice echoed, his message hanging in the air. It took a few heartbeats to process what had just happened. "Holy cow! He owns the largest paving and construction company in the north. I know Walkers do work for him." Peter was whispering, his tone tense with excitement.

"It's a fact that club members support each other. You might have to learn to play golf, Peter."

"Might be better if the pretty partner did," Helen said.

"If we can nail a contract with Dominion, we will be laughing all the way to the bank."

"He sure didn't mince words—just got right to the point, then left. Doesn't he own his own machinery?"

"Yes, Lois, he does, but he probably always needs more than he owns. By using other companies and operators, he keeps his overhead down and does not have equipment sitting idle." Peter's voice was edgy. "Also, by renting equipment, he can manage several locations at a time. I overheard that he is often caught in a bind when equipment breaks down and he has to bring it into Walkers for repair. That kind of problem can set a project behind by days if not weeks. Dominion is forever transporting broken machinery to Walkers from worksites."

"Maybe we can offer him something unique. Peter, do you think it is possible to have an on-site mechanic and operator?"

Peter leaned over the table, his hands waving in spiral circles. "Lois, that's a brilliant idea especially when the jobs are remote. Some time ago, while doing some repairs on a grader, I calculated how costly it was for the company to take it out of service, transport it to Walkers, pay for repairs and then truck it back to the job site. I mentally imagined an on-site service truck. Because I already have an idea of what would be required, I could put it on paper and give it some consideration. When we meet with him tomorrow, we will get a better idea of what he needs."

Chapter 22

My head is spinning. This could be the chance of a lifetime. Getting a contract with Dominion would help BDB pay off my loan sooner. However, I am thinking that if Dominion is offering a substantial amount of work, and if we are to be competitive, we will have to invest more money to make it happen. We may not have the necessary equipment and might have to decline the work. Crap, I am dreaming of climbing mountains; it is likely only one small job offer. Oh, I hope we can at least get a small contract—to be associated with Dominion would be incredible. Even a small contract could lead to bigger ones in the future.

Oh, my goodness, thoughts are racing through my head. Don't think I will sleep for even a minute. My stomach is doing flips and my head is buzzing with numbers floating in a spiral motion. The very thought of connecting with Dominion is overwhelming. Andrew Ford, for a small man, has a very commanding presence. Even though he walks with difficulty leaning on a cane, one forgets his physical appearance immediately when he starts to speak. His voice has a strong firmness that commands attention. He is direct and gets right to the point. I am sure that he built his company by controlling every minute detail and making positive decisions. Peter and I could learn a great deal by working with a man like that. Lordy, I have punched this pillow a hundred times and sleep simply will not come.

Chapter 23

Before heading to bed that evening, Norm had agreed to stay home with the twins in the morning, so Lois was free to meet with Dominion. Peter told Walkers he would be late. The way was clear for Peter and Lois to keep the early morning appointment. Lois took extra care with her appearance, choosing a simple tweed pantsuit. The soft beige allowed her skin to glow as did her simple white blouse. Lois smiled as she slipped pearl earrings into her ears that matched a string around her neck. "I am good to go." Lois put her hands together and issued a silent prayer.

The address on the card was on Notre Dame Avenue and they both arrived at 6:45 am. Peter had traded in his usual jeans for a trim navy blue suit, white shirt and simple striped tie. "Hey, partner, we clean up good." Lois did a double quick step to keep up with Peter. "Slow up there, fella. My legs are shorter than yours."

After identifying themselves to the receptionist, Lois and Peter were ushered into a massive office. Andrew rose from behind his desk and crossed the floor with his hand outstretched in greeting.

"You did not have to bring the little lady with you. My secretary will take notes of the meeting."

"Mr. Ford, I'm sorry, I'm afraid you have the wrong idea. Peter and I are full partners in BDB—he is the financial and mechanic side and I am the operations person. I am a fully licensed heavy equipment operator."

"Well, now, doesn't that beat all! A little lady driving those big machines!"

"I do."

"Not only does she drive them, but she is also extremely

capable and expert at handling the toughest of challenges." Peter felt that he had to come to the defence of Lois although she was facing Ford with steady, confident eyes.

When Ford laid out what Dominion needed, it was apparent that BDB would be fully engaged for at least six months.

"Sir, would there be a need for an on-site mechanic?"

"One of my biggest bugbears is every time a machine breaks down, we have to truck it to Sudbury to Walkers. You are likely the go-to guy there."

"Lois and I were considering rigging a mobile repair vehicle to have on site but need to crunch some numbers before we undertake such a large investment."

"My boy, if you and the little lady do that, I can assure you it will pay for itself within a year with what I need—a brilliant, brilliant idea. When you work out the logistics, come back to me. I lose hours and hours when a machine sits idle and that translates into mega dollars, all of it caused by broken-down machinery. If there were a way to repair on site, man, our expenses would drop and production would improve. Brilliant idea—you gotta make that happen for old Andy."

"So, little lady—"

"Lois, my name is Lois."

"Yes, little lady, I know."

The two BDB owners left the building and as they were crossing the parking lot to their vehicles, Peter turned to Lois.

"Well, little lady—"

Lois took a swing at Peter.

"I guess from someone else, it would be a derogatory statement, but when someone is offering a chance to put our company on easy street, I shouldn't complain."

"No shit, but I'm sorry. That label is going to stick where that man is concerned."

"He can call me whatever he wants as long as he comes through with a walloping big contract that translates into big cheques. Do you think he is related to the motor company Fords?"

"I heard he was some distant cousin. Why?"

"Nothing. Just something crossed my mind. I may have had a vague meeting with one of his long lost relatives, a ghost in fact."

"What!"

"Never mind. Let's see what you come up with to make a service vehicle a possibility."

Peter pulled all the numbers together to outfit a service van and purchase the vehicle. The numbers were staggering because not only would he have to have a portable hoist, he would need computer technology and all the necessary tools. Lois interjected by pointing out that a hoist could be eliminated because she could simply dig a pit, stabilize it and Peter could work beneath the machine. He worked with the accountant to determine return on investment and it was quickly determined that Ford was right. It could be making a profit within a year if Ford agreed to the hefty prices they would have to charge. It was a nervous pair that met in Dominion's office the next morning. Peter explained the scenario and set a page of cost estimates in front of Andrew. A few minutes of tense silence followed.

"Peter, you and the little lady just draw up the contract and old Andy will sign on the dotted line. Best thing ever for Dominion, yes, sir. Best thing ever."

Peter and Lois did not realize they were holding their breath until they both sucked in air at the same time.

"Well, sir, it would appear that we are in business together." Peter reached over Andrew Ford's desk to shake his hand.

"Andy, call me Andy—no sirs around here." Andy rose from his chair and leaning on his cane grabbed Peter and Lois's hands. "This is a deal that will bring us both prosperity. Now, Peter, how about you and the little lady join me at the club for lunch?"

It took several weeks to find a suitable trailer, plan how to outfit it and have a portable mechanic station up and ready by the time spring rolled around. Mary laughed that Peter was as proud of his invention as he was the day Jack was born.

"Not quite, but close," Peter said.

Lois wanted to remain working as a nanny mainly because she loved Barby and Grant like they were her own children and she was not ready to let them go. However, the twins would be going to kindergarten half days and, by the following year, would be in school full days. Peter and Lois worked a schedule whereby Mary took over minding the twins on Thursdays and Fridays since Peter was going to be staying at the work site and only home on Sundays. Helen didn't work weekends, so both she and Norm were delighted with the arrangement. This would leave Lois available to operate one of the machines three days a week and give her Sundays free too.

Small jobs kept them busy over the winter months and before they realized it, March was coming up fast. Dominion was gearing up to start the Manitoulin work by the end of the month. The revenue that had come in over the winter was enough for the bank to realize that BDB was moving toward being a profitable enterprise, so a loan was arranged to outfit the service vehicle. BDB had already bought a 4x4 that would be Peter's transportation and would haul the 16' service trailer he also bought. Peter was in his glory as he filed each and every tool in a specific place. This was his dream—not only to own his own business but to work with the latest tools. Lois bought a compact car to drive back and forth to the site two hours from Sudbury. She rented a room in Little Current that she and Peter could share—Peter would have the room Monday, Tuesday and Wednesday and sleep in the trailer on Thursday and Friday. Lois would use the room Thursday and Friday and drive home Saturday night as would Peter. At this point, the Dominion Construction crew had Sundays off. By the end of March, they were as ready as they could be.

The week started with everything working like clockwork.

There were no major repairs, but Peter kept busy with general maintenance. They had no idea that an ice storm would strike late Wednesday afternoon. Lois left Sudbury early in the evening and by the time she got to Worthington, she was crawling along the highway with her heater blasting on the windshield and peering through the defrosted portion ever mindful of black ice. She had to stop several times to clear the windshield wipers coated with ice before she got to the turn-off to Little Current. When she stepped out of the car to scrape the ice off the headlights, she had to be extra careful not to lose her footing. She felt sluggish from the heat cranked up full blast to keep the windows clear. She finally slid to a stop at the worksite to find everything at a standstill. Stepping cautiously from the car she slipped and slid, barely keeping her balance, to the office trailer to find Peter nursing a cup of steaming coffee.

"You are a happy sight. I was so worried about you driving in this mess. I tried to call, but your cell was out of service and I did not catch you before you left to tell you to stay put—you must have already left."

"I certainly would not have come had I known. The weather in Sudbury was clear and dry. I was already halfway here before I hit it, but I decided to continue. Not sure that was smart."

"Anyway, you are here now and safe. We cannot work in this weather so will just have to weather it." Peter handed Lois a cup of coffee laughing at his choice of words.

The storm set the work back a week. Water had gotten into some of the motors and the flash freeze created havoc. Peter's first week on the job was hectic and the first day after the storm was not an eight-hour day but a straight forty-eight hours to get the equipment up and running.

"It is amazing how strong water turned to ice can be. That expansion can crack a metal part in no time." Peter was turning over the motors and listening with a trained ear for any unusual sounds. He would not let any of the equipment be used until he gave it a thumbs up. Once satisfied with everything, he fell into the bunk set up in the trailer. He was sore, tired and happy. Right then, his cell vibrated. A slow smile spread across his face from cheek to cheek as he listened to the caller. Ford was over the wall with praise as he noted that Peter being on site had saved them from damaging equipment and at least another week's setback.

The following week, the weather finally cleared with not a cloud to be seen and a warm March sun beamed down on mud puddles and dripping trees. Work resumed and progressed at a steady pace. Dominion hoped to get as much done before the tourists started arriving at the end of June, so the traffic flow was not constantly disrupted. The most difficult problem would be getting the traffic across the bridge while construction continued. Stop lights were installed, so one side of the bridge alternated between coming and going traffic.

Andrew Ford and the corporate engineers inspected the work several times a week.

"My, that little lady can sure handle that big excavator. Why, I'll bet she could pick up a paper clip from ten feet away. Wherever did she learn how to handle those big machines?"

Peter just nodded but refused to explain. He was still very concerned about Lois not remembering her past. He had had to tell her that she learned all about heavy equipment from her father. She had dissolved into tears because she had no recollection of her father.

"Oh, Peter, I don't even know who my parents are. I have no pictures; I have no memories; I have no past."

Peter knew that it was a good thing they were so busy between the construction and excavation work. Running a new company and continuing with their daily lives allowed little or no time for Lois to get depressed. The doctor had explained that Lois might never regain her memory, or it might return in little snippets, or something could trigger it to return completely. He emphasized how important it was for her friends to be as supportive as possible. Helen and Norm became her new family, and Peter and Mary close partners and dear friends.

Helen tried every means she could think of to find a connection in Ottawa but without success. There was no trace of Lois on file at the obvious places. She constantly chastised herself for neglecting to get more information from Stacey. She didn't even have her last name.

The twins thrived under the new babysitting arrangements and competed to get Jack's attention. Jack in return wanted to do everything the twins did resulting in many funny moments as he struggled to keep up. When they ran, he crawled trailing along behind them. Mary enjoyed the children's swimming lessons and admitted she would not have thought to enroll Jack. It seemed that everyone's life was blending into a happy routine.

Chapter 24

BDB is moving ahead at such a rapid pace. I wake up juggling jobs and money—I am digging trenches in my sleep. Even when I am getting the twins breakfast, my mind is reeling with what has to be accomplished. Peter has become the ultimate partner—he rises to every challenge and comes up with a solution. I love driving the excavator and feeling the shovel dig deeply into the earth. I am always amazed by how smooth and easy it slips through layers of soil. One would think that it would be rough and bumpy, but on the contrary, it is like sitting on a cushioned sofa guiding the machine's movements. I love that I can be so precise with moving earth, picking it up and setting it always in the right place. Lifting tree roots with a gentle pull on the hydraulics or setting a boulder to the side with ease. I can't remember my father, but Peter tells me that that is how I learned to operate these big machines. Apparently, I helped my dad when I was a teenager. Try as I might, I have no recollection of my father or of helping him. That is very frustrating as I would give anything to remember his face, hear his voice or feel his arms around me. There must be a way I can remember.

The other side of that is—do I want to remember the awful part of my past that was so traumatic that my subconscious has suppressed it? Frankly, I do not have a choice now, do I? At least my life, as it is, could not be better. I have a beautiful family in Helen and Norm and the twins; I have a capable partner that is becoming a dear friend, as is Mary. I do have the oddest feeling whenever I see Jack, but Peter tells me that I told him that he reminds me of a child I used to look after. Ah, memories, or lack thereof, are a nuisance. Onward and forward—BDB is looking good.

Chapter 25

By July, Lois noted that BDB was paying down its debt at a steady rate and calls were coming in regularly for other job opportunities. Peter learned of another excavator that had come up for sale in Windsor. Both he and Lois knew it would be an asset to their company. The thought of plunging deeper in debt was frightening but likely not insurmountable. They gathered monthly projections and contracts that were pending to take with them when they crunched numbers with the accountant.

"Your debt is within reasonable margins comparing it to your expected growth rate. At the current time, you are barely viable because you lack machinery and workers to commit to additional projects. Where you want to take the future of BDB will determine the level of investment needed. Simply said, the company will not grow with your current holdings. That being said, you already have a successful and profitable operation, albeit your profits show a narrow margin."

Words were not spoken, but the simple nods from Peter and Lois said it all. They wanted to grow BDB and in order to do that, they needed to add machinery—they needed to borrow money in order to do so.

"Well, if I am heading to Windsor to see that hunk of machinery tomorrow, I'd better tell Mary to pack a shirt or two." He was currently wearing mud-spattered jeans, his BDB windbreaker and steel-toed boots. Peter shortened his step so Lois could keep pace with him. "Kind of nervous adding more debt. How about you?"

"There is no question that we are on the right track. No, Peter, I have complete confidence in our ability to make this work. You go to Windsor and I will tackle the bank."

Carrying a folder with all the information from the

accountant, Lois headed for the bank wearing a navy business suit with a cream, long-sleeved tailored blouse. BDB was set to enlarge its holdings and Lois wanted to look the part of an efficient executive. The bank asked numerous questions, examined the paperwork and nodded approval. It was good business for both parties. The bank was scrupulous at checking the bottom line and, the credit manager smiled and offered a preferred rate of interest. Without hesitation, he drew up a contract for the additional loan. Lois had signing authority, so the transaction was completed within an hour and a half.

Peter arrived in Windsor to sunny, high skies and found the company selling the excavator without any trouble. There were a few mechanical faults with the machine, but Peter's keen eye knew that the repairs were not difficult, but they put him in a good bargaining position. As a result, he was able to negotiate a price that was well below market value. Peter made a quick call to Sudbury and let Lois know that he would be buying the excavator. By the time he had arranged shipment, estimated time of arrival and how long the repairs would take, Lois had already booked it for the entire month.

By mid-October, BDB had grown from a single excavator, a grader, a bulldozer and a repair truck with trailer to a company of three additional graders, a dump truck and now another excavator. Dominion continued to be their best customer and smaller jobs kept the equipment in service day after day. Every time the corporate debt started to inch downward, a new opportunity arose to acquire more equipment. The field behind the motel still served Peter and Lois as a storage lot, but there was seldom anything parked there as the machinery was in such high demand.

"Peter, this has been a fast and furious ride, but winter is coming and I am worried about things slowing down."

"Dominion intends to continue through the winter months, so that, at least, will help keep the hounds at bay." Peter reached for his cell phone that was madly vibrating on his buttocks. After answering, he paused to listen.

"That's quite possible—here, let me hand the phone to Lois. She's the one who makes all our bookings."

Peter handed his phone across the table with a wink.

The City of Sudbury was looking to hire extra dump trucks and graders for the winter months for snow removal. BDB had already earned a reputation for not only having reliable equipment but for keeping it in excellent condition so that work would be done on schedule.

"A lot of our work is for Dominion and is away from Sudbury, so we would have to have a guarantee and a firm contract, not just be on an on-call basis. Yes, that might work. When can we meet?"

Once off the phone with an appointment to sign contracts, Lois leaped up and threw her arms in the air in triumph.

"Oh, my God, Peter. Can you believe it? The bottom line just went from red to black. The city will guarantee renting our three trucks for five days a week for December, January and February."

Peter strode across the room from behind his desk, swept Lois up and twirled her around in the air. The jubilant mood meant another celebratory lunch at the club. Peter was wearing faded blue jeans and a sweatshirt. Lois was also in jeans and a bulky-knit green sweater. They closed the office, headed home to change and met at the club. Conversation centred around the logistics of how BDB would manage the following months.

"Three trucks outfitted with plows. Peter, this means we are way ahead of our forecast. My only concern is if one breaks down. We only have the three, no backup and your repair unit is in Little Current."

Peter's repair truck was entirely contracted to Dominion, which meant Peter was away from home a great deal. Lois expressed concern that, not only was the repair vehicle totally reliant on Peter, but also there was no plan 'B' if he was unable to work.

"That is a huge problem. What if you get sick? What will we do?" Peter realized that Lois was right, so with a lot of consideration, Peter and Lois decided that they must hire their first employee. BDB had managed to date, but it was time to think about adding a mechanic. Peter placed an ad in the Canadian Mechanics Journal. In two days, they had thirty responses.

Peter quickly dismissed the bulk of them because the applicants did not have the right qualifications. One stood out from the rest. After a couple of long-distance conversations that answered Peter's targeted questions, they hired a mechanic on a trial basis.

Fred Buston arrived in Sudbury three weeks later carrying only a backpack and a guitar slung on his back. His references were exactly what BDB needed and he was willing to relocate from New Brunswick. Both Peter and Lois were nervous to meet Fred, anxious that he would fit in, anxious that he would apply himself to the job. When he walked through the door of the room BDB had rented from the motel to serve as the office, it was as if a presence filled the air. At 6'3", carrying little excess weight, Fred pushed the door behind him and turned with a smile that spread across his entire face. A halo of blonde frizz framed a broad, ruddy face and curled around his ears. He reached a hand with long fingers and grasped Peter's.

Lois stood up and approached Fred. "Lois Brenton-Douglas, the BD part of BDB. Welcome."

Fred towered over Lois, took her small hand in his, covered it with his other and said, "Man, this is the first time I have had a lady boss, but I reckon that means you run a tight ship. Nothing like female intuition and tenacity."

"Lois can handle any and all the equipment as well as, if not better than, most men."

"I just bet she can."

Lois laughed out loud. "A least Fred doesn't think I should be sitting behind a desk pushing a pencil."

"No, ma'am. My sister crews a lobster boat and has three more women in her team. She taught me that there isn't a single thing a woman can't do that a man can."

"Get rid of the ma'am stuff; it's Lois."

Fred Buston proved to be just what BDB needed. He knew his way around motors and was an accomplished mechanic. He was very taken with the mobile repair truck, and even made a few suggestions to improve it. Fred rented a room and stayed in Little Current, so he was always on call. This enabled Peter to be in Sudbury three days a week with his family and to help Lois with the paperwork. Fred settled in quickly and was soon playing his guitar and singing at the local pub. The fast tempo of the sea chanties were popular, but it was his renditions of rock-and-roll that had the crowd coming back again and again. He became a popular attraction in the small northern town and it was not unusual to see several young women hanging around the repair truck. However, Fred was all business and discouraged them being there much to Peter's approval.

Like Peter, Fred had a kinship with machinery and was adept at his job. Having Fred took a lot of pressure off Peter and he was able to divide his time between Sudbury and Little Current allowing him to spend more time with Mary and Jack. They were a close, affectionate family and the separation over the past months while BDB was in its fledgling stage was hard on Peter and Mary. Both recognized Fred as a godsend.

Winter hit hard in mid-November with record snowfalls. The city kept BDB's trucks working day and night, not just five days a week but seven. Lois was not impressed with the city workers; they were careless with the equipment and not only were fenders scraped and dented, but the cabs were also littered with coffee cups and other refuse. Based on this, Lois renegotiated the contract to include drivers provided by BDB. This meant Peter and Lois were busy interviewing drivers and subsequently hired four on a contract basis. They were able to offer decent hourly rates and enough work to make it worthwhile for the drivers. In return, each driver was obligated to undergo a training afternoon. Emphasis was placed on the drivers respecting the client, each other and their trucks.

Steady work from the city and Dominion continued through the following months. The months turned into years. Two years slipped by and BDB was by then well established as a Sudbury company.

On a dreary February afternoon, Andrew Ford walked through the office door and lifted his cane in greeting.

"Hey, little lady. Hello, Peter."

Peter rose and crossed the floor to meet him with his hand outstretched. "Andy, to what do we owe this pleasure? Can I get you a cup of coffee?"

Lois, too, approached with her arm outstretched, but Andrew used it to pull her to him and give her a big hug. Lois flushed in embarrassment but was soon laughing. "Can't be bad news with that greeting."

"Depends what side of the fence you are sitting on. I am bidding on a piece of land halfway between Sudbury and Little Current. There is gravel there that I want to extract; it would be a valuable asset for Dominion. The land borders the gravel pit of the company we are currently using. Right now, they are able to fulfill our gravel orders, but with the new contracts that we are bidding on, they have no way to keep up with our demand. I want to know if BDB has enough equipment to take on the job."

"You mean to run a gravel pit?"

"Hell, no. I mean to open it and move the dirt. Once it is opened, my guys can run the pit, but you will provide the machinery."

Lois and Peter spent the next two weeks doing site visits and crunching numbers. This opportunity went far beyond just digging and hauling gravel. A road would have to be built into the property and they would have to purchase or, if they were lucky, rent a stone crusher. It definitely meant they would be able to offer the temporary drivers full-time jobs and would have to hire another eight people. The numbers on paper showed that not only was it viable but lucrative. The accountant verified their findings and they took a proposal to Andrew Ford.

"Hell, little lady, BDB came in below my numbers. Are you sure you can you deliver my requests for this?" Andy was slapping his desk with the sheaf of papers.

"Well, we have built in a clause that covers us in the event there are unforeseen issues. In other words, we might have to renegotiate if problems arise apart from what you mentioned."

"Understood. Let me get back to you within a week. My lawyers are still hankering over some ownership details. Nothing is ever easy, is it?"

Peter and Lois left with their fingers crossed. This contract would turn BDB into a major industry with fifteen employees. It meant security; it meant profits that would stabilize operations. Every time the phone rang over the week, whoever was in the office said a novena that Andrew Ford was calling with good news. But the days dragged on and it was ten days before the call came. Both Lois and Peter happened to be in the office and Peter put the call on speakerphone. Andrew's gravelly voice seemed to fill the entire office space as he boomed his greeting.

"So it looks like BDB and Dominion are in the gravel business. Took that damn farmer long enough to sell that worthless piece of farmland. But he finally caved and we take possession immediately. When can you start on the road?"

Lois and Peter were both holding their breath and mouthed a silent 'whoop' simultaneously. "By God, Andy, you are going to make BDB rich." Peter was glowing with pride. His idea to own his own business and the plans for a company were now firmly in place and growing rapidly.

"No sense being the only rich guy in Sudbury, not counting

the mining industry, mind you. So I repeat, how soon can we get started?"

"Timing is perfect," Lois cut in. "We will be finishing our contract with the city in two weeks. That will free up four trucks and six drivers. The biggest problem will be spring rains and mud. Right now, the ground is frozen and the sooner we can get into the site and start getting the road built, the better. I have been looking into acquiring a crusher and other than old relics in sad shape, there is little available. We decided that this warrants purchasing a new one. There is one available in Michigan that can be delivered in two weeks. We can clear brush in the meantime. We can get the truck delivering the crusher to bring it to where the roadway will meet the highway and then we can drag it to the site on skids when it arrives. Once the road is built, the crusher will be leased to the gravel pit. So what I'm saying, Andy, is we can be moving forward as soon as Dominion takes ownership with the plan to start the road the second week of March." Lois punched Peter; as she was talking, a grin spread straight across her face. Peter, too, was one big, beaming grin.

"Little lady, you sure know how to make a guy happy. Meet you at the club in an hour to celebrate." He hung up.

Peter phoned Mary and told her to get a sitter and put on her glad rags. Lois called Helen on her cell and invited her and Norm to join them, this time on BDB.

Chapter 26

I can't remember ever feeling so fulfilled. Heck, what am I thinking? I still can't remember anything except for the past three years. Sometimes, I think a memory surfaces, but it is more like a déjà vu — when I try to bring it into focus, it just disappears. Like yesterday, I decided to make spaghetti and thought; why am I making spaghetti? It's not Friday. Whatever did that mean? I still love to cook and even though I have had to give up the cooking classes, I manage to still look after the twins after school by being connected to the office by phone. Most of the heavy construction work is in the early morning, so it is easy to manage from home in the late afternoon. I am still in awe at how rapidly the company has expanded and how quickly the contracts came in. I guess our timing was right and we just happened to start BDB at the right time. I can't believe that it was two years ago that we started a heavy-equipment rental company. Now we not only rent equipment but contract out to do all kinds of construction work. We have a staff that is working full time and many of them clock in overtime. Peter and I are both logging in long hours and seldom see a day off. But neither of us is complaining. It is all good.

My loan has been paid back and we are on track with the bank. BDB does carry a hefty loan, but according to business practices, it is quite within range of Return On Investment (ROI). Both Peter and I are now taking home a decent salary and are meeting a substantial payroll. There is always the fear of a disaster, either equipment failure or a construction accident. We carry significant insurance, but so far, we have easily coped with any unexpected issues. With Fred on staff, we have managed every mechanical crisis to date and been able to respond to Dominion's needs as well as the city's. I keep saying a little prayer to my gods that it continues.

Chapter 27

Two weeks later, Peter was standing by the roadside waving his arms and letting out sharp whistles as he instructed the tractor-trailer driver where to offload the crusher. The backup warning system was nearly drowned out by the roar of chainsaws, trucks and graders working at the site. Dominion had had a crew clearing everything from the planned roadway using their largest grader and one of BDB's bulldozers. BDB had rigged a flatbed skid to hold the crusher and it would be dragged, over the uneven ground to the edge of where the quarry would start, by the bulldozer. It was slow going and several times branches had to be trimmed back farther. They had reckoned for the width but not the height. There could not be any tree canopy left over the road. This meant it took two days to get the crusher to the site and set up.

Rock, of various sizes, was brought to the primary crusher by rear-dump haul units, or carried by a wheel front-end loader. Primary crushing reduces this run-of-mine rock to a more manageable size. The different types of primary crushers are jaw crushers, gyratory crushers, impact crushers and autogenous crushers. The jaw crusher BDB bought squeezes rock between two surfaces, one of which opens and closes like a jaw. Material enters the jaw crusher from the top. Pieces of rock, that are larger than the opening at the bottom of the jaw, lodge between the two metal plates of the jaw. The opening and closing action of the movable jaw against the fixed jaw continues to reduce the size of lodged pieces of rock until the pieces are small enough to fall through the opening at the bottom of the jaw.

The crew stood in quiet anticipation when Peter decided to start it up. The belt started moving. There were loud scraping noises and grinding gears—it seemed to take forever for the crusher to take hold and for the jaws to move. Then they did. The entire crew cheered. Fred had come to witness the event and be there if the machine was not working. He was there on his day off to help Peter, to help BDB. If an emergency arose in Little Current, he could be there in less than an hour. All the anxiety was dispelled when the crusher warmed up. The next step was to see if the rocks could be turned to gravel. Peter signalled a half-loaded dump truck to empty its load into the hopper. The noise was ear shattering, but the coarse rocks clattered and banged into the crusher and spewed finer gravel out the other end and a belt fed it into a funnel that poured it into the empty truck waiting at the other end. The whooping and clapping celebrated the moment.

The truck driver edged forward to the road site and the hydraulics raised the box just enough for the driver to expertly spread his load where the road began. Andrew Ford arrived just as the newly acquired roller tamped down the gravel. His small body stood silhouetted by the sun backlighting him. He raised his arms with a can of Coke in one hand.

"Watch you don't fall over, old man. Where's your cane?" The familiar camaraderie that had developed between Andrew Ford and Peter was evident.

"I christen you Dominion Pit Road." He poured the dark liquid on the new road and held up his other hand. "This marks the beginning of a new phase for Dominion. I want to express my gratitude to all of you who have worked so hard the past few weeks to make it happen. You have done a fantastic job. Now get the hell back to work." His good humour was greeted with nods and pleased expressions. With his arm around Peter, Andy just stood surveying his latest acquisition. "How soon can I start hauling gravel out of here?"

"Tomorrow soon enough?"

"What? You can haul tomorrow?"

"We can haul and build at the same time, but we need to limit the load and number of trips over the portion not gravelled to prevent it from turning to slick mud. I am thinking we can move ten partial loads using two trucks. The road crew will edge forward and we will use the other two trucks for that. The roller can keep up nicely. I think the road should be pretty well complete in three weeks. It will be rough, but that is all we need. As long as the crusher keeps pace, we can start moving back-to-back loads out of here daily."

"Oh, I forgot to mention," Andy turned to Lois with a grin, "Dominion will need that roller up at the new site as soon as it is done here. Better get a contract ready."

In the meantime, Lois planned a celebration party to mark the end of the second year of BDB being in business. She decided on an afternoon affair so the children could be included. Peter and Lois insisted the company be family friendly. All the employees brought spouses and children to the rented hall. It was picnic style albeit inside as warm April showers fell in torrents. Lois and Peter had worked together to come up with special recognition of employee's work. Peter dressed in a navy suit, stepped up to a mike and made a rousing speech.

"Not only has BDB expanded, it has become a company that Lois and I are proud to say has the best damn employees in the Sudbury area." Clapping exploded and friendly back slaps were exchanged. "I want to especially thank Andrew Ford for believing in a couple of newbies with big ideas–he brought the job offers to BDB and you folks rose to the occasion and brought it to where it is today. And we could not have made the advances we did without the support of our families. Our hours are long and we are often away from home, but each one of you went above and beyond to bring BDB where it is today. You have done your share and often more. Personally, I want to thank my wife, Mary, for her unwavering support and my partner, Lois, for her intuitive decisions and hard work; we make a great team. Please lift your glasses with whatever you are drinking and salute each other. Here is to success and teamwork." Lois's voice suddenly faltered as she shouted out, "hear—hear." Then she recovered quickly and turned to Helen. "I may not remember much before Sudbury, but my goodness, so much has transpired since that I have collected enough memories to make up for it."

The months flew by and BDB services were heavily in demand. Lois still split her time between the twins and the job sites. However, she was beginning to feel that she was being pulled two ways. On a warm May morning, Helen, wearing brown cut-offs and a beige T-shirt, beckoned Lois into the garden. As they stood by the tulips in full blossom, they both spoke at once–"Remember the two lips." They doubled over laughing. Lois had been with Helen and Norm for over three years. "It is impossible to think that the time has whipped by and how the twins have grown. There is no doubt they are going to be tall like you and Norm."

"Yes, and that is why I wanted to have this time together. Norm and I are taking the twins for the month of August to travel across Canada. What, I'm trying to say is...."

"You don't need a nanny after July."

"It's not that we are throwing you out. It's just that..."

"I knew it was coming and you know what? I am so pleased. You and Norm are the most wonderful employers–no, friends— and I love the twins, but it is time I moved on and BDB allows me to do that. In fact, I have been doing a little research and think I have found a house I want to buy."

"No way!"

"Yes, way. BDB has repaid most of my investment and I draw a good salary. Peter and Mary are also looking for a place. Not only is BDB expanding, but it seems Peter's family is too. Mary is pregnant. The house they are looking at is in that new subdivision near the college; it is a neighbourhood of young families, perfect for Peter and Mary. Peter and I have been searching the web for suitable houses for his family and that is how I spied the little house I am interested in. It is a converted cottage on Ramsey Road."

"Lakefront?"

"Yep. Acre and a half with 250-foot frontage."

"That has got to be pricey."

"Actually, it is quite within reason. The house needs lots of work and there are not many buyers for a one-bedroom, winterized cottage."

"Perfect for you."

"Perfect for me."

When Norm heard this news, he insisted that they all make an appointment with the Realtor to see the property that very evening. They knew it was vacant, having heard that the owner had moved to a retirement residence, and they hoped the agent could accommodate them. He definitely could. In fact, he suggested they pick up the keys and go on their own. As they drove up the driveway, the cottage stood on a barren piece of land looking quite dilapidated. Paint was falling off the trim and the porch sagging on the west side needed shoring up. Norm looked at it and frowned. He stepped out of his SUV and strode off on his own to circumnavigate the property. He then moved carefully through the house testing his footing and viewing everything with a critical eye.

"The windows are in need of replacing and the kitchen and bathrooms are far from modern. The house is still a summer cottage with heating. Not sure about the insulation."

"I know, but the living space was open and bright with an unusually large bedroom." Lois stood in the middle of the living room with her arms spread wide and smiling as she looked outside to the lake shore. "I will fix what needs fixing."

Helen was occupied keeping an eye on the twins, who were exploring the waterfront. Barby squealed in delight when she saw minnows. Grant was trying to catch a frog.

"It sure needs some loving and by that, I mean, it needs a hell of a lot of work. Lois, are you sure you want to take this on?" Norm was taking notes. "It is a formidable project. But, you know what? I like it. It has potential and good bones. I have an architect friend..."

"Whoa. Stop right there. You have friends in everything. My plan is to live in it as is and fix it up bit by bit."

"Norm always wants to jump right in and solve the problems of the world." Helen had just entered the kitchen door behind the twins and in time to hear Lois.

"Well, both of you got behind BDB and that was a good thing. I just don't want to over extend myself and I will have all the time in the world to make changes."

"Right, you're right. I should mind my own business."

"Norm, I love that you take such an interest in what I do. One thing that I will do right away is fix up the waterfront. With BDB equipment, it will be done in no time. You don't happen to have a landscaper in your back pocket, do you?"

"As a matter of fact..."

Helen and Lois burst out laughing.

"Listen to me. You would think I already owned it. Come on, let's drag the Realtor back to his office and draw up an offer."

After they left the Realtor's office, Helen suggested they pick up some nibbles and, after the twins were in bed, talk about the property over a glass of wine. Lois was pleased as there were some things on the listing that she wanted clarified and brainstorming over a glass of wine was perfect. She smiled at Helen and Norm, "you, not only have been the best employers I could ever have had, but I know we have become friends and I hope we will be lifelong friends."

Helen and Norm frowned. "Lois, you are more than a friend — you are family." Everyone drew together into a group hug.

It took three long days before Lois heard that the owner of the cottage had accepted her offer. It had a quick thirty-day closing, so Lois just had time to draw up some landscaping plans and order furniture. She also ordered a new stove. Now that she had her own place, she planned to cook up a storm.

Chapter 28

This is absolutely the best fun ever. I have been out to the house, which I dubbed "Shoreline Cottage," every chance I could to take measurements and to just soak up the atmosphere. Sometimes, I forget why I went and get lost in thought about how lucky I am. Then I made the mistake of going to talk to kitchen designers. Oh my, that was the turning point. I had to keep myself in tow—I wanted every luxury—but of course, that wasn't practical. I did decide to treat myself and do some immediate renovations and am delighted with what I chose. New kitchen cabinets will be installed as soon as I take possession.

I had planned to live in the house as it was, but once I splurged for top-of-the-line appliances, I knew that I wanted to modernize the entire kitchen. Maybe it was a bit extravagant, but what the heck? I deserve the best, don't I? Of course, I do. Funny thing, when I was looking at paint, I rebelled at yellow. Must have been something in my past that caused that—I like yellow but couldn't tolerate it in the kitchen. I had a couple of other odd reactions to some things like wallpaper and tiles. I rejected black floor tiles for the entrance way knowing they showed every little speck of dirt and dust. How did I know that? Anyway, I have made my choices and will be able to move in three weeks after taking possession. I'm lucky the owner has given me a key to come and go as I need. She is a delightful old gal and has no regrets about selling the house. She is settled in the retirement home and has many friends there and an active social life. She claims she is pleased that I am the new owner, as she knows I will love the house. I'm glad, and she sure has that right. I will have her over for a visit once I am settled in.

Chapter 29

Owning his own business turned out to be a seven day a week job and often twenty-four hours a day for Peter. He and Mary moved into their new three-bedroom house at the beginning of August. As the months passed, Peter was eager to be closer to home and Mary. She was not having an easy time with this pregnancy but was still able to help with Barby and Grant after they came home from school. She went to babysit three days a week for just a few hours until Helen got home from work. She looked forward to this little job as Jack was entertained and she felt she was contributing. She was, however, quite uncomfortable with lower back pain and lifting Jack was increasingly difficult. The baby was due the first week of December, not a good time as far as BDB was concerned—every piece of equipment was assigned and working full out between Dominion and the city. Road construction was booming and Dominion contracted all BDB's equipment except four trucks that were used for the city contract. They had to be staffed by BDB, so two more employees were added to the payroll. Lois found a bookkeeping company that took BDB on as a client and did all the invoicing and payroll. This freed Lois up to operate equipment and oversee the other operators. Fred took on an apprentice. It seemed everyone was helping BDB on the road to success.

Peter was in the office one late October morning when his cell buzzed. "Pete, help! Come quick!"

Mary's piercing scream for help sent Peter racing westward across Sudbury to find Mary lying in a pool of blood on the living room floor. Jack was safely in the playpen. Peter shook with fear; there was so much blood. He knelt beside Mary as he dialled 911.

"She's unconscious, bleeding. Hurry!"

"Sir, stay calm, we are here—the ambulance is on the way.

Can you cover her to keep her warm? Try to revive her by rubbing her arms and shouting at her to see if she hears you. The ambulance is only four minutes out. Stay calm; we will be there soon." The voice on the phone kept talking to calm Peter. But, to him, it seemed a lifetime before the ambulance arrived. "Is the front door unlocked?"

"Yes."

"Good."

When the medics pushed through the door, Peter stood aside and answered the paramedic's questions as he watched them examine Mary and gently lift her onto the gurney. After telling Peter that they were leaving for the hospital, they took off with sirens blaring, careful to avoid potholes and not to jar the patient. As the driver eased into traffic, the medic in the back inserted IVs and, as he monitored Mary's vital signs, relayed them to the hospital. It was determined that this was a critical case and the ambulance was to be met on arrival with a full crisis team. Peter headed for his truck to follow the ambulance when he realized that Jack was in the house.

"Oh, God. Jack!"

The next-door neighbour who had been watching what was happening suddenly appeared at his side. "Go, I'll take care of Jack."

With a weak smile of gratification, Peter jumped in the truck and headed for the hospital. Working all hours and being new to the neighbourhood, there had not been time to meet many of the people on the street, but he and Mary had met Tanya and Clark, who lived next door. It was fortunate that Tanya was home and stepped forward to look after Jack. Peter, distraught as he was, did quickly write down his cell number.

"My sincere thanks. Here is my card with my cell number in case you need me."

"Don't worry about a thing. I will bring my daughter over and wait at your house. Chandler is about the same age as Jack, so it will be fine. You just hurry after Mary. My prayers are with you."

Peter hastily said thanks, then with shaking fingers tried to call Lois while he was driving. "Come on, Lois. Pick up."

Lois was preparing a potential contract for the City of Sudbury. She needed to do a site assessment so was at the site doing a walking through of the property. She needed to estimate the time to clear the lot that would eventually be a parking garage. Her phone buzzed.

"Peter, calm down. I don't understand. What are you saying?"

When Peter explained what was happening, Lois ran to her truck and broke every speed limit as she raced south across Sudbury heading for the hospital. The entrance gate to the parking lot seemed to take forever to open and finding a parking spot was another challenge. Finally, she parked and headed for the emergency entrance. She found Peter rocking against the institutional green wall in a sorry state. She reached for his hand and drew him to her. With the flat of her hand, she wiped away tears that were spilling down his face.

"I'm here, Peter. I'm sure Mary will be fine."

Coaxing information out of Peter in a calm, soft voice, she learned that Mary had called his cell and simply uttered, "Pete, help! Come quick." When he got home, he found her unconscious lying in a pool of blood on the floor. He called 911 and tried to rouse her.

"All I know is I overheard the medic say she was in hemorrhagic shock with a heart rate of 140, weak pulse and pale skin. Lois, she looked like a wax doll. All the colour was drained from her face. I didn't know what to do. When the paramedics arrived, I just stood aside and watched. I have never felt so helpless. In no time, they had her loaded on a gurney and in the ambulance. Our next-door neighbour is looking after Jack and I came here. I haven't talked to anyone yet, except reception told me she was being examined and someone will come and talk to me as soon as they know what has happened."

At that moment, a doctor in green scrubs approached them. "Mr. Barto?"

Peter nodded.

"I'm Dr. Adams. Please follow me." The doctor led them down a hallway and into a small room. "Mr. Barto, please sit down so we can discuss Mary's condition."

Peter sank into a navy faux leather settee and Lois sat beside him automatically straightening her pant legs over her steel-toed work boots. The doctor pulled up a chair and sat to face Peter. "Mary suffered what is known as placental abruption, which means the placenta partially or completely separates from the wall of the uterus. In this case, it was completely separated and the baby suffered from lack of oxygen. Usually, it is not this severe and the treatment is bed rest. However, in Mary's case, we are dealing with another issue. When she fell, she tore more tissue and has lost copious amounts of blood."

Lois leaned forward and asked, her voice quivering, "How severe?"

"I do not want to give you false hope; she is in grave danger. I need permission to do a C-section to try and save the baby and Mary, although I am not optimistic."

Peter stared at the doctor with moist, glassy eyes and nodded.

"Please believe me when I say we will do everything we can to save the baby and Mary, but both have very weakened vital signs. I will keep you posted as soon as we have more information." Dr. Adams touched Peter's hand in a comforting gesture, then left the room.

The room was silent except for soft breathing sounds and the odd gulp for air. Peter stared at the wall; every muscle tensed. The wait seemed forever, but actually, the doctor returned in about thirty minutes. His demeanour was solemn and foreboding.

"I am so sorry, Mr. Barto, but she slipped away and there was nothing we could do to save her or the baby. Our staff worked tirelessly to resuscitate her, but every effort failed."

The wail that rose from somewhere deep within Peter's soul pierced the silence in an animal like noise. Tears rolled down Lois's face, falling unobstructed, soaking her jeans and her lap.

"Can I see her? I need to see her." Peter was lurching forward.

"Take a few minutes to process this information. Do you have any questions? Can I get one of our spiritual counsellors to stop in?"

"No. I just need to see her. I need to see her!" He was clutching at the doctor's sleeve, his voice getting more and more frantic.

"Please try to calm down, Mr. Barto." Turning to Lois, Dr. Adams asked, "Mary is still in the operating room. As soon as she is out, I will come back. Here are a few tranquilizers. I will get Mr. Barto to take two now. Then if you can, get him to take one every four hours. Here is a prescription for more." He turned to Peter.

"Mr. Barto, I want you to take these right now. It will help." He handed Peter two small pills and a cup of water and watched Peter swallow. "I will come by shortly to take you to see Mary. I am so sorry to have had to bring you this terrible news."

After the doctor left, Lois held tight to Peter's arm. "I can't believe it. How will we tell Jack? How will he be without a mother? This is too much. I should have called 911 as soon as she called me. It's all my fault."

"No, Peter. To begin with, you didn't know why Mary called. You got there very quickly. It is one of life's cruel twists of fate."

True to his word, Dr. Adams returned to take Peter to see Mary. While they were gone, Lois called Norm at the store and told him the news. She asked him to have someone come and get Peter's truck. Norm assured her that he and Helen would be there as soon as possible. When Peter returned, he was shaking and crying. A nurse followed him into the privacy room carrying documents that she explained had to be signed. The bodies— there were two since the C-section had delivered a baby girl— were to be transferred to the morgue until the hospital received funeral arrangements. The tranquilizer had calmed Peter and he listened to the nurse explain the documents and signed where indicated. Lois could see that he was functioning by rote and seemed to be numb and disconnected. Once the paperwork was complete, the nurse urged them to leave.

As Lois and Peter walked along the corridor to the exit, they saw Norm and Helen. Norm gathered Peter in his arms and Helen hugged Lois close. No words were spoken except to tell Lois to take Peter to their house. One of Norm's staff members was minding the twins and Helen would drive Peter's truck and pick up Jack on the way.

Norm took over the logistical things that had to be done. He contacted the funeral home and made all the arrangements, confirming with Peter every decision. Peter sipped a cup of tea, but it was obvious he was not aware of what he was doing. Jack sensed something was wrong and shied away from his father. The twins, too, knew to avoid the grown-ups and took Jack to the family room.

Mary had no family other than a cousin who lived in France. Peter had a brother in the military stationed in Afghanistan, unable to return. A small service was planned to take place at Jackson & Barnard Funeral Home. The visitation found the sanctuary filled to overflowing with representatives from BDB staff, the city, Dominion Construction, neighbours and friends. Peter was overwhelmed and almost unable to communicate but did manage to find comfort from the support. Lois made sure he took the tranquilizers the doctor prescribed which certainly helped. Fred moved into the house with him until the funeral was over and made sure he ate and got through each day.

The week after the funeral, Fred came to Lois. "I have an idea. Peter is going to need to hire a housekeeper and nanny for Jack and I may have a solution. My girlfriend, Belinda, wants to move here to be near me and I am anxious to have her with me. She is a great gal and has helped raise her wee brothers and sisters. She is one of eight, so she has had lots of experience. Anyway, here is what I thought. She could move into Peter's house and care for them, do the cooking and cleaning and whatever is needed. We are planning to get married later this year."

"Fred, that sounds perfect. But let me propose it to Peter. He is so out of it. I'm not sure he will agree to anything. Let's give him a week or so and see how he is."

Lois took every opportunity during the following week to stay close to Peter, Jack and the twins. She told Helen about Fred's suggestion and was pleased that she welcomed Belinda taking on Mary's hours with Barby and Grant. The twins were having a hard time understanding why Mary was no longer coming.

"Sometimes, sad things happen and we lose exceptional people in our lives. Mary was a very special person, but she got sick and died. That means she has left us forever and now is only a memory, a treasured memory. We can keep those memories alive by talking about her and looking at photos of her. The saddest thing of all is Jack no longer has a mommy to look after him."

"Will our mommy die?" Barby was snuggled against Lois, who was sitting on the sofa in the recreation room. "That is most unlikely. I expect your mom plans to be like your grandmother and come for birthdays of your children. Now, who wants to go to the park?"

The week dragged and Lois was glad she had the children to look after. They had a way of lifting her spirits and made her get on with each day. But Peter was slipping steadily into a deep depression. He wasn't taking care of himself and even with Jack, he was remote and withdrawn. He barely ate and the house was beginning to show signs of neglect. It was time for Lois to tell him about Fred's idea.

Armed with a bottle of wine and a bucket of KFC, she arrived at Peter's house on Sunday evening. It had been three weeks since Mary's death and Peter had not been out of the house. He was pale, a thick stubble was sprouting on his chin and he was wearing a sweatshirt and jeans that definitely had not seen a washing machine in a long time. Lois was not sure how to approach the subject. Should she be the good guy or the bad guy?

"Peter, we need to talk."

"Honestly, Lois, I just want to be left alone."

"What you want is not going to happen. BDB needs you, I need you and Jack really needs you. I know you have been dealt a rotten hand, but life does go on and believe me, Peter, you need to make an attempt to return to work."

"I can't. I just can't."

"You know what, Peter, BDB was your idea. You are my business partner and my dearest friend, but without you taking a hold of daily matters, we will be in trouble. Already there are some things I cannot handle. I need you and Jack needs you. You need to get a grip on things and this can only happen if a few changes are made. Fred has suggested a solution and I think it is a great idea."

Lois explained about Belinda. Peter just nodded.

"Okay then, I am going to have Fred send a message to her and bring her here. She is expecting the call so should be here by Wednesday."

Chapter 30

Being tough with Peter is the hardest thing I have ever done. Well, in the time I can remember, that is. It was weird that during the funeral, I kept seeing some woman in the coffin who wasn't Mary. That is crazy as it was a closed coffin, but I was as devastated to see that woman as I was about Mary. Was this a memory? Could that have been what I was running away from? Did I kill this woman? Oh God, I wish I could remember. Then, on the other hand, if it was so horrible that I have buried the memory, do I really want to recall my life before Sudbury? Dr. Frosst thinks it might have been someone close to me like my mother. I have no idea who my mother is. Don't you think if I loved my mother, I'd remember her and want to see her? I know I told Helen my parents were deceased. Peter told me I mentioned that my father taught me to work heavy equipment and I also told him that he was dead. That is all I know about who I am—basically nothing. I wonder who I look like, who I take after. Was my mother small like me? There are so many questions I have no answers for.

I have to find the strength to push Peter and make sure BDB does not suffer from this tragedy. One thing for sure, I am a stronger person now even though I am small in stature. Was I always strong? Somehow, I don't think so. Andrew Ford never calls me by name—it's always 'Little Lady.' I am getting used to it and in fact, rather get a kick out of it. I am looking forward to meeting Belinda. I sure hope she is all Fred says she is. She will have to perform miracles to make that house happy again. Fred was a blessing and now it looks like the love of his life will be another. I sure hope she can cope with the situation. Jack needs plenty of love right now; he is so confused that his mommy just disappeared. Peter is walking around in a fog, hardly functioning at all.

Chapter 31

The following Wednesday, Fred waited at the airport terminal shifting his weight from one foot to the other. He had taken extra care with his appearance—a newly trimmed haircut was shampooed and blown dry so that his blonde curls seemed to float around his head. He had exchanged his steel-toed boots for beige loafers and his khaki cargo pants were crisply ironed as was his green checkered shirt. He paced the length of the corridor, back and forth, counting his steps as if that would make the time go faster. Finally, the passengers started to appear at the arrival gate and Fred smiled broadly as Belinda walked toward the opening. He rushed to her and scooped her up into one big bear hug. Fred lifted Belinda off her feet, swung her high above him, then lowered and held her tight. She dropped her suitcase and it went crashing to the concrete floor but fortunately stayed closed. The pair were blocking the exit of the Arrival Gate yet nobody seemed to mind as they witnessed this emotional greeting.

"Set me down, you big lug." A grin spread across Belinda's face.

Once on the ground, Belinda pulled down her purple shirt that had been pulled away from her white jeans. Fred grabbed the suitcase and pointed her in the direction of the parking garage. They strode off grinning at each other every few seconds. When they got to Fred's truck, Belinda pointed to the BDB logo.

"You rate a truck? Have Lois and Peter any idea what a lousy driver you are?" Belinda teased Fred because he was given an award for driver's safety by his former employer.

During the twenty-minute drive into the city, the conversation never stopped even though they had talked on the phone three times that week and every week. Belinda leaned over and kissed Fred on the cheek time and time again. When they pulled into Peter's driveway, Fred cautioned Belinda that Peter was still very depressed and confused.

Fred had helped Peter prepare his son for Belinda's arrival and Jack stood in the vestibule on his chubby little legs clutching a spray of flowers. His pudgy face was pointed at the floor, his mouth drawn into a firm line.

"How wonderful! Are those for me?"

Jack glanced up at a smiling face and shoved the bouquet into her hands as he nodded. He hung his head again and looked at the floor, too shy to meet Belinda's smile. His round face wore a solemn expression, his lips quivering. He focused on his foot moving one running shoe back and forth, back and forth. He was dressed in denim jeans with a BDB sweatshirt made especially for him in a size two. Belinda went down on her knees to match Jack's height and put out her hand. "I'm Belinda; you must be Jack. I am very pleased to meet you."

Jack looked into a face that shone with warmth and affection; he forced a weak smile, then raced into Belinda's arms and hugged her with desperation.

Fred noticed that Peter had shaved and wore clean clothes. It was a start. Jack broke from Belinda and reached for her hand to pull her away to show her where her room was. Belinda was all 'oohs' and 'aahs' and before anyone knew it was getting Jack to help her find a vase.

"They will be perfect on the kitchen table where all of us can see them every day. But you know something, Jack? I haven't met your father yet. Do you think you could introduce me?"

She hoped Peter would be as accepting as his son. She was going to have to cook some special meals to fatten him up because his clothes were hanging off him. The air was tense but not unfriendly. It was filled with another presence that was missing. Belinda knew that a house that experienced death had to heal too.

Lois arrived a few minutes later carrying a grocery bag.

"I brought steaks and salad stuff."

Peter and Fred were still standing awkwardly in the hallway. Both turned and acknowledged her arrival. Jack, pulling Belinda, announced that he was hungry. Lois watched a tall, smiling, freckle-faced redhead, pretending she was completely in Jack's control, ease into the gathering.

"Well, your Uncle Fred is the best barbeque chef there is, so I vote he fire up the BBQ and get some steaks a-cooking." Reaching for Lois's hand, she introduced herself. Lois smiled her most welcome smile and pulled Belinda into a hug.

"Belinda, we are so glad you agreed to come, especially Fred. But myself, Jack and Peter need you and I need Peter." Lois watched Belinda scoop up Jack and set him on her hip. She was still wearing bling-studded white jeans and a loose purple chambray shirt. Lois was in standard denim jeans and a red T-shirt. Belinda's long legs had her across the hall and out into the backyard in half the steps it took tiny Lois to get there. Within minutes, she had Fred firing up the barbeque, Lois shredding lettuce, Jack putting utensils on the picnic table and Peter buttering a loaf of French bread while she added spices to the meat. "You sure can get things organized, I see." Lois did a thumbs up to Belinda. Peter didn't join in the conversation other than to nod his agreement to some comments, but he did eat—a good start. After dinner, Jack insisted that Belinda tuck him into bed and as Lois was leaving, she heard a sweet low voice singing the Cape Breton Lullaby.

Peter arrived at the office the next morning. Lois was already there and tried acting as if nothing had changed or that Peter had been absent for a month. She walked him through the active accounts and suggested he might want to do a site visit to the gravel pit as she was uncertain if the operation was operating at peak. Peter nodded and pulled his cap on as he headed out the door. Forty minutes later, Lois's cell dinged.

"Lois, it's Peter. I'm in the ditch."

"What! Where?"

"Just after the entrance ramp onto Highway 144."

"You're not even ten minutes away. How come it took so long to call?"

"Stopped for gas. Then when I went into the ditch, I did a walk about and tried to get out myself. Not going to happen. I need a tow."

"Okay, I will be there in a few minutes."

BDB had purchased a tow truck when they moved to the new office-garage space. BDB was entering its fourth year of operations and had moved out of the motel. It had served them well, but BDB was now a large corporation and needed proper offices, garage space and storage. This led them to purchase a two-acre parcel in the industrial area west of the city. The offices were in a large six bay building with excellent ventilation and boasted an employee lounge. Peter had designed a repair shop complete with a paint and body shop attached. This meant BDB was self-sufficient and wholly independent.

Lois drove across the city and eased the truck to the side of the road where Peter's 4x4 was nose down an incline. She backed up to Peter, who reached for the winch and pulled it to reach his vehicle. "Peter, how the hell did you end up down there?" Lois called out the window. "The road is straight. Did some jerk force you off the road?"

Peter looked at her with sorrowful eyes and muttered, "no, just was distracted."

Lois knew what that distraction was. She was sure Peter was lost in his own thoughts about Mary. Once she hauled the BDB's 4x4 back onto the road, she motioned to Peter. "Okay, I am only going to say this once. I know you are seriously grieving, but you need to come to terms with what life has dealt you and you have to do it NOW! If that guardrail had not been there to stop the truck, we would likely have another funeral. Jack needs his father. I need my friend. BDB needs its partner. Peter, you have to get a grip. You are too valuable to lose."

Peter nodded, his lanky frame slumped into submission. "I...I. Lois, I just can't seem to ..."

"Well, Peter, my friend, you wanted your own business and together we have built an enviable one, but we are still borderline profitable and if I don't have you on side, I will lose it. Damn it, Peter. I can't do it alone. Belinda is not Jack's mother, so his father is doubly important to him. You need to reach out for help when you need it and you need to pull yourself together. I know it is difficult, but you have to move forward. Now, are you going to get your act together and be able to continue to the pit or not?"

A bruise was starting to appear on Peter's forehead and as he rubbed it, he nodded. "I think I needed that lecture and I know I need to finish this task, so, yes, I will go to the pit."

Lois watched her friend and partner, wearing his company shirt and cap with jeans that hung loosely on him. He had lost so much weight since Mary's death. He got into his truck and headed west. Her chastisement had been brutal but seemed to have done the trick.

Spring came, then turned into summer and Peter seemed to improve and poured himself into work. He let Belinda manage the house and took little notice of what transpired there. Belinda confided in Fred and expressed her concern about the distance that was growing between Peter and Jack.

"He just doesn't pay any attention to his son." Belinda was snuggled up to Fred on the sofa. "He gets home late and Jack is often already in bed and Peter is up and away before Jack wakens. A boy needs a father, Fred. Jack needs Peter."

"Okay, here is what we will do. On my days off, you and I are going to take in the sights. Peter will have to get home in time for you to leave. With a little planning, I can set it up so the both of us can be away from the job site as long as I am on call. We can start with Saturday. The Northern Lights Festival is on and I, for one, want to take in the entertainment."

"What is this festival?"

"My girl, the Northern Lights Festival Boreal is Canada's longest continually running outdoor music festival. Over the years, it has grown from local talent presenting the diverse energy of Northern Ontario's artistic community. It started in 1972 and the guest artists have grown to feature Gord Downie, Broken Social Scene, Rita MacNeil and Shania Twain to name a few. It is one hell of a musical party and you and I are going."

Peter stayed home on Saturday and on Belinda's suggestion took Jack to the afternoon portion of the festival. She had learned that clowns and children's entertainers were going to be there. Jack pulled Peter from one clown to another, stuffed himself with cotton candy and was spellbound with the stilt walkers and giant puppets. The Party Cannon Pirate Cruise delighted both father and son. Peter took photo after photo of Jack in his pirate hat wolfing down candy floss. A supper of hot dogs and French fries was the grand finale before Peter and Jack headed home exhausted.

As Peter tucked his son into bed, a sleepy voice insisted they go again the next day. Of course, that was not to be, but Peter vowed he would spend more time with Jack. He admitted to himself that he had enjoyed the day and realized that he missed spending time with Jack. It was different without Mary, but Peter knew that now it had to be a father and son relationship—a closer father and son relationship.

Chapter 32

I am so glad that Peter is back to functioning mode. He has fallen into the daily routine and, thanks to Fred and Belinda, spends most evenings with his son. Renovating my house has been the best thing ever. Living in it over a year without any renovations other than the kitchen allowed me to get an idea of exactly what needed to be done and what I wanted to have done. Norm and Helen were surprised when I mentioned that I wanted specific brands of tile and flooring. They asked if I had been researching them online. I haven't. So how do I know so much about building products? Is this a clue to my past? I do know a great deal about lumber and building stuff—where did I learn that? Maybe I worked in a hardware store when I went to school. Yes, that must be it.

I am delighted at how the house is taking shape. All the grading and landscaping I did before moving in has settled as if it was there forever. The new windows that I had put in last week make a difference. The baseboards painted that sparkling white set off the buttercup walls. Tiling all the floors was one of my better decisions because the twins and Jack are forever racing through from playing in the sand or paddling in the lake. I know I spent a fortune tearing apart the front exterior wall to put in that huge picture window, but I simply love staring out at the water. I think I remember telling Norm that I was going to live in it the way it was and fix everything in good time. Not the case—I have been living in a construction zone for the past six months. Well, one thing just led to another. I do love my kitchen though. Heck, I love the whole house. Next, I need to design a deck so I can sit out there with a glass of wine. Speaking of wine—

Chapter 33

Sixteen months later, Belinda and Fred took Labour Day weekend and went back to Nova Scotia where they planned a small intimate family wedding. They had delayed the wedding by a year from when they had originally planned it, but the situation in Sudbury demanded both of them be there constantly. It was not a small event as both came from large families and in the Atlantic Provinces, families were all important. The ceremony, however, was intimate. It was held in Belinda's parents' backyard looking out over the ocean. Commanding a bluff overlooking the Atlantic, the two-storey weathered clapboard house, boasted a new coat of white paint with black trim done especially for the occasion. On an unusual serene day with high blue skies, the ceremony was held outdoors with the preacher's back to the ocean as Belinda and Fred took their vows looking out over the endless blue water. The setting could not have been more appropriate for the betrothal to take place. Belinda, clutching her father's arm, walked down the improvised aisle, created by rows of chairs for family and a few friends. Her ankle-length, white satin gown glowed in the early afternoon sunlight, making her seem like an apparition, an angel. Fred caught his breath as he watched her approach, then straightened his back and stepped beside her to say the words that would bind them together as husband and wife. Fred's sister, Alice, choked back tears of joy. She did not look like a lobster fisherman. Like Fred, she had a mop of blonde curls that tumbled down her back. Like her brother, she was tall and slim, but that didn't stop her from wearing high-heeled shoes. Her cheeks glowed from being exposed to the ocean breezes and she wore a smile a mile wide. Fred and Belinda held a special place in her heart—to now have Belinda as a sister-in-law was her wish come true.

Even though they would be miles away in Sudbury, there would always be a closeness. Once the vows were exchanged and congratulations were offered by each and every one, tables magically appeared and were immediately loaded with food. A busy group of mothers, sisters and cousins moved as a team and within minutes had filled the tables to capacity. Selections of salads, chicken, seafood, breads, rolls and pies, cakes and much more spread across the tables. Happy chatter was constant. Barrels of beer and bottles of wine were set at a suitable distance from the food tables, so the drinkers were not hampered getting a refill. Faint scraping notes of a fiddle being tuned created a buzz. Several guests gathered their instruments and joined the fiddler. Fred watched as more of his buddies arrived toting their instruments. Within minutes, the backyard was full of neighbours and friends ready to celebrate the occasion in true Maritime fashion. Peter and Lois were enthralled with the whole affair.

"Okay, folks, hold it right there." Fred held up a hand to quiet the crowd. "I have something to say and my way of talking is in music. This is where I may get a little sentimental." Holding the neck of his guitar, Fred joined the other musicians, nodded to them, then turned to the backyard full of guests.

"Today, the most special day of my life, I stand here incredibly proud to be a husband, a husband to the love of my life. I know it is traditional for grooms to make a speech and toast the bride, but I want to honour my girl with a song I wrote especially for her. It's called 'Belinda.'"

A hush fell over the crowd and Fred sang of their courtship and his love. As he sang, he strolled to stand beside Belinda and stared directly into her adoring eyes. When he finished, someone handed him a glass of champagne.

"To the love of my life—I will love you forever." Then ignoring the tears dampening her cheeks and her runny nose, he bent and kissed her.

The party continued into the small hours of the morning when the guests straggled away. Fred and Belinda crawled into the bed in their honeymoon suite reserved at the local hotel at 4 am, a little drunk and a whole lot happy. The following day, a number of friends and family members returned to Belinda's family home for the opening of the wedding gifts.

Belinda was overcome with the amount. "Fred, we will have to hire a truck to get this stuff to Sudbury."

"Not really." Fred then handed a small wrapped parcel to his bride. "My gift to my love."

Belinda eased the wrapping off the box and lifted the lid to reveal a key. "What is this?" Her puzzled expression was met by a beaming Fred.

"Our wee cottage on the Atlantic. I bought that old cabin out on the point that you are so crazy about. We can be miles away, but it will always beckon us home—our holiday retreat." Belinda nearly bowled him over when she lunged at Fred and threw her arms around his neck.

They spent the rest of the week at the cabin completely alone together. They did have to make family dinners and write thank-you notes though. Alice dropped by to assure them that she would check on the cabin regularly while they were in Sudbury, but that was just an excuse to be with her brother and sister-in-law again.

When the newlyweds returned to Sudbury the following Sunday, a week after Lois and Peter had returned, it was to another celebration in Peter's backyard. The yard was packed with coworkers and friends. Belinda, a head above most, smiled until she felt her skin would crack. Andrew Ford raised his voice to get everyone's attention. "Thought this occasion would be a good time to recognize Fred's hard work and commitment to BDB and Dominion." Leaning heavily on his cane, Andrew, dapper in a silver grey worsted suit, hobbled up to Fred and handed him a small parcel. "My gift."

Belinda leaned over as Fred opened the envelope. "Fred! It's a picture of a car."

Andrew then handed Belinda the keys. "Yep—red to match that flaming head of yours." At that moment, a blaring horn was heard from the front driveway as the dealership delivered a brand new Ford Mustang.

"Holy shit, Andrew! This is way beyond anything."   Then with tears streaming down his face, Fred smothered Andrew in a bear hug.

"Put me down, you crazy oaf, before I belt you over your head with my cane." Laughter exploded throughout.

"Well, I guess the cedar chest full of linens and the new nuptial bed won't compare, will they?" The employees had taken up a collection and had outfitted Belinda's room with state-of-the-art furnishings.

While the couple was in the Atlantic Provinces, Peter and Norm had redecorated Belinda's bedroom and turned it into a bridal suite. They were to continue to live with Peter and Jack.

Jack was a high-energy little boy, who ran full tilt everywhere he went. He grabbed Belinda by the hand demanding a ride in her new car. The car seat was removed from Peter's 4x4 and Fred, Belinda and Jack took off for an inaugural ride, waving as they drove away. When they returned, they were all smiles. The next thing Fred knew was someone handed him his guitar. The evening finally broke up close to midnight with everyone saying they had to work the next day.

Weeks followed weeks and months passed until another year was behind them. Peter improved and lost himself in work. BDB continued to win lucrative contracts and was busy six days a week, sometimes working through the night. Lois took some time off and joined Helen and Norm on a return holiday to Greece. The twins would celebrate their eighth birthday when they returned and like before, their grandmother, even though she was a little frail now, would arrive for the celebration. On this trip, Helen and Norm took the children with them on most excursions and Lois booked herself on day trips when she didn't join them.

One day Norm took the twins off to explore a cave and Helen and Lois kicked back at the cottage.

"Lois, do you ever wonder what your life was like before Sudbury?"

"Sometimes—no, nearly all the time. But then, I think about what the doctor said that most cases like mine are caused by traumatic or sordid events. I may be one very lucky person that I've forgotten what I've forgotten. I do wish I could remember the happy times though. Surely, there were some."

"I sure wish I could find Stacey. She would have the answers. It's been almost five years since you arrived and try as I might, I cannot fit the pieces together. I sometimes think I have failed you. She was such a convincing person and recommended you so highly that I never even asked her for her last name. How stupid is that and me with a masters in engineering."

"Oh, Helen, never, never call yourself stupid and in my case, I am delighted that that Stacey person was so complimentary. Otherwise, I would never have met you, Norm and the twins. You and Norm have been the best friends anyone could have."

"Including Peter? I notice you two seem to be getting very close."

"It's almost as if we have just blended together. But I can't replace Mary and at this point, we are simply extremely close friends."

"Lois, I think you are avoiding the obvious. Peter adores you, more than as a friend. I see love in his eyes."

"Between you and me, Helen, I am frightened of getting involved romantically. What if in my past I was a criminal, or married or in love with someone else? That is when I would like a glimpse of who I was. Then, maybe I could return Peter's love, but this way, I can't."

"Norm wanted to get you to tell us your problems and I convinced him to leave it alone. Now I wish we had pressed. Our sole reason was to be supportive and perhaps help. But I am someone who respects one's privacy and this time it backfired."

Lois had experienced some odd dreams and déjà vu moments, but they didn't result in real memories. She still kept regular appointments with Dr. Frosst and whenever she had one of those moments, she discussed them with him but to no avail. The memory block was just that, a total block.

Chapter 34

I am definitely faced with a dilemma. Peter and Jack are so important to me yet I always live with a nagging fear because my past is forgotten. Dr. Frosst encourages me to let the past go and concentrate on the future. In a way I do. I am fully engrossed in the business, have dear friends, love my little house and can't imagine home being anywhere but Sudbury. However, I should take up Helen's suggestion and take a trip to Ottawa to see if that will break through the memory block. Truth be known, I am terrified to go alone for fear of what I might find out and I am reluctant to drag Peter, Francis or anyone else with me. Probably if I do decide to go, I will ask Peter. I don't know why I'd choose him, but I feel safe when I am with him. He knows me well and would probably assess any situation realistically. Anyway, I have too much on the go right now, but when I get back to Canada, I will discuss the idea with Dr. Frosst. I think in order to move ahead, I need to find my past.

There is no doubt that I am attracted to Peter in an emotional and physical way, but Mary was a dear friend and I find myself reluctant to even consider Peter as anyone but a business partner. I do envy Fred and Belinda and wish my life was not so complicated. Even if I do get my memory back, I am not sure I can consider a relationship with Peter. It seems as if I am betraying her memory. Peter has moved on and is, perhaps, ready for a relationship, but I may not be the person he needs.

Chapter 35

When Lois returned to Sudbury from Greece, she delved into business schedules and site applications that had piled up in her absence. Once she was on top of everything, Peter took Jack to Disneyworld and when he returned, Fred and Belinda left to spend two weeks in the Atlantic Provinces. There was no time to consider taking a trip to Ottawa or anywhere else. The equipment was in steady demand as were the drivers. She had no time to think of anything besides BDB.

"Peter, what do you think about making Fred a corporate manager? He is acting the role anyway without the recognition."

"We are so in each other's head. I was thinking the same thing."

"Mr. Barto, Mr. Ford is on line one." Stella, their shared administrative assistant, knocked lightly on the open door and tucked her head hair around the office door. Her shoulder-length, straight brown fell softly forward. She pointed to the phone and held up two fingers to indicate that Peter should pick up line two.

"Andrew, what's up?"

"I want you and that little lady to meet me in my office tomorrow morning at nine."

"Can I ask what it is about?"

"Nope. Just be here."

Peter looked at Lois. "Hmm, he didn't sound angry, so maybe he has another contract he wants to talk about. You know how he is—short on words, long on command."

"Yes, and without him, we would still be struggling to get one or two jobs—in fact, we might not be in business."

"Nah, I think we would have done better than that, but he sure put us on the fast track."

At a few minutes before nine the next morning, Lois and Peter greeted Ford's receptionist at Dominion's head office on Beech Street. They were ushered right into Andrew's spacious office. Lois never failed to be impressed with the view of Science North and the lake beyond from his tenth-floor office. The walls were a soft taupe, the perfect background for his outstanding collection of native art. She recognized the artist's style of two large paintings; one by Norval Morrisseau and one by Benjamin Chee Chee. Andrew grasped both their hands, drew them each into a bear hug and released them with a gentle slap on the back. Andrew motioned Peter and Lois to the deep maroon leather sofa, and leaning heavily on his cane, walked across the room to sit in the matching leather chair facing the sofa.

"Coffee and donuts are on the way. Good to see you both this morning."

Lois noted that somehow Andrew appeared smaller, frailer, but his smile was larger than life. Even though Andrew Ford was not large in stature, he was an impressive figure who commanded attention and got it. In order to run Dominion Construction and all the burly types that he employed, he had to always be in control and he revelled in being able to do that. The coffee arrived and Lois continued to observe Ford. His charcoal worsted suit was tailor-made and his tie, in mellow tones of wavy blue stripes, sat perfectly against his pale blue shirt. His hand-carved cane was leaning against his chair; his highly polished, black shoes were crossed at the ankle.

"Well, little lady, you are looking right pretty this morning. I like the new haircut."

Lois had made an appointment with her hairdresser immediately after Andrew's call the previous day. She had her hair cut in a soft layered bob and had her highlights redone. Whenever she was nervous about a meeting with this man, her hairdresser performed miracles that gave her self-confidence. She knew she always had to fight against a desire to be a shrinking violet. Running a heavy-equipment company meant she had to be decisive and confident, but sometimes it was a real struggle. She managed to overcome her fears and always put up an appearance of being self-assured. This morning was no exception. Peter and Andrew would think her strong-minded, but she was nervous and afraid of what was coming. All BDB needed was to lose Dominion as a client. Then they were in trouble, big trouble.

Andrew leaned forward and placed his elbows on his knees and looked right into the faces of the two young people sitting across from him.

"There's a matter I want to talk to you about."

Lois felt her stomach muscles tense and waves of nausea rise.

"As you know, I am a widower and me and the misses never were lucky enough to have a family. That means that I have to make some decisions about Dominion since there is no heir. I thought about selling it."

Lois flinched. If Dominion was sold, it might mean the new owner would not work with BDB.

"So, I did some figuring and talked to my accountant and lawyers. Here is what we came up with. We thought, no, *I* thought if Dominion amalgamated with BDB, it would make one fine joint venture."

Peter let out a breath he had been holding and sunk against the sofa back. Lois stared at Andrew in disbelief.

"I don't understand why you would want to do that."

"Yes, well, I figured you would think that. So let me have my say. Without becoming maudlin, I have become rather fond of you two and if I'd had children, I'd have wanted them to be just like you."

"But..."

"No buts. Don't interrupt—as I was saying, I kind of wish I had raised kids, and if the missus and I did, I'd want them to be just like you. I know I've helped you along the road, but both of you deserved and earned my respect as hard-working business people. What I'm proposing is a company comprised of a Board of Directors with shares divided proportionately. Probably take six or seven months to work out all the kinks; from what I've discussed with my legal beagles, it's a doable thing. It would relieve me of some of the decision making and I'd know that when I decide to leave this planet, all that I built up over the years will be in good hands. Now there, I've said my piece. What do you think?"

Neither Peter nor Lois said a word. Andrew's pronouncement hung like heavy air pressing them deep into the furniture. Conversation stagnated. Everyone's breathing slowed. Peter finally spoke. "Uh, I guess we have some thinking to do. I am sure I speak for both of us when I say we are flabbergasted. There is no way to say how honoured we are. There is so much to consider. Lois and I need to talk." Peter was rising as he spoke. His heart was hammering so loudly in his chest that he was sure Andrew could hear it. "We will just go now."

"No, wait. You haven't had your coffee yet." Andrew was chuckling. He knew he had thrown a curveball and he was enjoying seeing it slide home. He was not surprised when Lois joined Peter and said that they would be in touch in the next few days when they had had time to digest the offer. They needed to talk everything over between themselves and speak to their accountant and legal firm. At least, they were considering the proposal. Andrew handed them a large envelope.

"Here is my proposal and all the numbers. You take your time and work your way through them."

When they got back to BDB's corporate offices, Peter and Lois sat at their desks deep in contemplation. A paper clip came flying across Lois's desk; she looked up.

"You know what? I need a drink. What say we head on over to the club for lunch and order up a bottle of wine?"

Lois nodded as she rose and headed for the door. Peter

reached for her and held her by her upper arms. He looked deep into her eyes, then gently bent and kissed her forehead. A shiver ran down Lois's back and heat raced up her inner thighs. Shrugging away from Peter, Lois smiled, then slugged Peter in the arm. Putting his arm gently around her shoulders, Peter ushered Lois out the door. The sky had become overcast and a brisk wind was whipping the branches—nature was promising rain, but nothing was about to dampen their mood. It had been a dry, hot summer, so the change in weather would be most welcome.

"So, initial thoughts?" They were walking across the parking lot to Peter's Silverado.

"I don't know what to think; it is almost too overwhelming. You are the one who wanted to own your own business. Do you think this takes away some of your proprietorship?"

"Yeah, it might. On the other side, we stand to be part owners of one hell of a big company. That is a formidable challenge and I am not sure we are up to it. It is slightly overwhelming. We've learned a hell of a lot by BDB growing leaps and bounds, but Dominion? Holy cow—we would be looking at millions in annual revenue. Too much money, too scary. Let's weigh the pros and cons over lunch. Then if we are at all interested, make an appointment with our accountant and our lawyers."

Lois ordered a frittata and Peter a cheeseburger. They had already emptied a large glass of Merlot when the food arrived. Refilling their glasses, the waiter left. Both Lois and Peter nibbled at their food but drank the wine quickly, and refilled their glasses.

"Okay, this is not getting us anywhere. We need to speak to the powers that be to see what an amalgamation would look like. I'm afraid we are in over our heads and have no idea what Andrew has in mind."

The next six weeks were spent in consultation with lawyers, accountants and meetings between Dominion and BDB. The final outcome outlined a corporate structure that was incorporated and financially diversified through a shareholder arrangement. The pros far outweighed the cons, so with most of their concerns dealt with, the amalgamation moved forward. Lois and Peter insisted that Fred be a small shareholder in accordance with his contribution and dedication, and Andy's foreman was awarded the same consideration as well. The new company, fully incorporated by November 31, became Dominion BDB Inc. The Board of Directors consisted of Andrew Ford, CEO, Peter Barto, President, Lois Brenton-Douglas, Vice-President and six members including Fred and the lawyers and accountants of both firms. Andrew held forty percent of the shares as did Lois and Peter between them. Fred held six shares as did Mike Follows, Dominion's foreman. The rest were divided between the other Board members. Norm French was able to buy into the company as a single share shareholder. Between the legal aspects and the financial considerations, Lois and Peter were always in meetings. Even though there were now more meetings, they were scheduled to allow Lois and Peter to continue to work as usual. Regardless, they still needed to be hands-on wherever their skills were required. The mobile repair truck had paid for itself over and over by time saved and machinery being kept in top condition.

The newly formed partnership, really a newly formed company, was not yet made public. Andrew was determined that it called for a celebration that included all the employees of Dominion and BDB. Andrew reserved the club and Lois arranged the food and entertainment. In fact, their assistants did most of the work, but the ideas came from Andrew and Lois. It was decided that it would be a combined family Christmas party and corporate amalgamation party. The official announcement would be made during the evening and everyone would receive navy peak caps with the new Dominion BDB logo. It had been difficult to keep the partnership a secret, but Andrew wanted to announce it to all the employees at the same time. There had been some questions muttered around the room, early in the evening, as to why the employees of Dominion and BDB were holding a combined Christmas party, but the consensus was that they worked so closely together that they might as well play together.

As the guests were called to their tables, a hush fell across the room. Andrew strode up the middle aisle to the stage. Andrew reached the podium, tapped the mike and the squawk of the speaker feedback got everyone's attention. In his most eloquent manner, Andrew announced the joining of the two companies, and informed the audience that the amalgamated company would be called Dominion BDB. At first, the silence in the room was stifling—then a single clap was joined by a thunderous roar of clapping and table banging.

"I am so pleased that this news is being received in such a positive manner. Peter, Lois and I have been busy for many weeks working out the logistics and legal crap, getting all the documents signed and setting up new offices for our team. From this day forward, every employee in this room will receive their paycheque from Dominion BDB Inc. and you city folks will have to change your cheques and make payments to Dominion BDB Inc. We all know how government systems work—could take months." A roar of laughter filled the hall.

There was an easel standing beside him draped with a navy cloth trimmed with gold. Inviting Peter and Lois to join him, Andrew asked each to take a corner and lift the cover away on the count of three.

"One, two, three—"

A rendering of the Dominion BDB logo was revealed. Flashbulbs erupted from all around the room. This was big news for Sudbury and the media had been alerted that there might be a special announcement of note. It was also big news for the employees of both companies. After introducing the Board of Directors and assuring all the employees that there would not be any job losses, Andrew stepped off the stage with Peter and Lois to mingle with the crowd.

Lois looked radiant in an ankle-length, strapless gown with a deep blue, paisley pattern; she had a navy Pashmina shawl draped over her shoulders. Even in four-inch heels, she still was diminutive, barely reaching Peter's shoulder. He kept a protective arm on her waist as they greeted employees, city dignitaries and friends.

Jack was standing up on his chair with his hands firmly set on his hips looking for all the world like a victorious imp, his Dominion BDB cap crowning his curly, black hair. He cheered when everyone clapped, getting caught up in the spirit of the moment.

The corporate table was humming with conversation between the Board of Directors and their families—the champagne flowed freely and, in honour of Fred, Surf 'n Turf was served.

"I want a hot dog," Jack announced in an ear-shattering shout.

"Shush, you have to learn some social manners." Belinda, with her forefinger pressed against her lips, leaned into Jack's face. "Where Fred and I come from, we pile lobster into a hot dog bun. Wanna try that?"

"NO! I want a hot dog!"

The waiter leaned over Belinda and assured her that hot dogs were available.

"So there."

"That lad will not take 'no' for an answer. Ladies and gentlemen, meet our future CEO." Andrew Ford raised his glass in salute.

"You better watch it, Andy. You might be cultivating a monster."

"What I want to cultivate is a Board that is a hard-working family. I want everyone to feel they are a contributing member; I want every aspect of Dominion BDB to be important. And you know what? I know this is a team to be reckoned with. Please raise your glasses and drink a toast to the biggest little company in the north."

"You know, little lady, this was exactly where this all started." Peter was grinning and hugging Lois. "I can still see Andrew Ford hobbling across the room and dropping his card on the table suggesting we call him. What an amazing lot of stuff has happened since then." He planted a kiss on Lois's forehead.

Helen and Norm smiled a knowing smile as they watched Lois blush.

Chapter 36

My head is swimming and I don't think it is entirely from the wine. The whole evening just seems such a blur—almost too much to absorb. It is a relief that the staff was so receptive to the changes in the corporate structure. Really, Peter and I had not completely considered their reaction. We only looked at the bottom line and the legalities of forming the partnership. We should have given the employees more consideration but, as it is, there was already a bond between Dominion and BDB and we were working so closely together that it just meshed so well. The whole transaction will be smooth.

Andrew did an amazing job of blending the two companies—it was a seamless transition. So now look at me— I am a big wig in a big corporation. My goodness, I am sure I will not get a minute of sleep tonight. My thoughts are swirling with the magnitude of the whole affair. Even though we have been working with lawyers, accountants and shareholders for weeks, it didn't seem real until tonight. I am so glad that Helen and Norm bought a share. It somehow brings them even closer to me. Jack and the twins are so close now, almost like cousins. Oh, that little monkey is so independent. I am sure Belinda has encouraged him to openly express himself. Andrew sure made a fuss over him just like he was the grandfather. Well, since he mentioned that he considers Peter to be like his own family, that makes him a pseudo grandpa. I think Peter will have to curb how he spoils the child. Andrew has such a generous side to him. Peter and I have to be the luckiest people in the world to have been brought under his wing. Oh, my! My thoughts are rambling. Peter was so attentive during the whole evening. It was as if we were connected at the hip. He is the best partner and friend a gal could have. I wish my past was not an issue—I really could let myself...

Chapter 37

The following day, a Saturday, Helen took the twins over to Lois's house for coffee early in the morning. Helen had a dozen freshly baked Danish from the grocery store bakery. The smell was mouthwateringly tantalizing.

"Helen, we will never eat all those. Besides, I am sluggish and perhaps a little hungover. The party last night was amazing. I shook so many hands, kissed so many cheeks and drank way too much champagne. I was so wound up that I didn't think I would be able to sleep with all those thoughts racing through my head, but I think I fell asleep mid-thought. I'm not sure, but maybe you are right. A sugar rush might be just what I need. Bring on the Danish. Yes, pastries might be just the thing—but so many?"

"Barby and Grant will eat two each as I am sure you and I can match, so that leaves four for Peter and Jack."

"Are they coming over too?"

"I kind of expected that Peter might drop by after last night."

"Whatever for?"

"God, Lois, do you need a whack on the head? He was doing everything to get you to look at him as a special person, a person to love, not just as a friend or partner. He is becoming very attracted to you. He was almost drooling over you last night. That man is so over-the-hill in love, he is pathetic. Lois, you need to smarten up. Peter definitely wants more than a business relationship."

"Helen, if I was interested in getting involved, Peter would be my first choice. In fact, I cannot imagine my life without him and, yes, I am seriously attracted to him. But, that fear of what I have forgotten and do not know keeps me from letting myself get involved. I simply cannot allow myself to get emotionally entangled."

"Lois, you need a life partner and a business partnership just doesn't cut it. It's just not enough. The past is behind you. Let it go. Give Peter some indication you care, that you might love him given time. You deserve each other. He needs to move forward with his life. He is one hell of a great guy and you are going to lose him if you do not reciprocate."

"I'm sorry, Helen, but I just can't."

Grant was reaching for his third Danish and Helen grabbed his hand in mid-reach. "Young man, you have had enough. Let's get your skates out of the car and try that patch of ice at the side of the house." The twins scrambled off their chairs and eagerly waited for their mother to get their skates organized. "Think about it, Lois. Don't close the door on Peter. Talk to him."

It had never dawned on Lois to tell Peter how she felt, but the thought that perhaps Helen was right and her conflicting emotions and undeniable fear of the unknown needed to be addressed. A truck horn sounded from outside.

"See, Peter and Jack are here." Helen's knowing grin beamed across the kitchen counter.

"Did you bring your skates?" The twins yelled as they ran to meet their best friend. Jack nodded and held them up by the laces. "Eat your Danish. Mom brought them. Your dad can put on your skates. Mom is going to help me and Lois will help Grant. Isn't it fun to have our own private rink right here at Lois's house?" Barby talked non-stop.

Lois watched as Peter lifted his son to a stool at the counter. He handed him a pastry while he took a monster bite out of one he had scarfed for himself; he dropped it on the counter. All while he was pushing Jack's foot into a skate with the other. The whole scene was orchestrated as if to demonstrate the perfect family moment.

"The perfect Norman Rockwell."

"What's that?"

"Oh, I was just looking at this whole scene and thinking it

would make a perfect Rockwell illustration."

"Yeah, I hope it does not include my screwed up face as I am trying to get this damned knot out of these skate laces."

"Here—let me. I have a knack for releasing knots. Grant is good to go." She edged close to Peter, thighs touching as she wrestled with the skate lace. The heat that rose from where they connected caused her to turn beet red. She sprang back and a startled look passed between Peter and Lois.

"Great idea to build a rink, Lois."

Lois had had two of the construction crew come over several days during the previous week to build and flood a low section of the side lawn so the children could skate. She had continued to flood the area for several nights. While she dragged the hundred-foot hose across the yard, taking a deep breath, she relished the exertion. Standing alone in the brisk cold air while she carefully sprayed the water over the surface of the ice was peaceful. The weather had turned just cold enough and stayed at the right temperature, so the ice froze smooth and hard. Truth be known, she wanted to give it a try too. Peter had told her he played hockey all through high school and loved to skate. She made a mental note to purchase a pair of skates during the week. She decided to get night lights installed. She watched Peter with Jack, both of them with a pastry jammed in their mouths. A wave of emotion flushed through her again. Maybe Helen was right and she should encourage Peter's advances.

"Why not?"

"Why not, what?" Peter was pulling the skate laces tight.

"Oh, nothing. Just something Helen and I were discussing earlier."

The twins took skating lessons so were very confident on the ice, but Jack slipped and fell repeatedly. Peter had put soccer pads on his knees and a helmet on his head. His small body seemed to roll in a heap each time he fell, but he struggled up again and again with a determined shrug of his shoulders. He would strike out with long strides, manage to get, at most, three in before he lost his balance and toppled. Barby and Grant figured out his problem and got on each side of him. They held him by his elbows and guided him forward. After their cheerful suggestions and a few demonstrations, Jack was taking slower, more leisurely, strides and did indeed stay upright. The three adults cheered as they watched from the kitchen window each holding a fresh coffee and Peter another Danish. Peter downed the last of his coffee, then slipped on a pair of skates and joined the children. He pretended he was chasing them and when he caught them would swing them in the air. The laughter was infectious and Lois and Helen were holding their aching sides. With rosy cheeks and bright smiles, Peter and the skaters eventually came in for hot chocolate.

"These kids have had enough sugar this morning to have them bouncing off the walls."

However, they settled on the living room floor to play Candyland.

The morning ended with Helen announcing that she wanted Jack to join her and the twins for a program about beavers at Science North, that is, after they stopped to get some lunch.

"Can I, Dad? Please."

"Sure, as long as Helen promises that the lunch will not have any sugar."

"I want a hot dog."

Peter rolled his eyes as he laughed. "What else?"

Lois held the door open as Helen herded the children toward the SUV. This left Peter and Lois together to clear the counter, pick up the game and wash the mugs.

"Lois, I need to ask you something."

"Sure, Peter. Anything."

Peter moved beside her and held her hands in one of his. With the other hand, he cupped her chin turning her face to him. "We have been together as classmates and as business partners and have ultimately become friends, very close friends. This closeness, for me, is becoming something more than a friendship. I know you do not date and have never pursued a romantic interest. Why, I don't know, because you are one special gal. You are beautiful in every way. No, don't pull away until I have had my say. Lois, I am attracted to you and would like our friendship to move to the next level. I am falling in love with you." Lois recognized this as a well-rehearsed speech and noted beads of perspiration on Peter's forehead.

"Peter, stop right there. First, let me say, I treasure every moment with you and nothing would make me happier than to be able to love you back. In many ways, I really do love you and Jack too. But I have issues. I have no idea who I am. All I know is that my life before Sudbury was so traumatic that I lost it. What if I was married, what if I was a criminal, what if I ....?

"It doesn't matter. I love you with all your issues and I simply cannot see you as a criminal. But, that is a past life and you can't let whatever it is keep you from enjoying a full life now."

"The odd thing is that there is no record of me before I came to Sudbury. What if that means I came here under a special police protection program to escape someone that is trying to kill me. What if they find me? That would put you and Jack at risk and I would never do that. There are too many ifs—and much as I would like to let it all go, I can't. Sorry, Peter."

Lois turned finished loading the dishwasher, pushed the button and started it. Peter came up behind her and turned her again to face him. He looked deep into her moist, blue eyes, lifted her chin and kissed her softly and deeply. Lois felt a rush rise from her knees to her groin. Her heart was skipping crazily and her breathing shallow. She leaned into Peter and felt their bodies blend. Peter pulled her close, his arousal obvious. Then placing his hands on the side of Lois's head, he looked into her face for approval. Soft eyes met his and her slight nod made him lift her and carry her to the bedroom.

Their bodies blended in passionate waves, climaxing together again and again. Exhausted, they finally lay back, each with their own thoughts.

"Oh, my God, Lois, you are amazing. You are so much more than I ever dreamed. We are so perfect together; you complete me. I love you and want you to be beside me forever."

"Peter, I can't replace Mary."

"I know and you are right. She will always be a part of me, but you belong to a different part of who I am. I need you. Besides, Mary would approve. I just know it."

"Right now, I am in heaven, but it is a heaven I am not sure I deserve. Give me some time. I need to go back to Dr. Frosst. I am very confused right now. Please, this has been so special, but I need to deal with my head and give this whole attraction I have for you deep consideration. Don't be upset. I can't handle a relationship if I don't know where it will lead."

"Okay, I respect that, but Lois, I want to warn you. I can't not love you. What is, is."

"Oh, my dear Peter, what have we gotten ourselves into?"

Lois made an appointment with Dr. Frosst for Wednesday of the following week. Once she explained her reason for needing additional assessment, he suggested she hire a special investigator. She might then learn about her past even if she had no memory of it. At least knowing would allow her to move forward.

Following this advice, Lois thought about how to find the best person to handle her case. Ian Shields came highly recommended. Of course, it was Norm who found him through people he knew.

"I can't believe we haven't thought of this sooner. It just makes so much sense. He is a former detective and consults for one of the largest firms in Toronto. He is highly recommended for his researching skills and has ways of accessing police files."

Lois called his office, spoke with Ian at length and asked for his résumé after inquiring if he was available. Because she was taking this initiative, Lois decided to have a heart-to-heart with Andrew. She had never discussed her concerns with him although he sometimes asked some leading questions. He did know she had lost her memory; it was common knowledge.

She invited him to her home and plied him with home-baked cookies and herbal tea. She filled him in on the whole story, as much as she felt necessary.

"I have no idea what the investigator will find. On one hand, I do hope he locates the truth. On the other, I'm afraid of what he might find. I felt that you needed to know that my past might flush up some unsavoury facts. There I said it—now you know."

"Well, little lady, it sure as hell won't change how I feel about you. And, now that I know that you make such amazing cookies, I will never allow anything to get in the way of my thinking you are one fine little lady."

"Andrew, seeing as we are business partners, don't you think it is about time for you to call me Lois?"

"Nope, little lady, I sure don't."

Chapter 38

I woke this morning with the strangest thoughts in my head. I was in a kindergarten classroom with children swarming me singing Tar-ar-a-boom-de-ay. Now it is like an earworm. It simply won't go away. I know I did not learn that song since being in Sudbury. Is this a missing piece to my past? Well, it is a happy song, so I must have had happy moments. Maybe I was a teacher or went to camp and learned it around a campfire. There must be happy moments to remember—I do so wish I could. I need to get back to Ian Shields; he thinks he has the resources and can delve into my past and find out who I am. He is confident that there are not many people by my name, so searching records should reveal something. And if it was changed under a police protection program, he might be able to access that information through a contact he has. He indicated that he likely could do a thorough search within six weeks.

Oddly enough, the closer I am to Peter, the safer I feel and am a little less frightened to learn about the life I left behind when I left Ottawa. No matter what the circumstances that had me fleeing to Sudbury, I am ready to face them. The thought of building a relationship is certainly appealing especially with Peter. After that afternoon we found ourselves in bed, I think of him constantly and not in a business sort of way. My body sure responded—wow, I was so passionate. Did I always love sex so much? Maybe I was a hooker. I sure did seem to know what to do. It was so fulfilling and now I am secretly hoping we will find a way to be together again and again. Just thinking about it has my body quivering.

Chapter 39

Winter, once again, took a firm grip on Sudbury. Dominion BDB had their road crews on the go 24/7. Due to the weather, construction had slowed. Peter and Fred were happy to have the machinery in for maintenance repair and paint renewal. The design company had come up with an improved logo and was pressing for the company to display it everywhere so that the branding would be consistent. It was all about raising awareness. As soon as the logo was authorized by the Board members, each piece of equipment had the logo printed on it. Jackets, crests and hats were issued to all employees.

It was a cold, dreary November day and both Peter and Lois were busy in the office.

Andrew walked into Lois and Peter's office, which was still a combined suite. "Little lady, Peter, there is someone I want you to meet." Trailing him was a middle-aged woman a head taller than Andrew. She was wearing a bright red, down-filled jacket, opened to reveal a brown plaid shirt and cargo pants. Even in steel-toed boots, she moved with the grace of a panther—rugged in appearance but regal in carriage.

"This is Amanda Elliott. She and I go back a bit. Her husband owned a garage over in Kearney. When the wife was with us, we often shared a few drinks and a few laughs. Amanda lost her hubby a few months back. She was devastated at the loss but had to get on with life. It is a good thing she is one busy gal. She keeps her hand in and runs the garage on her own, so she has little time to get depressed. She is not a mechanic but can do the office work. She has always been involved in the community and it has been very supportive at this difficult time. Anyway, I have asked her to come with me to talk to you about what she does for the community. Amanda has a proposal to make. She has my support. Not that I want to put pressure on you, but I think she should have yours as well."

Lois and Peter exchanged puzzled looks. Offering coffee, they directed Andrew and Amanda to the conference room.

"You got any homemade cookies on hand?" Having learned that Lois was an avid cook and that there were always special treats available, Andrew never failed to request them. "The first thing this little lady fixed up in her broken-down house was the kitchen; she loves to cook."

"My house isn't broken down; it just needs some more loving." Lois smiled and placed a plate of hermits on the table just as their assistant brought in coffee.

"Amanda's crazy about dogs, but not just any dogs. In fact, she is one crazy dog person."

"Excuse me, what do you mean she is one crazy dog person?"

"Well, for one thing, she breeds dogs."

"Oh, how many dogs do you have?" Lois had turned to face Amanda.

"Eight."

"Eight! Do you own a kennel?"

"Well, yes and no. I do breed them, but what is more important, I train my dogs and others for dog sled races."

"There are dog sled races here? I thought that was only in the Northwest Territories."

"Oh, yes, sledding is big here and that is the reason I want to talk to you. The Kearney Dog Sled Races take place in February and are an international event. We get pretty broad media coverage locally and have a committed following. We, I, think Dominion BDB would find this an event worth sponsoring." Amanda sucked in a deep breath after delivering her pitch.

Andrew leaned forward. "This is the largest dog sled race in Ontario and one of our employees, Rod Easter, has a team and competes every year. He is one fine musher."

"Well, it does sound interesting. What are we looking at?"

Amanda placed an attractive folder with the heading Kearney Dog Sled Races and a picture of dogs pulling a sled on the coffee table.

"Kearney was originally a logging town and those logging roads still exist and became the dog sled race trails and continue to be today. Even back twenty years ago, there was enthusiastic support for the annual event from local residents, cottagers, businesses and, of course, mushers. For the past twenty years, The Kearney Winterfest, otherwise known as The Kearney Dog Sled Races, has been a member of the Ontario Federation of Sled Dog Sports. Twenty years ago, the race was affiliated with the Quad Crown. In its first year running, Kearney hosted a four-mile, four-dog race, a six-mile, six-dog race and the ever-exciting thirty-mile, eight-dog race. That first year, they hosted twenty-four teams from all over Ontario and the prize purse for the first year of the races was a total of $3,000."

"Well, that's a tidy purse, but I do not know a thing about this sport."

"Today, the prize is considerably higher, five times higher, and one of the reasons we seek sponsors. The event runs over two days and competitors come from all over North America. Most arrive a couple of days before the races to rest their dogs and introduce them to the terrain. As you can imagine, this is good for local businesses."

Peter was scanning the brochure and looked up. "I am not quite sure how this works. I see various categories and there are different lengths of races, right?"

"Yes, sled dog racing is one of North America's oldest winter sports. Natives who inhabit the northern regions of the North American continent have always been associated with and dependent upon man's best friend. Their dogs have played a leading role in their lives and economy by providing faithful companionship, assisting in the hunt and, more importantly, by being the sole means of transportation during the long winter season. One of the most incredible events of the era was the hastily organized relay of native and mail teams to carry lifesaving serum from Anchorage to the diphtheria stricken village of Nome in 1925."

"Impressive," said Peter.

"Records of formal racing events date back to 1908 with the running of the first 'All Alaska Sweepstakes', a distance of four hundred and eight miles from Nome to Candle and back. At Kearney, we recognize the history, but our races are much shorter."

"Do many people attend the days the races are run and are all the dogs Huskies?"

Amanda threw back her head and let out a laugh that rippled with mirth. "It is not uncommon for visitors to have to park a mile from town and hike in even though there are wagons running constantly to transport guests. The town is packed with young and old. There are many events other than the races—the dogs can be purebred or mixed breed. Both of the sprint races held over the weekend include purebred and open categories. Dogs in the open class are usually a mixed breed, utilizing any combination of Alaskan Huskies, German Short-Hair Pointers, Greyhounds, et cetera. The emphasis is to breed the race dogs for speed and stamina, as well as more general considerations like climate. The purebred class is generally thought of as the more traditional sled dogs, such as Siberian Huskies, but we've seen teams of Border Collies, Setters, and even Spaniels compete in past years. This category is satisfied by any dog team that has purebred papers."

"So, tell me how we can help and a little more about the event."

"One of the most popular activities is put on by the SugarDogs Adventure Company from Sundridge. They offer a chance to experience riding in a sled over a thirty-forty minute trail. They are coming back again this year to provide dog sled rides during the Race Weekend. Everyone of all ages is an aspiring musher. During the event, everyone becomes an authority and thinks they are a musher or know everything about dog racing. When I mention mushers of all ages, one of our favourite races is the children's race. It is a short course and the children, aged six-thirteen, race a small sled with two dogs. Often the dogs are not well trained and the event turns into a comedic event—just one heck of a lot of fun, hilarious, in fact."

"Can one sponsor that activity?"

"Yes, but I want you to be familiar with all of the events before you decide. There is public skating at the arena with a roaring bonfire to sit by and sip a cup of hot chocolate. One of the other popular races is not a dog sled but Ski-joring. Ski-joring is a winter sport that originated in Scandinavia. One or two dogs will pull a person on cross-country skis by means of a mountain climbing harness. Our Ski-joring race is a sprint with high speeds involved, making it exciting for spectators and racers. Ski-jorers must have strong cross-country skiing skills to manage to stay on their feet. Some of our past racers have previously competed in cross-country skiing world championships. Television stations show up in droves to catch this event. The action is furious and there's always the chance of a serious accident. We have emergency crews stationed at strategic locations in the event one of the skiers has a nasty fall."

"Okay, I am already excited about that one."

"Of course, our major event is the Six-Dog Sprint Race. This sprint race consists of a six-dog team and includes both purebred and open categories. The same course, utilizing the same dogs, is run by the mushers on both Saturday and Sunday, with the total time from both days determining the winner. In previous years, we have had racers from Ontario, Quebec, several Northern States and even as far away as Jamaica competing. Yes, believe it or not—Jamaica!"

"Now, that is hard to grasp."

"There are also short course races with sleds pulled by two dogs. Where we see BDB partnering with us is as the overall race sponsor—this entitles you to numerous benefits, but the main one would be the entire event would carry your corporate name for a cost of $25,000. Instead of The Kearney Dog Sled Races, it would be called the Dominion BDB Dog Sled Races and would appear on all promotional material."

Lois nodded, then looked at Amanda with a thoughtful expression on her face. "You know, Amanda, Dominion BDB is a local corporation. I'm not sure it needs that kind of exposure. Peter, how do you feel about being involved?"

"I see where you are heading and I think this event is one we want to support. Andrew agrees since he brought Amanda here. My take on this is, since it has been in existence for so many years and is known across North America as The Kearney Dog Sled Races, I see no reason to change the name—I think a tag line 'sponsored by' is the way to go. Let's do it."

Amanda sat down hard in the nearest chair. "Oh, thank you. I thought I would have to give away everything to convince you to step up to the plate. You have just made my day."

"See, what did I tell you?" Andrew draped his arm across Amanda's shoulders.

"Can we sponsor a specific team as well?"

Peter's question had Andrew straighten up and grin from ear to ear. "Jacob Belcher works for us and is a serious six-dog team contestant. We can approach him."

"Not sure that is a good idea. It might smack of favouritism if he wins. What might work better is if his fellow workers simply cheer him on."

"Nope. I want him decked out in Dominion BDB colours—we will take a chance on how it is perceived. After all, it is a race and may the best team win." Andrew thumped his cane on the floor in defiance.

Everyone laughed.

"Well, I guess I know where I will be February 7th and 8th. I sure hope the weather is clear and crisp. You know—I am excited about this partnership." Peter ran his hands down the side of his jeans, then rubbed them together in glee. "I wish I had dogs to train for Jack to enter the kids' race."

Amanda stood up and touched Peter's arm. "Bring your little guy over to my place next Saturday and I will show him the ropes and introduce him to my dogs. I have a couple of young ones that have never raced so would qualify for the kids' race. If Jack likes the dogs and the sport, then we can have a few training days before the event."

"My friends, it is lunchtime and I propose we head to the club and have a champagne lunch to celebrate." Andrew could never resist an opportunity to eat at the club. There was no objection though and since Lois and Peter would be returning to the office, they hopped into Peter's truck.

"You know, I think this is going to be fun, but apart from that, it is a good corporate move. It is time we were a more community-minded company. I can think of a number of ways to involve our employees and their families. We can host a corporate family event with lots of hamburgers, chili dogs and beer."

"Great idea. We should set up a meeting with Fred and get his input."

"No doubt he will have some entertainment ideas."

"Lois, on another topic—have you contacted that private detective yet?"

"No, not yet. I did meet with Doctor Frosst and he encouraged me to move forward with the private investigator but wanted me to go back for regular visits with him so he can be supportive for whatever happens."

"You know I am here, don't you?"

"Of course, but Doctor Frosst does not have an emotional stake in who I am. He is only interested from a professional standpoint."

"I don't care who you were. I love who you are and I want us to have a life together."

"Don't say it, Peter. I have this terrible confusion when I have no idea what transpired before my memory loss. I am trying to sort it out and, yes, I have very strong feelings for you and Jack. I just don't want to start something that might come crashing down on us. Let's take it a day at a time." Lois leaned across the seat and planted a kiss on Peter's cheek as they pulled into the club's parking lot.

Chapter 40

So many confusing thoughts are racing through my brain. Peter has become so precious to me and I want to return his affection, but every time I go in that direction, I simply freeze at the thought. Not knowing who I was and what drove me to escape to Sudbury is a major deterrent. I have avoided pushing for the answers because I am terrified what I will find out. Now, I have no choice. I am falling deeply in love with Peter and nothing would make me happier than to become Jack's mother. No matter what I discover, I must have the courage to face it full on and overcome the obstacles. Surely, I can do that. I certainly have lots of support and special people who believe in me. Like the mushers, I need to have faith, find the trail, guide myself to the finish line. I may not come out the winner, but I will, at least, know what I am dealing with. And for that matter, learn about my background and life before Sudbury. First and foremost, I have to get up the courage to contact the detective. Tomorrow, I will make the call.

Night after night, I sit and try to remember what drove me to start a new life in Sudbury. Yesterday, I sat at my computer and pored over a map of the city of Ottawa. Nothing jumped out at me, but I was familiar with the main streets and even remembered, or thought I remembered, some of the buildings at some of the intersections. I searched the major events to see if I reacted to any one in particular. Nothing. It's as if I had no connection with that city at all.

Chapter 41

Ian Shield's raspy voice answered Lois's call. "Shields Investigative Services."

"Mr. Shields—"

"Ian—I never go by Mr."

"Ian, it's Lois Brenton-Douglas. We spoke several months ago. I don't know if you remember, but Norm French suggested you might be able to help me."

"Hey, of course, I remember. My goodness, I haven't seen Norm in a dog's age. How the heck is he?"

"Fine. I wonder if I can make an appointment to speak with you."

"Sure. Your place or mine?"

"Oh, it doesn't matter. Here might be better if you don't mind, but I am in Sudbury."

"As long as that Norm fellow can free up for lunch, I'll head north. Probably more comfortable anyway—my office is a bit of a hole-in-the-wall."

"I think my partner might want to sit in on the meeting, so it's better here. Do you know where Dominion BDB headquarters are?"

"Hell, I don't even know *what* Dominion BDB is! I am overdue to visit another friend of mine up there, Owen Davis."

"I know Owen. I am only a few blocks away. How about we meet next Wednesday?"

"It would have to be late afternoon; I am tied up in the early morning and couldn't get there until after three."

"How about three forty-five?"

"That works."

When Lois told Peter, he was pleased she had included him. Although he was familiar with the details of her amnesia, he was interested in how a detective would perceive the information.

Wednesday afternoon found Lois pacing the office floor. Peter closed the door quietly and stopped her mid-stride.

"Nervous?"

"Yes, and I have no idea why. It is simply an interview, but that old nagging doubt creeps in and I get very restless and almost scared. Crazy, isn't it?"

"No, it's totally what one would expect."

At that moment, the buzzer on Lois's desk sounded. Her assistant announced that Ian Shields had arrived and Lois told her to bring him in.

When the door opened, a tall, grey-haired man with sharp features stepped through. Lois couldn't help noticing his highly polished, brown loafers and sharply pressed gabardine trousers. He wore a tweed jacket over a beige turtleneck sweater. He wasn't what one would call handsome and a nasty scar pulled his mouth into a permanent sneer, but he definitely had a commanding appearance.

Lois walked across to meet him, reached her hand out and, as Ian reached to shake it, Lois noticed that his middle finger was missing. "Ian, I'm Lois and this is Peter Barto, my partner and friend. Please have a seat. Would you like a coffee or another beverage?"

"You wouldn't have a cold beer on hand by any chance?"

"You know, it *is* that time of the day. Peter and I might join you."

Peter was already opening a cupboard that concealed a mini-fridge and pulled out three Coronas. He knew Lois liked a glass, but Ian indicated the bottle was fine. Peter reached into an overhead cupboard and quickly took the wrappings off a prepared dish of crackers and cheese.

"So, Lois, what can I do for you?"

Ian's voice was as raspy in person as it had been on the phone.

"This is kind of a tricky one. You see, I don't know who I am."

"Half the time, I don't know who I am either, so let's start with what you do know."

"I arrived in Sudbury to work as a nanny for Helen and Norm seven years ago. That is the earliest memory I have. The first summer I was with them, Helen suggested I take my holidays on Manitoulin Island. I had an unfortunate accident and suffered a head injury that resulted in dissociative amnesia. According to diagnostic analysis, this probably means I erased some traumatic occurrence in my life by simply erasing my past."

"You mean you have no recollection of anything prior to arriving in Sudbury?"

"That's right—although I sometimes get weird flashes one that comes often is a red door. I have no idea why. Helen told me I was in Ottawa before coming to Sudbury. She has tried to reach my former employer, but the contact info she had is no longer applicable."

"She does have her name though, right?"

"Yes, but only her first name—Stacey."

Ian was taking notes as Lois was speaking. "Sure haven't got a lot to go on what with a red door and a partial name, but it is something. I will try to locate Stacey. How did you end up in the construction industry?"

Peter grinned, leaned forward and set his Corona on the table. "Well, Lois and I were enrolled in an adult education program together. We ran into each other one day where I was working on repairing a bulldozer and Lois asked if she could help as she knew how to drive one."

"Now that is a valuable clue. Where do you think you learned that?"

"I helped my father—he worked in excavation. I sometimes drove for him."

"Well, now we have something. What was your father's name?"

"There again, I can't remember. I sometimes have a vision of a short, muscular man whom I feel affection for, so it might be my father, but nothing more."

"Peter, did Lois tell you any other details about her father?"

"Not that I remember."

"Well, think about it and if you remember anything, no matter how insignificant you might think it is, let me know."

"Once I find Stacey, the rest should be easy. Probably only take a few days to find her. Even though we only have a first name, it is not that popular, so I will start there."

As Lois and Peter saw Ian to the door, Peter noticed that Lois was clenching and unclenching her fists.

"Hey, partner, you okay?"

"Oh, Peter, I do want the answers, but the very thought of maybe finding out that I had committed a crime or suffered a heinous assault or some other sordid traumatic thing scares the hell out of me. I am not sure how I will handle that. And the fact that Ian thinks I will know within weeks just makes me more scared."

Peter put his arm around Lois and drew her to him. "Listen, I will always love you no matter what. You need to know that you have loyal friends who will be there too. Besides, once you know what you are dealing with, or what you ran away from, remember that it does not need to be shared with anyone but me."

"You're right, but it is still frightening."

"Come on, let's dash through this downpour and head to the club for a calorie-loaded plate of burgers and fries."

The weeks flew by and Lois was in regular contact with Ian Shields, but he was having little luck finding anything.

"First of all, there are no missing person's reports that match your name or description for the time period when you disappeared. So I expect that you are not defined as a missing person. I can find no records of anyone with your name attending school here. I can't find that there ever was a mailing address in Ottawa or the surrounding area under your name. There are no police records, but my friend did find a possible connection in the protection program. He is getting the files. It may take a week or so. I will call you then."

When Lois disconnected the call, she started to shake. Peter came into the office. Seeing how pale she was and that she was in distress, he gathered her in his arms.

"Oh, Peter, Ian thinks I might be in a protection program. I am terrified. This whole thing could turn out to be a sordid mess. Now I am worried for you, Helen and Norm, the twins and all my friends. What if someone wants to kill me?"

"Lois, Lois, you are taking the grim approach. It has been almost seven years since you arrived in Sudbury. Whatever was the cause for alarm at that time is likely not relevant anymore. Just because you may learn about your past does not mean that the person or persons that meant to harm you will find out. You have been safe for all this time; you will likely remain safe."

"Oh Peter, I am so scared. Ian will not have the files for another week or so. How will I be able to concentrate on anything else until he calls?"

The call came five days later.

"Lois, this file paints a picture of someone who is very different from what I perceive you to be. That being said, time can change people. Due to the nature of the case, there are no pictures of the woman, but she sounds like a bit of a rough number. The one defining item is that she has a tattoo. Do you?"

"No, I don't. Could I have had it removed?"

"That is possible, but even so, there are nearly always traces or scarring left. It was on her left shoulder. Do you have anything there that might be healed over?"

"No."

"There is one other thing. She had a hysterectomy."

"Then that is definitely not me. I still have all my bits and pieces."

"Okay then, I will try another way, but I am sure running out of ideas. I am planning to head to Sudbury for the dog sled races; hopefully, I will have something for you by then."

"We are the main corporate sponsor. Come as our guest."

"Now that is an offer I will not turn down."

The opening morning of the races dawned crisp, cold with a nasty wind that was penetrating and bitter. Andrew, Lois and Peter stood on the stage to officially open the event.

"My bloody teeth are chattering."

Once the official ceremony was over, the three sponsors were bundled into a sled, wrapped in warm blankets and handed a hot cup of cider. By noon, the weather decided to cooperate. The wind died and the temperatures rose to a more tolerable level. By evening, Lois was hoarse from yelling and cheering. Andrew kept himself warm with a Hudson's Bay blanket and a flask of scotch. Peter busied himself by volunteering with the dog teams. On the Sunday, Peter brought Jack all decked out in a BDB outfit. He was scheduled to race right after lunch. Helen and Norm came with the twins. Fred and Belinda joined up with Lois and the Frenches to cheer Jack on. Peter acted as Jack's coach and proud dad. There were ten participants and watching them line up was hilarious. The dogs wandered around not the least bit interested in the starting line.

Finally, the coaches, parents mostly, held the teams. The gun went off, the leads were handed off to the mushers and the race was on. The whole affair was a comedy of errors. One team simply sat down at the starting line and no matter how hard the little musher pulled and pulled, they would not move. To call it a race was taking licence with the word. There were a few comedic spills and some dogs, along with their mushers, wandered into the crowd to visit people they knew. Five teams got to the finish line. Jack was one. He trailed two others but was third across the finish line. His smile was radiant as a green ribbon was pinned on his sleeve.

"Oh, my God, I laughed so hard, I nearly peed my pants. That was too, too crazy." Belinda was bent over double from the exertion of laughing.

The twins were chanting "Jack, Jack, Jack."

Peter helped return the dogs to their crates and Jack gave them each a hug and a special treat. "Dad, can I do this again next year?"

It was a happy group that wandered the site and took in the various things going on. The activities were so well paced that there was something to do every minute. Of course, Peter brought his skates and took to the ice with Jack, Barby and Grant while the others watched the six-dog race. The Dominion BDB team, cheered on by a significant number of coworkers—Ian, Norm and Helen—placed second.

It was generally agreed that the whole event was well worth sponsoring and as the races drew to a close, Peter signalled to Amanda to join them.

She was greeted by rosy cheeks and beaming faces. "Amanda, we want to congratulate you and your team for putting on one hell of an event. We wanted you to know that Dominion BDB will commit to being the lead sponsor for the next three years."

"Even though I am dog tired...."

Everyone broke into fits of laughter at the pun.

As she was returning to Sudbury with Peter, Lois told him that Ian had not found anything and was withdrawing from the case.

Chapter 42

I don't know if I am relieved or not that Ian Shields was unsuccessful. It means I am no further ahead, but it also means I can likely dismiss any criminal thoughts I had. It appears that I left Ottawa without worrying anyone. Or, so I think since no missing person's report was filed. In a way, that makes it better, and in a way, it makes it worse. Did I not have anyone who cared about my whereabouts? Maybe I simply do not have any relatives or family. In one way, that would make it easier yet in another way, that is sad. Surely, I had a friend or two at least. Now, I am in a real quandary. At least, if Ian had found something out about my past, I could decide how to deal with it. This way, it is almost other worldly—a damsel without a past. I had to have had a past. But I have no idea how to find it when such a reputable detective as Ian Shields cannot. Maybe Peter is right and I should let it go and get on with life. Life with him and Jack. That wouldn't be so bad; actually, that would be damned fine. Besides, Belinda and Fred need to move onward too. Goodness, I hadn't thought of living arrangements. What about my house? I love my house. Now that spring is approaching, I can't wait to get at the flowerbeds.

I want a little gazebo by the lake and a path of flowerbeds leading from the front walk to it. I researched the type of plants that need to be planted along the lakeside. Conservationists are encouraging planting to conserve the shoreline. People used to strip away all the foliage and that resulted in shorelines being washed away. I want to maintain a healthy property. The trees at the edges are perfect. I will tuck in crocus bulbs and lots and lots of tulips.

Chapter 43

At the club, the topic of table conversations was the constant spring rain. The downpours never ceased. The golf course had not been able to open the season on schedule, as the greens were sodden. There were flood warnings on the River Stour from Kedington, near the creek near Haverhill and the Sudbury River. Similar warnings soon followed on rivers across both Suffolk and Essex. Peter turned to the television to watch the news in time to see water flowing over Coniston Creek Bridge on Government Road. Trees were jammed against the bridge and debris was washing swiftly down the river and piling up along the banks. His cell phone rang.

"Yep, Peter speaking."

Lois watched as concern washed over Peter's face.

"Lois is here with me. We can get some equipment to you within hours. I was just watching it on the television."

Peter ended his conversation and looked over at Lois. "The city wants some machines over at Coniston Creek. The engineers think they can divert some of the overflow by digging a channel to one of the deep drainage ditches. Excavator 2 and 5 are in the yard as is the Casey bulldozer. I will call Fred and see what else is available. In the meantime, can you call the shed and have them get the excavators and the bull fuelled and loaded on trucks? You and I need to head over there right now."

Lois was already reaching for her raincoat as she dialled the service manager.

They had their food packaged to go, then headed out the door.

An hour later, they were standing on the banks of the creek going over diagrams with the city engineers. A temporary shelter had been set up with a table and a couple of chairs. People were coming and going with cell phones at their ear. The plan was to divert the flow and capture the debris before it collected at the mouth of the Sudbury River. Opening a channel from a bend in the river to the farmers' fields would ease the flow and divert stuff the river was collecting along the way. The river, which usually meandered through picturesque countryside, was now a raging torrent ripping away the banks and everything near. Trees toppled into the water; brush got caught up in the rush and waves threw debris into the air. Everyone was shouting over the roar of the river. Lois pulled out her cell and moved away from the river so she could direct the trucks to the river bend. Once she finished the call, she and Peter left and headed to meet them.

Peter waved the trucks to the side of the road beside the field nearest the drainage ditch. The plan was to open a channel between the river and the ditch breaking through to the river once it was dug. Definitely, the water would do some damage as it spread over the fields, but it was the only option to prevent further flooding down river. They needed to divert the water as one of the bridges in its path was threatened. Lois pulled her hard hat onto her head and saw Peter do the same as they climbed onto the excavators. The ground was already sodden and the ditch almost full, but the work progressed quickly because luckily, they were in an area of deep soil, not the usual rock of the area. This had been a definite concern that the plan to dredge a channel might not work as Sudbury was noted for rock and more rock. Lois started moving dirt from near the river and Peter from the ditch. It was estimated that it would take four to five hours to connect the dredged ditch.

Lois dipped the bucket, filled it with dirt, raised it, turned it and emptied it into the back of a truck to carry the dirt well back from the area. Again and again, she lifted bucket after bucket elated at the quick progress. "Hey, Peter, this stuff is easy going at this end. Yours?"

Lois's voice in Peter's earphone made him smile. This could

have been a difficult job, but he was lifting dirt at a rapid rate too. "Easy here too. I'm munching on my hamburger and chucking fries as I work."

"I was so engrossed in digging that I totally forgot my lunch. See you in a bit."

In a little less than four hours, Peter told Lois to head back to the river and he would open the rest of the channel. By the time she broke through to the river, he would have it open the rest of the way. The river was due to peak by morning, so their progress was timely.

Lois rumbled across the muddy field toward the riverbank. Before she got too close, she stopped, stepped out and surveyed the landscape. Walking it off to make sure the heavy equipment was safely situated on solid ground, as the banks were starting to crumble under the force of the water, was typical procedure to make sure it was safe. Finding a solid rock shelf at just the right distance from the channel and the river, Lois took the extra precaution to secure an anchor chain to a large oak tree. She knew that once she broke through to the river, the power of the water surge could and would be dangerous. Satisfied that she had taken every precaution, Lois, once again, stepped up on the excavator's track and into the operator's cab.

A wave of nervousness washed over her as she raised the bucket to take the first bite out of the riverbank. It gathered a tree trunk and mud. She raised it and swung away to deposit the load to the side, then turned back again. As she lifted the second full bucket and turned to deposit it, something caught her eye. One of the engineers was standing close to where she was depositing the loads. He lifted his arm and signalled her to stop. Lois stood to get a better view of what he was looking at. A limp body of a small girl tumbled from the bucket. Dirt fell away from her clothing to reveal Dora pyjamas.

Lois started to scream as she jumped down off the machine. "Lois! Oh, my God! Lois!"

She stumbled and staggered toward the body, but Fred, who had arrived at that moment, caught her and held her as she screamed and screamed.

"Lois, calm down. What has gotten into you?"

The city engineer came up to her, a cell phone at his ear.

"I called the police. No one is to go near the bucket. They are on their way. What is wrong with Lois?"

Lois was struggling with Fred and crying hysterically. "What have I done, oh, God what have I done?"

"Lois, it is likely that kid is the one who went missing from First Street last week. Take it easy. Take big breaths. Try to calm down. Here's Peter."

Fred stepped aside as Peter gathered Lois in his arms. She didn't seem to notice who was holding her as she was led over to the tree.

Peter was whispering in a soothing voice trying to find out what happened.

"Lois, sweetheart, it's okay. You didn't do it. We think it was the little girl who went missing last week. She must have wandered all the way to the river and fallen in and drowned. It is a terrible thing. The police are on their way. They will want to talk to you. You need to take a deep breath and calm down."

His words started to take on meaning. Lois looked through teary eyes at Peter.

"What have I done?" She grabbed a tissue from her pocket.

"It's okay, Lois. You didn't do it."

"Yes, I did! It's all my fault. I've lost them, abandoned them."

As Peter tried to hold Lois to comfort her, she flew into a rage. She pounded his chest with her fists and was screaming, "Lois, Dougie, Brent, oh, my babies, what have I done?"

Peter held her tighter but was no match for her flailing arms. She pummelled him with her fists.

"Let me go! I have to leave. I have to find them!"

Fred came over and when he saw the state Lois was in, he

went for a medic.

The more Peter tried to calm her, the more frantic she became kicking and punching him with her fists.

When the medic arrived, having been filled in by Fred, he realized that Lois was so out of control that there was no restraining her in her current state. She was hysterical. Asking Fred to hold her arm as Peter held her bodily, he administered midazolam, a sedative often used when medics were confronted with a case of severe agitation.

"It will take a few minutes to take effect and once it does, we will transport her to the hospital. Have you any idea what triggered the episode?"

She was the operator of the excavator that dredged up the body. It just set her off."

Lois rolled her head back and forth frantically and started to mumble, but before she said anything, she fell into a deep faint. Peter barely managed to catch her before she fell to the ground. Her hard hat fell at his feet.

"Why don't we get her out of the rain and into that tent over there?"

"No need. I have called the ambulance to come over. Since the child's body will be transported by the coroner, there is no need for us to stay here and this lady does have to be taken to the hospital." After taking Lois's vitals, he confirmed that she was in shock. Peter arranged for Fred to handle the site and followed the ambulance to Sudbury.

As the medics were offloading the gurney at the emergency entrance of the hospital, Lois started to regain consciousness. She appeared confused. Peter stepped up beside her and grasped her hand.

"You have had a shock—you are at the hospital."

Tears poured down Lois's cheeks. "I remember. Peter, I remember. I thought it was Lois."

"Sweetheart, you are still a little confused. You are Lois. The little girl was likely the one that went missing..."

"No, Peter. I mean I remember who I am. I remember everything. I made a terrible mistake. I have to go home."

Lois was shaking and sobbing. A doctor gave her another mild sedative and she drifted into a deep sleep. Peter was alarmed by her statement and went in search of Doctor Frosst. If Lois did regain her memory, then Dr. Frosst needed to be there when she wakened.

An hour and a half later, a drowsy Lois wakened to find Peter and Dr. Frosst at her bedside. Peter held her hand as Dr. Frosst asked her gently how she was.

"I thought the body was Lois."

The doctor looked at her with concern. "No, you are Lois. You have had a shock. Just tell me ..."

"No, you don't understand. I need to explain. I remember everything. I have a daughter. Her name is Lois. The last time I saw her, she was wearing Dora pyjamas, and she was four years old. When I saw that child in Dora pyjamas, I thought it was Lois. The last time I saw Lois, she was wearing identical pyjamas."

"Okay, easy now. Did you lose your daughter?"

"No. My daughter lost me."

Lois burst into tears again. "I ruined everything! I lost my family. I lost everything."

Both Peter and the doctor were alarmed at the intensity of Lois's distress. Peter stroked her hand and kept assuring her that everything was all right.

"No, it isn't all right. I have ruined my life and my children have lost their mother. Oh, God help me! What have I done?"

Dr. Frosst took Lois's other hand and softly asked if she was responsible for their deaths. It was a likely reason for the amnesia and if this was the case, she was going to have a difficult time dealing with the grief all over again.

"No, they are alive. At least I hope so. It is a long story. I walked out on my husband and three children. I only wanted —

no, needed—a short break, but then I had the accident. Oh my God, my children! Seven years, I have been away for seven years!"

Peter slumped in his chair. He loved Lois with all his heart. He had lost Mary and now he lost Lois. She was married.

Bit by bit, Lois told them how she left Ottawa and changed her name so she would not be found. She told them that she had incorporated her children's names to become her new surname. She said she had been on the verge of suffering a dangerous depression and feared committing suicide. She told them that she came to Sudbury because she thought it likely to be the last place anyone would look for her.

Dr. Frosst convinced Lois to work with him over the next few days to see how to resolve her dilemma, reunite her with her children and address how she felt about the changes in her person. The last thing he wanted was for Lois to rush off to Ottawa without fully understanding every aspect of the situation. He made arrangements for Lois to stay in the hospital overnight, then encouraged her to go back to her house. Peter called Helen and Norm and asked them to join them at Lois's house, so she could tell them her story. Dr. Frosst suggested that Peter continue to be supportive and loving and not to give up hope of her love.

"In fact, the more you can talk about the whole situation," Dr. Frosst said to Lois, "the more comfortable you will be with how we can resolve it. And, Lois, you are not to blame. Not only were you dealing with loss of self-respect, but your body was depleted from one pregnancy after another—you were likely dealing with post-partum depression as well. Fleeing from your situation may not have been the most sound decision to make. However, over the years, you have become a better person. We will have to assess both the good and the bad to determine how to proceed. Believe me, the more you can talk about the whole seven years here and your life in Ottawa, the better."

Lois nodded. The whole realization of who she was and what she had to face made her tremble.

"Peter, I want you to stay with Lois every minute. She must not be alone. She is still in a fragile state and I do not want her to do anything rash. And, Lois, promise me you will not phone or try to get in touch with your family until you and I form a plan. A few more days won't make any difference in the circumstances. I need you to work with me to rationalize what you left behind and what you are likely to find. I want you to imagine every scenario of meeting your husband again. I want you to be strong and confident when you meet him and your children."

"How can I be after what I have done? How can I put off seeing my babies, oh, God, Lois is twelve years old! I missed her growing up. Dougie was a wee baby—I- I am scared. What will they think? How can I possibly tell them I am their mother? I can't do it. I simply am not strong enough."

"Lois, you are one of the strongest people I know. We simply need to merge what you know about your past with who you have become."

The following morning, Peter drove Lois home.

"When I left the hospital, I went back to the river. The police still have it cordoned off, but we were able to open the channel from another location. Sorry, kiddo, but I still have to deal with the flooding situation on top of all of this. I am going to tuck you in a cuddly blanket, light the fireplace, heat up some soup, then call Fred to see what is happening."

Lois smiled for the first time since the body fell from her bucket.

Fred's first concern was for Lois and once assured she was home, he told Peter that the body was indeed that of the missing child. It had been removed and because of the flood emergency, the excavation had been completed. They were now scooping up rubble from the river, so it wasn't carrying as much debris beyond the channel they had dug.

"By the way, the channel worked. Mind you, the farmer will have flooded fields, but he claims it's not a huge bother. His words: other farmers will help him clear them when the water recedes."

"Good work, Fred. Lois and I appreciate how you were able to step up at a moment's notice."

Peter hung up the phone and returned to sit on the sofa beside Lois.

"Peter, I loved Randy and I love you. I don't know what will happen when I meet Randy face to face. It is hard to believe that so much of my life has been lost. Lois is twelve, almost a teenager. Brent will be eleven and my baby Dougie will be almost eight. I missed them growing up. I love them. I love them so and I ruined our lives because I was so selfish."

"No, Lois, you were not selfish. You were desperate. You never planned to stay away this long. It was because of the accident. And I have to say, since I have known you for almost the entire seven years, you have grown as a person, become confident and a very astute businesswoman. That is the woman I have grown to love. I can't lose you."

The doorbell chimed and Peter opened the door to Norm and Helen.

Helen rushed over and knelt beside Lois. "What is this? You remember your past? Are you okay? Can you talk about it?"

"Slow down, Helen. Yes, I can talk about it. It is somewhat of a mess, but Dr. Frosst said the more I talk about it, the better I will be at dealing with it and the memories will increase. First, I want to apologize for lying to you. I am Stacey, not Lois. Well, I am Lois now as I legally changed my name right after I started to work for you."

"You are Stacey!"

"Yes, I lied to get away from a verbally abusive husband. I didn't realize how abusive until I saw how compatible you and Norm were together. You made me see how a relationship could be, should be. I saw how you completed each other. I am really sorry I deceived you."

"Honey, you were and are the best person regardless of how you had to deceive us to be a part of our lives. We love you, the twins love you and that is not going to change."

Helen leaned forward and gave Lois a big hug. "And that goes for both of us."

Peter came out of the kitchen with a tray with glasses of red wine and a plate of crackers and cheese that Norm had brought from the store. "Looks like I have been courting a married lady."

The hurt in his voice was picked up immediately by Norm.

"Oh, Peter, I am so sorry. This is such a mess."

Once Helen and Norm were apprised of the whole story, Norm took hold of Lois's hands and held them to his heart. "Sometimes, life leads us down paths we cannot control. You have travelled one heck of a route. What I am about to say is for both Helen and me. We love you with all our hearts. You are more than a friend; you are family. The fact is, one way or another, your life is going to change and we still want—no, need—to be a part of it. I want you to know you cannot go back to being who you were. You are who you are now. When you meet your children, you will still be Lois Brenton-Douglas—that is who you have become. Stacey no longer exists."

Lois stared at Norm. He was right; there was no going back to being Stacey. But, how could she not be? How could she face the rest of her life without her children? Lois looked at the faces of her dear friends. They had been her family for seven years. They had supported her when she strove to educate herself and stood close by as friends and advisors to build a thriving business. Now, even though they now knew that her whole being was a lie, they were there to support her still.

Two weeks later, after a session with Dr. Frosst, Lois had made the ultimate decision—she was going to return to Ottawa.

To be as prepared as possible for what she was apt to

encounter, Norm contacted Ian Shields, filled him in on the whole story and tasked him with finding out everything he could about Randy and the children. At Dr. Frosst's suggestion, Lois met with her lawyers.

Chapter 44

My thought are whirling. When I regained my memory, my first reaction was to jump in the truck and head to Ottawa. Now, I am glad I didn't. Dr. Frosst has made me realize that I need to prepare myself for what I will face. My children will not know me and may well reject me altogether. Randy could be hostile. That I find hard to believe—he is not a cruel person. Dr. Frosst thinks his papa bear protectionism will surface and that he will be difficult. I countered everything he said and told him that I knew Randy and that that was simply not a part of his personality. Maybe Lois will remember me. She was five when I left. I do hope so. Every time I think about holding my children, a wave of warmth washes over me and gives me strength. Yet, the fear of rejection looms there as well.

Dr. Frosst suggested that I engage legal counsel before I meet with Randy. I was surprised that they, too, thought I might encounter a hostile reaction from him. They also advised me to remain as inaccessible as possible. Until I know what I might be dealing with, I can't let Randy know how to reach me. I need to be distant and in control for what I am about to encounter. They recommended not to warn Randy ahead of time. That took me by surprise, as that is exactly what I planned to do. They explained that by giving Randy a heads up, he might put barriers in the way. They put me in touch with their Ottawa team, and Felicity Arthur, a family lawyer of some renown, was assigned my case. Deep down, I felt all this was unnecessary but thought it a good idea to have a plan 'B.' With all these safeguards in place, I should be able to handle whatever happened. I thought of scenario after scenario of meeting Randy again after seven years apart.

Chapter 45

Stacey eased the mud-caked Silverado to the curb vaguely aware of the tires rubbing against concrete. She pulled her navy peaked cap with BDB in gold lettering low over her forehead and watched the front door. The house looked the same—nothing had changed except the truck in the driveway was a newer model. The two-storey was the typical suburban home of the 1990s with red brick facing on the front and off-white vinyl siding covering the rest. Large bay windows on either side of the recessed front door were the main features of the otherwise bland design. Early morning sun glanced off scattered puddles left on the street by showers during the night.

A flash of yellow in Stacey's peripheral vision prompted the front door to fly open; the school bus signalled, slowed and stopped, lights flashing. Three children streamed out of the red door. A tall string bean of a girl in multi-coloured leggings and a dark green, very short, pleated skirt was followed by a chubby boy with his hooded jacket wide open to the chilly March morning dragging his green backpack along the damp pavement. Walking slowly reading a book, a curly-headed boy wearing glasses and carrying a guitar case came next. Hardly able to breathe, Stacey swallowed threatening tears and watched her children—she was watching her children that she had not seen for years. She watched Dougie reach back and slam the door shut while still reading. His jacket was a black and white plaid that hung half on and half off. Even though he was immersed in his book, he walked confidently to the bus and climbed on after his brother and sister.

Stacey held her hand firmly over her mouth to prevent herself from yelling out—calling to her children that more than likely would not remember her.

I remember deciding to paint that door red—red doors meant good feng shui, a sign of welcome and that joy and love dwelt within. Stacey walked out through that door seven years ago and had not returned until this morning.

Steeled for this moment, Stacey took a deep breath and watched the bus pull away taking a significant piece of her with it. White knuckling the steering wheel, it was all she could do not to leap out and rush toward them, tell them who she was and hug them tight. Instead, she watched the bus disappear around the block carrying them away. A choking breath escaped as Stacey reached for the SUV's door handle and released the catch. Easing across the leather seat wiping tears that had trickled down her cheeks, she jumped down to the road landing on legs that almost failed to support her. Her diminutive stature looked out of place emerging from the blue Silverado 4X4.

Randy's truck with Martin's Lumber Yard scrolled along the side in the company's maroon and grey lettering dominated the driveway indicating he was home. Her humorous side toyed with just opening the door and calling out "I'm home, honey." She had imagined and rehearsed numbers of ways she would greet him—none of them easy; none of them stopped her tense muscles from clenching and her hands from shaking. *Just do it, girl. You have come this far and there is no going back.* Reaching forward, Stacey started the truck and eased it into a parking spot around the corner out of sight from the house.

Stacey took off her cap, flung it up on the seat and loosened her salon-highlighted curls. Standing facing the truck door, she glanced at her reflection in the side-view window. A full mouth set in a determined line was perfectly outlined and coral lipstick carefully applied; wide blue eyes and high arched brows stared back at her. "Okay, girl, you can do this." She slammed the door, turned and headed for that red door, firm steps belying her roiling stomach.

Once again, she paused with her finger trembling over the

doorbell. "There's no backing down, girl. Just do it." Even her voice quivered. Her breath hovered in a white cloud on the morning air drifting toward her finger as she pressed the button. A melody of chimes flooded her with memories—memories of answering it to guests, salespeople, neighbours and friends she had greeted time and time again. Her thoughts were interrupted by the knob turning, the door easing open and facing her was Randy. His eyes widened and his mouth froze open in the midst of the unuttered greeting. Moments later, he blinked.

"Stacey?"

"Hello, Randy."

"What ..."

May I come in?"

Opening the door wider, Randy mumbled, "I have to go to work."

"Might want to call in sick—I doubt you will be very productive after finding me on your doorstep." Stacey surprised herself at her self-assured, confident tone.

"Um, yes. Good idea."

Stacey watched her husband's awkward movements and backward glances. This was exactly the reaction she had hoped for—she wanted him off guard and confused. She needed to be in command of the situation, which was the reason she had not given any notice of her arrival.

"A cup of coffee would be welcomed. Do you still make a great brew?"

"What? Oh, yes—come into the kitchen."

As they walked along the narrow hall to the kitchen, Randy regained some composure, pushed his uncombed morning hair off his forehead and anger welled up. "Where the hell have you been? What do you mean bursting in here after seven years without a single word?"

"Some of it, I can explain. Most of it, I can explain. You may or may not believe it, but it is true. I need you to try to understand no matter how difficult it is."

"How the hell do you expect me to understand anything when you just up and out of here seven years ago without so much as a whisper? No, Stacey, I do not understand. And what about the children? You think you can just waltz back into their lives and they are supposed to understand too? I don't think so. You always were unable to do anything properly—"

"Randy, just shut the heck up. That kind of statement was what drove me away in the beginning. You never gave me credit for one single thing. I was always a burden to you and you made sure I knew it. I loved you with all my heart, but you were too selfish to return my love."

"What! I'm not the one at fault here, so don't go laying the blame on me. I was a good provider, good father and—"

"Lousy husband. Randy, I did not come back to berate you, but there is no way to explain why I left and what happened without telling you how you drove me into a state of depression. Yes, depression. You were abusive. No, not physically, but verbally and emotionally. I lost all self-confidence and self-respect."

"Well, you sure seem to have plenty now!"

"Thanks, Randy, that's the nicest thing you have said to me since you got me to drop my pants when I was seventeen."

"What do you mean? I married you, didn't I?"

"Yes, you did. This is not about that; I wanted us to be married and happy. I tried, but Randy, I was a kid, pregnant and married. You thought all you had to provide was a nice home and food for the table. You had no idea what a marriage was all about. Whether you want to believe it or not, you drove me away. But, it was only to be for a few months. Then I had an accident and lost my memory."

"Oh, yeah, that sounds like a crock of lies."

"Randy, I have all the medical records to prove it. Now I am here and you can either listen to me and try to comprehend what transpired, or I will take legal action to handle this another way. Two weeks ago, I recovered my memory and since then have been going through therapy to enable myself to meet with you."

"Legal action! What the hell would you know about the law? You didn't even finish high school."

"Actually, I did. College too. You thought I was too stupid to help with the company books, so let me tell you, I have a degree in administration and own a very lucrative company." Lois took pleasure in watching Randy look back in complete surprise. "By leaving here, I created a problem that won't go away. However, I do have a proposal to make if you will let me finish telling you what happened and who I am now."

Randy topped up their coffee cups and sat down. He picked up his cell phone and called the office to tell them he would not be in. A look of resignation washed over his face and he slumped in his chair in an "I'm listening" pose.

Lois proceeded to tell her story leaving out where she was living, her new name and the name of her company. She told how she had planned to return the week following the accident. She explained what the type of amnesia was called and how it manifested itself. She told him about the little girl in the flood and how it had jarred her memory to return.

Randy made no comment but stood up and walked to the patio doors, opened them and stepped outside. He walked down the steps and across the yard. He stopped and didn't move for several minutes.

Lois took advantage of his departure to visit the washroom and wander around the house. She hesitated at the door to their bedroom, then stepped quickly to the dresser where a crowd of pictures of the children were displayed. She picked up one after the other, tears flowing unstopped. She had missed it all. Her children would not know her—they would probably reject her. She became aware of Randy's presence before he said anything.

"I never doubted that you would give our children love and

affection—that is the one thing that allowed me to walk away in the beginning. You were and likely still are a great father."

"I tried. It was not easy. I had to hire a housekeeper to replace you."

Those words slapped Lois harder than any physical wound. Randy didn't love her, couldn't love her, if all he needed to replace her was a housekeeper. The years living under this roof became clearer as she saw how Randy saw her role in it. She realized that he visualized that his duty was just that, a duty. His lust was just that—lust. He loved his children but not his wife.

"Randy, did you ever love me?"

"Sure, I married you, didn't I?"

"When I left, how did you feel?"

"I was angry. What did you expect?"

"Besides being angry, I understand that, but how did you feel emotionally?"

"Well, I needed to think about the children. They were upset without their mother. Lois cried a lot. When you didn't come back in a couple of weeks, I told my parents. They helped a lot and we soon found a housekeeper. Now that all the kids are in school, she doesn't get here before 3 pm."

"And me—did you think about not having me there beside you?"

"Of course I did. It was not easy to figure out what to feed the kids and the house got a little grubby before Anna started working. She was great, had us all in spit spot shape in no time. Mom helped find her. Mom never did understand why you left— still doesn't."

Lois looked at Randy and saw him for the first time as he was, a spoiled son of a lumber company owner and his wife. When he married her, it was not for love but to protect the family name. He was a dutiful son. She was supposed to be the dutiful wife. Well, she had sure messed that up!

"Randy, can you call the housekeeper and tell her not to come today? I would like to meet my children." Even though Lois's voice sounded firm, she clenched her hands tight to stop them from shaking. "I would like you to help me explain everything. I promise I will not blame you but take full responsibility for leaving. I do expect you to let me explain though and not be corrected with demeaning excuses. I promise, I will tell them only what I think they need to know. If you interrupt, I will tell them why I left. Understood?"

"Well, Stacey, I don't think that is going to happen. I raised our children and you are not going to walk back into their lives and claim any ownership at all. You gave them up and that is the way it will be, so I think you might as well leave and never return."

Lois had not anticipated this reaction because she had firmly believed that Randy had loved her. Fortunately, Dr. Frosst had predicted that she might meet this reaction, so even though she was shocked, Lois quickly gathered her wits and countered, "Randy, I have all the medical documentation to support my claim and I have witnesses who will stand behind me with respect to how you treated me, so I am prepared to fight this, if that is how you want to proceed. However, hear me out. I know you are a good father. I know my children are happy, thanks to you, but they deserve to know what happened. They deserve to be reintroduced to me; they deserve to have a loving mother. I have no intension of taking them away. I have no intension of returning to you, but I have every intension of helping my children reach maturity with a mother and a father. I have every intension of being a part of their lives from this point onward."

"That is too bad. It won't happen. I refuse to let you see them."

"Randy, I am a tough businesswoman, with a formidable legal team. I warn you; if you take this stance, I will not only have limitless access to my children but can and might move to be granted legal guardianship. I would be kinder than you though. I would allow you visiting rights."

"Yeah, right, as if I believe you."

"Randy, believe me. I am very wealthy, more than you could imagine and I have a team of legal beagles that are brilliant. If I wanted to execute my right to take the children and go that way—it would go in my favour. I guarantee it."

Randy started to appear a little uncomfortable; the woman standing across from him was not the shy, backward Stacey who had left seven years ago. This Stacey had walked in wearing designer clothing, confident, in control, a woman of the world. She spoke as if she knew her way around the business world.

"So, what are you proposing?"

Lois saw Randy's indecisiveness and a small glow of victory showed in her eyes. She had never stood up to Randy before and now she saw she was winning. An inner smile crept to her face. She cleared her throat and spoke in a firm, steady voice.

"Randy, all I want is to explain to my children what happened to me. At their request, I would like to be a part of their lives again. I have a nice life; I would like to share my friends with them. I am proud of what I have accomplished and I would like my children to be proud of me. I would give the world to hear them call me Mom. But Randy, I have no intensions of taking them away from you. I am not that cruel."

"Not a hope in hell any court would allow that anyway."

"Randy, I am not here to play hardball, but believe me, if you pushed me into court, you would lose."

"Hah, how on earth would you do that?"

"I would illustrate how you drove me away. I can prove that you undermined me to the point of severe depression. My lawyers would prove that your personality is such that you do not know how to love and would, therefore, deprive our children of love and affection. Do I believe this? No, but if you push me to court, I *will* take the children away from you. Frankly, that serves no purpose but to hurt them and you. I am not here to seek revenge. I am here to right a wrong, or should I say—to explain my absence and reclaim my position as mother—a caring mother. In order to do that, I will need your support. Can we not resolve this in a civilized manner?"

"I need to talk to my parents."

"Understood. I will go into the city and return at two. Just so there is no confusion, you had better be here. I know you will call your lawyers, so here is a card from my lawyer. She knows I am here. She knows my intent. She knows your name even though you do not know mine—ah, I see surprise. The reason you were never able to find me was I changed my name. I have this lawyer here in Ottawa and I am sure your firm knows of her. She is rather well known."

Lois had sought legal advice from the Dominion BDB's legal firm before returning to Ottawa. In order to keep her identity hidden, for the time being, it was decided to involve a lawyer from a branch of their firm in Ottawa – the company was high powered and handled some of the most prestigious cases in Canada. Lois knew that the firm used by Morton Lumber was no match for the one she employed. Randy had reacted exactly as Dr. Frosst had predicted, so she had prepared herself for that possibility.

Chapter 46

I am now relieved that I did not rush here and bungle this whole meeting. Because Dr. Frosst and Felicity had prepared me for the least expected consequences, I think I handled it well. I don't think Randy was aware how shaky I was. Thank goodness, I learned how to appear in control when I confronted difficult construction obstacles and had to sort out many a burly type. It sure came in handy today. Two o'clock can't come soon enough. I am as nervous as can be. Having seen the children this morning, at least I know what to expect now. Lois looked so confident. Well, she was that way at five, so I guess I should expect her to be that way now. And Brent, oh, my, he looks so studious and Dougie looks like a typical seven-year-old boy. How they will receive me is a different matter altogether. I have practised and practised what to say and somehow must handle this in a confident way. If only the butterflies in my stomach would settle down. What I need is a good girl-to-girl chat and a stiff drink. No, I can't do that. Meeting my children smelling of alcohol would not do.

I need to get my head together. I want to drive by the school and once I stop shaking, I am going over to Emily's. Oh, my, she is going to be one surprised lady. I do hope she is home. Let's see; it is Tuesday. If I remember correctly, it is her housework and baking day. I hope she is still a creature of habit. Well, here I go. I am nearly at her house. Good. There is a car in the driveway, which means she is likely home.

Chapter 47

When Lois left her house, she glanced back, straightened her shoulders and headed for the truck that she had driven and parked around the corner before walking back to the house. She did not want Randy to see the logo on the door. She had five hours to put in and she decided to reconnect with Emily and her cousin Edna. Driving familiar streets, Lois pulled into Emily's driveway behind a maroon SUV. She saw the front curtains move. Then seconds later, the front door flew open. Emily stood there with a querulous look. Lois opened the truck door and stepped down to the driveway. She waved. A frown crossed Emily's face. Then as recognition dawned on her, she fled to greet Lois.

"Oh, my God! Stacey, it is you! Where have you been? I have been crazy with worry for the past six years. You just fell off the map. Oh, my God, you look incredible—I can't believe it is you—come in."

Lois let out a laugh as she hugged her dear friend. "Lots to tell you and lots to explain."

With their arms around each other, they went into the side split bungalow, stepped on the 'WELCOME' mat before entering and Emily closed the heavy dark green door. Lois smiled at her friend who had changed very little over the seven years since she left. She towered over Lois and wore her auburn hair long and straight; the splash of freckles across her cheeks always gave her an impish look especially when her eyes lit up when she smiled. She wore brilliant orange leggings with a thigh length, soft yellow, long-sleeved top. Even in casual attire, Emily could always look elegant.

"Love the new car—so much better than the old banged up one."

"Well, I came into a little money when Dad passed. Also, I have a part-time job. Stacey, Stacey, Stacey–I can't believe you are standing here. Come into the kitchen. I need a coffee and to hear all about what happened to you."

"Emily, I am so sorry to hear about your dad. I guess it was to be expected, but painful nonetheless. I wish I'd been here as some support."

"Thanks. I did have an amazing support group. Do you know that Annie and Lois are still best friends?"

"That I am delighted to hear, especially now when Lois is going to need all the support she can get. By the way, my name is now Lois too."

The puzzled look on Emily's face led Lois to explain away seven years.

"That is far beyond whatever I could have imagined. How difficult for you. What are you going to do now? Change back to Stacey and move back?"

"No. I have a new life, a new identity and, just for your information, I am a very successful businesswoman."

"No way! But I am not surprised. I always knew you were capable of much more than the life you were living with Randy. So tell me more, what business, where are you living?"

Lois filled Emily in on the missing bits. "Emily, can I ask a huge favour?"

"Sweetie, you can ask anything at all–if it is in my power, I will do it."

Lois explained that Randy might push the whole issue into court. She said that it was the last thing she wanted and that she just wanted to be reunited with her children and have shared custody. But if Randy pushed it, she was prepared to demand custody and would need character witnesses to substantiate that Randy had undermined her in many ways.

"Randy should be pleased that you are prepared to share custody. Bullheaded as he is, surely he can see that you are being reasonable. Just for your information, Lois and Annie talk about you all the time. Lois pines for your return. She will be ecstatic. Of course, you are a big mystery to her now as her memory has faded, but she always carries a picture of you."

Lois felt moisture on her cheeks as her eyes welled over; she wiped them away with the back of her hand. "I so want to wrap her in my arms. How I wish I could make the lost years disappear. It is like reading a novel right up to the climax to find there are missing pages. I have so much to make up to all three of them. However, I realize that our relationship will never be one of a family settled in one place. I will not return to Ottawa but will have to content myself with being an away mother. Of course, I hope they will be with me for extended periods."

"Stacey—ah, er–Lois, is there a special other in your new life?"

"I was always afraid to get involved because I had no idea what I had fled. But, that being said, yes, my business partner, Peter, and I have a serious bond and that will lead me to ask for a divorce from Randy. Peter has a seven-year-old son."

"Well, I sure don't envy you what lies ahead and regarding your question–I hope it does not go to court, but if it does, you can count on me."

"One other thing, Emily. Please do not let anyone know my new name or the name of the corporation. Until I know exactly what Randy is going to do, I would rather not be accessible."

Lois hugged her friend, both of them mopping away the tears. Lois had hoped to see her cousin, but the time with Emily had flown. Emily hastily put a plate of cold cuts, cheese and buns on the table. The two friends continued to catch up on the missing years.

"My life is like a story that one begins, then a whole bunch of pages go missing in the middle. I need to rewrite those pages, make it up to my children and let the rest of the story unfold."

"After hearing what you have been through and accomplished, I have no doubt that everything will work out."

However, that was not what transpired when Lois returned to meet Randy. He met her at the door and refused her entry.

"As far as I am concerned, Stacey, there is no way you are entering this house unless it is to return as my wife and the mother of our children."

"Randy, that is not going to happen. I have changed. I am a different person—one that you would never tolerate. You need to be in control and I no longer can be controlled by you. We need to come to an understanding whereby we can share raising our children."

"Yeah, like that would ever happen. Stacey, just a little reminder—you abandoned us and now face the consequences—you will never see your children again. My father and mother are currently collecting them from school and taking them someplace that you cannot access. I am telling you that as far as I'm concerned, you left so you can stay gone. We have adjusted and do not need you in our lives."

Lois felt her knees falter. Her world was slipping away. She had lost.

"Randy, you are not a cruel person. How can you do this?"

"You were always incapable of doing anything right. You always managed to mess up and this is no different. You did a stupid thing when you left; so live with it—once a dunderhead, always a dunderhead."

His demeaning words forced a well of anger to overcome Lois. "We could have resolved this in a reasonable fashion. Now you are forcing me to take action that I don't want to do. Randy, think about it. We could resolve this in a reasonable way."

"As far as I am concerned, it is resolved, period."

"In that case, my lawyers will be in touch." Lois spun around and headed toward her truck that was, once again, parked out of sight.

"There is no way the legal firm you said you had is yours as they only have wealthy, important clients. I am calling your bluff."

Randy's words shouted at her as she headed down the sidewalk, made Lois stand straighter and her steps deliberate. When she reached the truck, she started to tremble and it took every effort she could muster to turn the key and start the truck. She drove three blocks, pulled to the curb and crumpled over the steering wheel. The tears fell in torrents as she punched at the numbers on her cell phone, heard it ring and the familiar voice answered.

"Peter, I need you. I can't do this alone."

Peter convinced Lois to return to Sudbury and together with their friends, doctors and legal team, they would formulate an action plan. Driving back to Sudbury, Lois went over and over her encounter with Randy. All the love she thought she held for him melted away like an ice-cream cone dripping away in a messy slush. She saw Stacey as another person entirely, someone she could never return to being. "My darling children looked so different. I don't know how they will accept me without Randy's support. If only I could take a swing and knock him flat to try and drive some sense into his stubborn head." With steely resolve, she gripped the steering wheel, put her foot down on the pedal and put the miles behind her as she broke speed limits heading home.

As soon as she got in, she reached for her phone to call Peter. She had neglected to set up the hands-free phone in the truck and had turned the buzzer off when she planned to meet her children and talk to Randy again. Right away, she noticed that the voicemail was flickering.

"Lois, where are you? We have been trying to reach you for hours. Andrew Ford took a spell and was rushed to the hospital. The results aren't in yet, but it looks like he may have had a stroke. Go directly to the hospital—I will meet you there."

"Oh, man, my life is getting far too STRESSFUL. Dear God, please don't let me lose Andrew." She shouted her request to the roof of the truck willing it to reach the highest power.

She pulled into the parking lot of the hospital and rushed to the emergency desk. A message was waiting for her and she was directed down the hall to a waiting area. She hesitated as she recognized the area as the same place she and Peter had been when Mary was admitted. Definitely, not good karma.

"Lois, over here."

Peter looked in control and even had a weak smile to greet her. He stood and gathered her into his arms and kissed her forehead. "You okay?"

"Outside of feeling crushed at how things went in Ottawa and worried sick about Andrew, I'm barely managing. How is he?"

"The doctor left a few minutes ago and the news is better than expected. The medics were there in record time and that is crucial when the patient has had a stroke. He has lost some mobility in his right arm and his speech is garbled. That is how he recognized that he had a stroke. He was in his office and managed to hit the 'call' button for his assistant. She called 911 and made him lie down. An ambulance was only minutes getting there. We are fortunate the response was so quick. Right now, he needs professional care and rest. We cannot see him. The doctors don't want him to be alarmed when he starts to speak and nobody can understand what he is saying. By tomorrow afternoon, we will be able to visit. His speech will not likely have improved, but he will have an understanding of why he is having difficulty, so it will be less stressful."

"Oh, Peter, I was so worried. Now I am somewhat hopeful. Do they expect a full recovery?"

"Well, his age is certainly a factor, but he is in good health otherwise, so, yes, we hope so. He will need rehab and probably will be out of circulation for some time, but the prognosis is quite good."

"Has anyone told Amanda?"

"Amanda? Why would we tell her?"

"Oh, Peter, you dolt. They have been keeping close tabs on each other for years. She is as close to being his girlfriend as possible. Since her husband died last year, Andrew has been her strength and support. Neither had children, so their friendship grew in a different way."

"Well, the old duffer! I would never have guessed he was getting some on the side."

"Peter, that is crude. Anyway, she needs to know. I will give her a call."

"What about you? Are you going to be okay?"

"I guess I didn't handle things in Ottawa as well as I might. It is going to be an up-hill battle. I certainly would rather we could have come to some reasonable arrangement. But it is what it is. It was strange how I saw the man I was married to for five years. There was no appeal for me anymore. I just see him as an adversary and an obstacle standing in the way of my seeing my children."

"Now, that is great news for me. I dreaded how you were going to react when you saw Randy. I was afraid you would realize how much you loved him and I would be out of the picture."

"Peter, you will never be out of the picture. I do love you so. Come on, let's get out of here and snuggle up in front of my fireplace."

Chapter 48

Sitting here cuddled up to Peter feels so right. Even though my trip to Ottawa stirred disturbing emotions, I have to approach this whole mess I created in a logical and professional manner. The hardest thing will be being at a distance where I cannot explain to my children what happened. That is the cruel reality. Right now, I am barred from even approaching the children or trying to call them on the phone.

The funny thing is, I am no longer Stacey. I can't even relate to her. I am Lois, a strong businesswoman and now I am on a mission. Tomorrow morning, I will consult with the lawyers. Hopefully, they will have another solution rather than taking the case to court. I'm afraid that that would alienate the children and I would never get them back. Randy didn't believe that high powered team of lawyers would represent me—maybe once he realizes that they will, and his lawyer explains that I have a formidable case, he will relent and we can come to a reasonable agreement. My mind keeps replaying the scene of the three of them getting on the school bus—so familiar yet so strange. Every time I mentally visualize them, I want to reach out and grasp them to me. I hurt so deeply in my heart. This kind of pain is far worse than healing from the fall. Lying here in Peter's arms feels so right. Somehow I have to mesh my two lives—I have to reach my children. I will make it work. There has to be a way.

Chapter 49

Between visits to the hospital to see Andrew, meetings with lawyers and Dr. Frosst in addition to managing a very complex company, the days dissolved into weeks. The good news was that Andrew was improving daily and was to be moved to a rehab facility. Amanda sat by his bedside daily and it was she who informed Peter and Lois that it was unlikely that Andrew would return to work. The additional work fell to Peter and Lois. This meant that Lois was working entirely in the office. Even though her mind was torn in several directions, the days slipped away.

Three weeks later, late in the afternoon, Lois's phone rang.

Lois answered as she was walking around her desk.

"Mommy." Lois fell into her chair.

Peter was at his desk when he saw her stagger and rushed to her side. She reached to grasp his hand as she spoke. "Lois, baby, is that you? How did you find me?"

"Annie told me you had been at her house. I nearly drove her mother crazy until she dialled your number."

"Oh, sweetheart, I love you and your brothers over the moon, but there are complications. I want to be with you so, so much, but your father has a problem with that."

"Annie told me you had an accident and lost your memory. That's not your fault. You need to come home."

"Oh, Lois, sweetheart, it has been seven years. I have changed and have a new life. But that does not mean I love you any less. I just got my memory back. I know this is a lot for you to understand. If only your father would let me try to explain to the three of you what happened and what can be done."

"You need to come home. I need you."

"Oh, how I wish it were that easy. It isn't and I can't. I do want to get to know you from this point on and return to being your mother due to circumstances though, it will have to be different. I have to stay here."

"Where are you? Annie's mother dialled the phone and wouldn't let me have it until after you answered."

"She did the right thing. Lois, I need you to be very grown up right now. I live far away and have a new name. I don't want your father to learn where I am right now."

"Why? What did he do?"

"Sweetie, this is not something I will discuss with you. He does not want me to have access to you or your brothers, so until the matter is settled in court, I should not even be talking to you."

"What do you mean 'court'? Are you going to jail?"

"Far from it. Courts decide other issues than criminal ones. In this case, it will be to make your father let me see you children."

"Why won't he let you see us?"

"My dear, you will learn that life is sometimes very complicated. I want more than anything in the world to see you. However, if I am not careful, that privilege might not be granted. Oh, how I wish I could just hold you tight and never let you go."

"I need you to come home. I want you to be my mommy again."

Lois could hear the sobs across the wires. Her daughter was confused and hurt and there was nothing she could do at this point. It was evident that she would have to speed up the process.

"Lois, here is what I want you to do. Please, keep our conversation a secret and I will try very, very hard to see you as soon as possible. Now can you let me speak with Annie's mother for a minute?"

"Emily, how did you allow this? I am so concerned that Lois will be more confused than ever."

"Stacey, if you could have seen her pleading, you would understand why I caved. Annie, the cheeky little mite, overheard me telling her father about your visit and it went from there. I am so sorry."

"You know something, don't be. Being able to talk with Lois was amazing even though it may complicate the whole affair. Can you be her support and tell her that I am trying everything to see all three of my children?"

"Of course."

When Lois hung up the phone, she burst into tears and fell forward onto her desk. Peter quickly wrapped his arms around her and just held her without saying anything.

True to an emotional twelve-year-old, Lois blurted out to her father that she had talked to her mother and he was just mean to keep her away from them. She told her brothers that she had spoken with their mother and all three children ganged up on their father. To them, it was a simple solution. They wanted to see their mother, so Randy had no right to prevent it. Randy tried to explain that Stacey had walked out on them and had no right to see them. Lois yelled that he was unreasonable and that Stacey still loved them. She stomped out of the room stating that she would never talk to her father again.

Randy kept asking how Lois had found her mother and how she had spoken with her. Lois realized that by telling her father how she got in touch with her mother, she would inadvertently make it difficult for Annie's mother, so she refused to tell him. She decided that to tell the boys how she found her mother would be unwise as well.

Angry and alerted, Randy called his lawyer to tell him what had transpired. He was certain that this would harm Stacey's case.

Days went by. Lois refused to speak to her father and the boys kept asking him if they could talk to their mother too. The atmosphere in the house was tense and storm clouds seemed to hover near the ceilings.

The lawyer representing Lois laid out the terms of reuniting Lois/Stacey with her children. Randy's lawyer impressed on him that the terms were reasonable and he should consider them. He reaffirmed that Stacey's legal team was a formidable firm and that he personally was not anxious to come up against them in court.

"Randy, the terms are reasonable. Please consider them."

"No fricking way! She abandoned them and me. She has no rights whatsoever. I want a restraining order so she can never see them — ever!"

In the meantime, little Lois had Emily call her mother again. The conversation was not much different than the previous one except her mother did express that she was concerned that Randy knew about the call.

However, the reason for the call was quite different than had even been imagined. Annie and Lois had conspired to find where her mother was. As soon as the call ended, the girls hit redial.

"Dominion BDB Construction, how can I help you?"

The call was immediately disconnected and the two girls, smirking at their success, ran to Annie's room and fired up her laptop. Once they googled Dominion BDB Construction, not only did they find out where it was located, but they also discovered a picture of Stacey, now Lois.

"She used our names! That proves she loves us. She's beautiful. She's important — see, she is an executive."

Annie and Lois were giggling at how clever their detective work was and swore to each other that their success was to be kept a secret. The secret turned into a plan for Lois.

When she got home, she turned on her computer and checked out where Sudbury was and how to get there. She had enough money in her bank account and was allowed to withdraw it. The next day, her brothers had soccer practice and she was always home alone for a little over an hour. When her father left with the boys, she grabbed a suitcase that she had packed the night before and took the city bus to the Fallowfield train station. She had bought a ticket to Sudbury online without being questioned. The schedule was perfect for her and she boarded almost immediately. The difficulty lay in the fact that the trip would get her into Sudbury near midnight. She had not planned what to do at that point.

A very sleepy twelve-year-old disembarked at the Sudbury station. She expected she might have to stay there until morning but decided to phone the number she had for her mother's office. It was answered.

"Dominion BDB Construction emergency line. How can I help you?"

"Oh, I need to get a message to Lois Brenton-Douglas right away. It's very important."

"I'm sorry, but this service is for construction emergencies only."

"This is an emergency—this is her daughter and I am at the train station."

"I'm sorry, dear, but Lois does not have any children. You need to stop playing telephone games. Phoning emergency numbers is against the law."

"No, no, this is real. Please, please let her know." The line disconnected.

The operator that answered the phone had second thoughts. She was reluctant to call Lois at near midnight. Instead, she knew that Peter was out on a call to fix a grader and he was not far from the railway station. She called him.

"Holy shit!"

"Pardon, sir?"

"Sorry. I just reacted. I will call Lois and go directly to the station. I'm glad you called. You did the right thing."

In the meantime, Randy was frantic. When he got home, he found a note stating that Lois had gone to see her mother. He called the police. When he told them she had run away to see her mother, the police were reluctant to respond. Randy insisted and finally got in touch with his lawyer, who contacted the police. They finally arrived at the house four hours later. It did not take them long to search Lois's computer and find the search for rail transportation to Sudbury and the ticket purchase. Within an hour, they had confirmation that she had used the ticket.

"Well, sir, what is her mother's name? We will tell her what has happened."

When Randy could not tell them, the reaction was immediate.

"You don't know your wife's name!"

"She changed it."

"Well, that changes things. The train is due there within the half hour. I will try to get an officer to the station and see if he can intercept her. That's the best we can do at this point."

"You have to find her. She is only twelve and travelling all that way on her own—I am fearful for her safety. I hope she is okay."

It took several minutes for the officer in Ottawa to be routed through to the Sudbury detachment and by the time the situation had been fully explained, the arrival time for the train was imminent. The Sudbury police promised to go to the station but explained that the nearest patrol car was forty minutes away.

Peter had finished fixing the grader when the call came in, so he grabbed his toolbox and ran to the truck. Within minutes, he was headed for the train station. He called Lois on the hands-free.

"Lois, we have a little problem."

"Peter, we always have little problems. That is why we have you and Fred—"

"Not that kind of problem. Your daughter ran away and I am on my way to the train station to pick her up."

"What!"

"She called the office and the emergency operator took the call. She had the good sense to call me."

"Oh, my God! Randy will be frantic."

"Whatever. Except, right now, you need to be ready to meet your daughter."

Peter pulled into the station parking lot, hopped out of the truck and headed for the waiting room. As soon as he opened the door, he saw a replica of Lois sitting curled up on a bench. He took a deep breath and slowly approached her.

"Lois, I am Peter Barto. I work with your mother. The operator you spoke with called me. Please, come with me and I will take you to your mother."

"I'm not sure I should go with a stranger. Why are you here and not Mommy?"

"You are smart to be cautious. I was working nearby and your mother is almost an hour away. Here, let me call her and you can talk to her."

The phone call convinced Lois to gather her suitcase and follow Peter. As they turned onto the main road, a police car was turning into the station parking lot.

Lois called Randy and told him she just learned that Lois was in Sudbury. She explained that she had absolutely nothing to do with this, but Randy railed at her anyway. He stated that he would drive to Sudbury and get Lois. Stacey/Lois gave him her address and phone number, and told him her new name.

When the truck pulled into the driveway, Lois flew to the door keeping her shaking hands clenched. She watched as Peter stepped down from the truck. Then the other door opened and Lois got out. Her mother ran across the grass and gathered her daughter into her arms.

"Oh, sweetheart, you better come in. You must be exhausted."

"Mommy, I just had to see you."

"Lois, this was a crazy thing to do. Your father is insane with worry. He will be here in the morning. You had better be ready for one good dressing down."

"He wouldn't let us see you. He is mean and I don't want to go back."

"Your father would never be mean to you. He loves you as much as I do. Now, let's get inside and make the most of the time we have together."

Peter had gone into the kitchen and come back with hot chocolate and cookies. Lois explained to her daughter that Peter was not only her business partner but her friend as well. Peter excused himself and left the two girls on their own.

"Is he your boyfriend?"

"That is a complicated question. Before I regained my memory, I wouldn't even consider getting into a relationship because I had no idea who I was. You need to know the whole story and if you are not too tired, I would like to tell it to you."

"I slept on the train, so I am wide awake."

As Lois told her story, she was careful to leave out any reference to Randy's belittling. Her daughter listened to every word.

"Well, you did complicate things by taking my name. Now, how will we tell each other apart?"

Lois laughed. "You have a point there; I hadn't thought of that one."

"I know—Annie calls me Lo. Why don't you call me that too?"

Around four in the morning, Lois insisted that they get some sleep. Since Randy was not expected until late morning, they would have some time together before he arrived. Lois called Helen, told her the situation and invited her for breakfast, the twins and Norm included. She then sent a text to Peter and told him to bring Jack for breakfast. She was up at daybreak and soon had a coffee cake in the oven and the table set. Breakfast turned out to be a lively affair with everyone chipping in with their side of the past seven years. Lo heard story after story about her mother.

Lois watched her daughter as she fit in with everyone—it was as if she had known them forever. Everyone called her Lo and the morning was filled with happy faces.

Chapter 50

Watching my daughter interact with my favourite people is so heartwarming. She is so beautiful, taller than me with an impish smile that is so warm and she fits in like she always knew everyone. How on earth am I going to be able to let her go back to Ottawa knowing I may never see her again? This rotten situation I created is one God awful mess. But right now, I am going to drink in every little thing about my Lois, Lo, as she insists she be called. I am so in love with my daughter. She is part and parcel of my soul. When I see how she relates to Jack, I know how she is with Dougie. All the years I have missed can never be replaced. My children have grown and without my help, their personalities have developed and formed. If the other two are anything like Lois, I have to thank Randy. I was not wrong when I told myself he would be a great father. That was the one comforting fact that I banked on when I abandoned my family. If the boys are anywhere near as delightful as Lois is, I was right.

Whatever happens, I have to understand that it was all my doing. I may have to pay the ultimate price of never seeing my children again. Oh, my gut is constricting at the very thought. Why can't Randy be reasonable? Right now seeing Lois here, I want to fight for custody, the right to have my children, the right to be their mother. I wanted to find a way to share them; I never wanted to deprive Randy of his fatherhood. Now, having Lois here, I know that even if Randy did relent and allow me access, being a part-time mother will make me miss them more. Thank goodness for Skype—what am I thinking? Randy is determined to forbid me any contact and he might win even though I have the best legal representation. How can I not fight to the bitter end? Just watching Lois makes my heart leap.

Chapter 51

Randy set off for Sudbury before daybreak having arranged for the housekeeper to come in early to get the boys ready for school. It was a dreary April morning with steady rain. Randy cranked up the heat in the truck to take the chill off and headed for Tim Horton's for coffee and donuts. Once back on the road, he put his foot down on the gas determined to put the miles behind him as quickly as he could. Not an hour into the trip, he was pulled over for speeding but managed to talk his way out of a ticket when he explained the circumstances.

"Sir, Mr. Martin, the roads are slick and greasy, so if you want to arrive in one piece, you better slow down."

Driving carefully after that encounter, he talked to himself as he often did in the truck when he was alone. "I have to confess that at least she had the decency to call me. That stupid little Lois is in for one hell of a lecture, that is for sure. How could she be so inconsiderate? What she did was dangerous. She is still a little girl and I shudder to think what might have happened with her traipsing off like that. Thank God, she is safe. I can't imagine how she got it into her head to do such a thing. Kids her age are so impressionable and react without thinking—she could have been accosted or kidnapped. Well, at least she is safe. Over the years, she kept saying how she missed her mother. How could she? She surely can't even remember that much about her. It has been seven years; she was little more than a baby when Stacey left. I made sure there were no pictures of Stacey left anywhere and never mentioned her except when Lois asked occasionally. I always answered that her mother didn't love us and left. You would think that that would have been enough to make Lois forget, but, no, apparently she didn't. Somehow, she kept asking for and about her mother. Funny how little minds work. I guess

I was only thinking of myself and didn't realize how much she did miss her mother. The boys were too young when Stacey left, but Lois did remember some things about her. Maybe I need to rethink this whole situation. Stacey has not demanded custody but says she might if I take this to court. My lawyer thinks her demands are reasonable and that she has a good case. How can they be? She bloody well walked out on us. I think my lawyer is afraid to come up against that high profile team. Can't imagine how Stacy is going to pay their fee. Lois is just like her stupid mother rushing off to Sudbury. Sudbury of all places. Why on earth would she pick a mining city? I would never have thought of looking there. Maybe that is why.

No, Lois is not stupid, just eager to be with her mother. Was I as hard on Stacey as she said? I guess I did criticize her sometimes, but who can't take a little honest, positive criticism? I only wanted her to improve herself. She was not the best wife— I hated having eggs for lunch. Surely, she could understand that. I can't begin to understand women."

The miles rolled by and the lush vegetation of the Ottawa Valley turned into scrub bushland and rock outcroppings. Six hours later, Randy pulled into Sudbury. Easing to the side of the road, he punched Stacey's address into the GPS and followed the directions. He drove through what was a newly developed area and merged onto a bridge that took him past the museum toward the lake. He found the address and turned into the lane. He was surprised to see a beautifully landscaped cottage on a lake. He pulled up behind a big 4X4 with Dominion BDB Construction on the side.

"Well, I guess she has a man—a man in construction giving her a nice home and sharing her bed. Of course, she has probably been shacked up with him for the past seven years. I should have known. Of course, she couldn't have managed on her own—she even had trouble coping with running a house and home. I can just imagine the crude dolt she has hooked up with. That would not be a good example for our children. I don't want some rough construction type influencing them. I know the type since I work with them every day. I'm sure the courts will take that into consideration."

He stepped out and took note of the tidy little house, then with a sure stride approached the door. His daughter opened it and invited him in.

Randy reached for Lois and told her to get in the truck.

"Wait a minute, Dad. I'm sorry I put you to so much trouble and made you worry so much, but I want you to listen to Lois."

"Lois?"

"Well, Mom changed her name and took mine. Isn't that cool?"

"No, it is not cool. It's stupid. Now get your things, so we can get out of here."

"Dad! Listen to me. I want to be able to see Mommy. She explained everything and how she told you it could work. I understand and even though I would like her to come home, I know she has a different life here, so she can't do that. But, the boys and I could spend some time each year with her and talk on the phone every day. Why won't you go along with it?"

"Yeah, well for your information, she has a different life with a man I know nothing about—that's why she won't come home. There's no way I'm letting my daughter spend time with a construction jockey that's banging your mother."

"Dad! That's a horrible thing to say. Mom doesn't live with anyone."

"Lois, open your eyes. His truck is in the driveway. Where is he anyway?"

"Actually, Randy, that is my truck and I am the construction jockey as you called it." Lois walked down the short hall to greet Randy.

"Excuse me. What did you just say?"

"I am a principal owner in one of the largest construction companies in Ontario. Dominion BDB Construction is mine. It's my truck in the driveway."

Randy looked at this woman, this woman who was his wife, this woman whom he did not know at all. She was certainly not the same person as the woman who left as Stacey. He stood there looking bewildered.

"See, Dad. Mom is terrific. I met some of her friends. I want to be able to visit her. Please try and see it her way. She told me all about what happened and I understand."

"She told you I made her depressed?"

"No. Did you?"

"Randy, don't do this. Why I left is between you and me. It is none of the children's concern. Look, let me get some lunch before you and Lois get back on the road."

"No. We will grab something on the way. Come on, Lois." He picked up the small suitcase by the door.

Lois gave her mother a big hug and promised to call the minute she got home to let her know she was safe. Her mother gave a querying look at Randy and his nod made her smile. At least, she would have some communication with Lo. It was a start.

Lois went back to the kitchen and phoned Peter. "I need one very big bear hug."

"I'm on my way with both arms aching to hold you."

All the way back to Ottawa, Lois talked non-stop filling her dad in on the people she had met, the facts she had learned about the past seven years and how her mother regained her memory. Some of it Lois had already told him, but hearing it again from his daughter's point of view gave Randy a whole new perspective on the issue.

"Dad, what did you mean when you said you made her depressed?"

"Honey, I think your mother was suffering from something called post-partum depression. At least, that is what she said the doctors mentioned. She was very young when we got married and I think she may have had too many babies too fast. I guess I didn't realize she wasn't happy."

"We can make her happy now. Please, let her be our mom again."

When they got back to Ottawa, true to her word, Lois called her mother. Randy asked to speak with her.

"Stacey, er… Lois, thanks for calling me to let me know Lois was safe with you. I was worried sick. However, remember that you left and created a very difficult situation. I am having trouble understanding and I may never, but Lois is adamant that you be a part of her life. Perhaps I was too stubborn and there might be a way we can work this out." Randy uttered a chuckle. "Lois is jumping up and down because I said that, so I guess it better be true. I think I will have to swallow a great deal of pride to work through this, but I will try. Do you Skype?"

Lois was nodding her head up and down as her mother confirmed that she did.

Within minutes, Skype was connected and Lois met her two sons. The conversation was cautious and Lo kept butting in with bits and pieces. It was agreed that Lois Benton-Douglas would go to Ottawa the following week to meet her sons. Lo sent air kisses, then a big smack on the computer monitor to end the conversation. They had agreed to talk daily via Skype.

When Lois disconnected the call, she hugged herself and yelled at the ceiling.

"I am the happiest mother in the whole blooming world!"

The beginning

About the Author

Living in a century-old, three-generation, farmhouse in rural Ontario, Molly hovers over her laptop downing coffee after coffee while she goes on a journey with her characters. Primarily known as a writer of short stories, *When Secrets Become Lies* was her first novel, published in 2015. Previously, she published a collection of short stories, *Fourteen Cups*; a creative memoir, *Wandering Backward*; and a children's book, *Snow Business*. Her stories appear in five *Chicken Soup for the Soul* anthologies, three OIW anthologies, NYMB, magazines and newspapers. She gives writing seminars, is often a guest speaker and sings in two choirs. In her spare time, she can be found hiking the byways in Ontario and the ranges in Arizona with her camera strung around her neck, all the while thinking where her protagonist is heading next.

While She Was Gone is her second novel. An avid believer that women are limitless in the roles they choose to play, Molly places her female characters in non-traditional professions challenging the alpha male dominance factor. She also enlightens the reader about little discussed mental anxiety and depression issues. That being said, her work is about story-telling, she buries the issues in a fast paced novel. She captures the reader right from the first page and takes them on a journey of discovery.

Acknowledgment

While She Was Gone was a solitary process, however, a few people stepped forward to encourage my efforts while writing this novel. Steve Dodge shared his expertise on First Responders and the actions they would undertake in an emergency. My dear friends, Jessie Hunter and Joan Grayer lent their ears and eyes to my efforts. Karen Ely helped wade through cover ideas to come up with the right one. A big thank you goes out to Sigrid MacDonald, who did a fabulous job editing the manuscript. Bruce Moran who guided me through the publishing process.

CPSIA information can be obtained
at www.ICGtesting.com
Printed in the USA
FSHW010420130319
56313FS